THE LAST ELECTION

Copyright 2011 © Kevin C. Carrigan

All rights reserved

D1737726

To my children

Part 1
January 28, 2012

Chapter 1

"The president has ignored the most basic principle of our constitution, which is American citizens are served by the government, not the other way around!"

There were two thousand strong packed into Columbia's Metropolitan Convention Center cheering, "A.K., A.K., A.K.!" The tightly packed crowd seemed to move like a rolling tide as supporters cheered and waved their banners and flags. The enthusiasm in the air was electrifying.

The crowd was a mix of supporters from all walks of life. Successful businessmen stood side by side with blue-collar workers and farmers. Middle class soccer moms cheered together with elderly gentlemen wearing VFW garrison caps. Young men and women who weren't even old enough to vote were proudly in attendance. They had all come to the convention center with the shared purpose of supporting the man they believed should be the next President of the United States.

"He came into office with control of both houses of congress, with a filibuster-proof majority in the Senate, and look where we are now. Unemployment is higher than it's ever been, our economy is teetering on the brink of collapse, our allies feel alienated and our enemies are laughing at us. When I am elected, Americans will be back to work, our economy will be restored, and America will once again be the unquestioned superpower of the world!"

"A.K., A.K., A.K.!" roared the crowd. Those who had signs with the words 'No More Years' plastered over a picture of the president's face held them high.

Senator Alexander Kirk soaked in the moment. He had won the presidential primaries in Iowa, New Hampshire, and today South Carolina. *Three for three!* Kirk knew that winning the South Carolina primary was a given, but taking his home state still tasted sweet. He had waited patiently his entire career, his entire *life,* for this moment. He had always known in his heart and soul that one day he would be the President of the United States of America. Momentum was on his side. *There is no stopping me now.*

Kirk gave a thumbs-up to some cheering supporters who were close to the stage. He laughed as a group of young ladies started chanting, "We love you A.K.!" Even though Kirk was in his early sixties, he still had the handsome looks that turned the heads of women of all ages. He was a tall man with a solid chest and broad shoulders that filled out the country western suits he wore most impressively. His facial features looked like they had been carved out of granite and he had a perpetual tan. His thick brown hair stood high on his head, and his brown, neatly trimmed goatee had a touch of gray around the edges. His frosty gray eyes sat beneath thick, bushy brown eyebrows. His colleagues in Congress often teased him about being the best looking guy on Capitol Hill.

Kirk waved to the ladies and went on. "I want to express my deepest appreciation and thanks to you, my fellow South Carolinians, for delivering a decisive victory in our party primary. You have shown the nation, just as Iowa and New Hampshire before you, that the Democratic Party wants and needs a new direction!"

For the last three years the direction of the country had been straight downhill. Senator Kirk and many of his fellow Democrats in Congress laid the blame squarely at the feet of Emmanuel Bonsam, President of the United States. Once he took office and rammed his ill-conceived policies through Congress, the country's economy became increasingly unstable. Kirk felt that in Bonsam's own delusional mind, Bonsam believed everything he touched turned to gold. However, when things went badly it was never his fault, oh no. To Kirk, Emmanuel Bonsam gave a whole new meaning to the word megalomania.

"Now, there are some in Washington who would like to see a monument built to honor President Bonsam," Kirk told the crowd. He was referring to Bonsam himself. He could hardly hold back a grin as the crowd laughed, then booed. "The only time the word 'monument' should be mentioned in the same breath as President Bonsam is when you are talking about monumental failure! During his time in office, he has delivered one monumental failure after another!" The crowd was simmering with excitement.

Kirk drove on. "Economic policy, monumental failure! Tax code reform, monumental failure! His handling of the Iran-Israel crisis!" This time the crowd joined in. "Monumental failure!"

Throngs of supporters were cheering so loudly that Kirk paused for a moment and stepped back from the podium to clap along with them. Bonsam had never recovered from his blundering attempts to take decisive action when Iran and Israel started shooting at each other. Thanks to Bonsam, America's allies and enemies alike might never again take America seriously in world affairs. *That is, until I'm elected.*

Kirk stepped up to the podium and continued. "The war in Afghanistan...monumental failure!" The roar was deafening.

Bonsam had allowed Afghanistan to slip into a political quagmire of nightmare proportions, and it was the American troops in the region who suffered the most. Kirk was by far the biggest critic in the Democratic Party of the president's decisions when it came to the military. Kirk made his decisions based on the intelligence reports from the commanders on the ground, whereas Bonsam, Kirk thought, made his decisions based on poll numbers, world opinion, political pressure from within his own party, and perhaps even an Ouija board.

Of all of the president's national defense disasters, Kirk thought that his handling of the war in Afghanistan was, without compare, his greatest disaster. Kirk had fought hard in the Senate to give more support to the troops, but was blocked at every turn by Bonsam loyalists who, in Kirk's mind, were just as spineless as Bonsam himself. Every time Kirk saw Bonsam waffling on military strategy, the bile would rise to the top of his throat until he almost choked. *More troops, less troops, Girl Scout troops. Make a damned command decision and stick with it, Commander-in-Chief.*

The Kirk family went all the way back to the founding of the United States. Kirk's ancestors had fought in the Revolutionary War, the Civil War, and both World Wars. He himself had served with distinction in Vietnam as a member of the Special Forces, and he had seen combat at its worst. He had taken two bullets in the leg from a North Vietnamese Regular soldier, who shortly thereafter received a .40 caliber round between the eyes.

What bothered Kirk most about Vietnam was that he had seen his comrades killed on senseless missions in a prolonged war that was never about national security. Vietnam was about politics. Politicians turned their backs on the suffering in the region and the needless spread of violence into Cambodia, and as a result thousands of American lives had been cut short because war pigs in Washington were more concerned with their legacy than victory. The U.S. could have left Vietnam, taken the loss, saved lives, and not threatened American security. The North Vietnamese weren't terrorists capable of flying large commercial airliners into American skyscrapers.

Afghanistan was completely different, but the painful feeling of *déjà vu* that the president and his administration were unleashing regarding Afghanistan was just as reprehensible. Kirk knew it would be disastrous to pull out of Afghanistan before the military eliminated the Taliban and Al Qaeda. To leave before the job was done would surely lead to another 9/11. Yet Bonsam politicized the war in any way he could, and his decisions on when and when not to use military force were based solely on pleasing the voters who would support him. For Bonsam, it was all about being reelected.

"And we all remember what happened in the mid-term elections of 2010."

"Boo!" The crowd shouted in unison.

"The Republicans pounded us and they now control both houses of congress! Never before has there been voter backlash of this scale against a president in the mid-term elections. How could this happen?" Kirk asked.

"Bonsam, Bonsam, Bonsam…" chanted the crowd disapprovingly. Kirk was on fire now.

"And all the so-called political experts from the 24-hour news networks now say that there will be a Republican victory in this year's presidential election. Do we want that?"

"Hell no, hell no, hell no…" the crowd chanted.

"We all remember what a splendid job the last Republican president did," Kirk exclaimed, and the crowd erupted in laughter.

"Unless we take a stand, here and now, to take back the Democratic Party, President Bonsam *will* be defeated by the Republicans in the November election. During the last presidential campaign President Bonsam spoke of hope and promises, but those promises were nothing more than castles in the air. The American people, as well as the majority of his own political party, are tired of the broken promises. *My* promise to you is to bring back the dignity and respect on which our party was founded!"

Loud cheers rang throughout the center. Kirk looked directly into the cameras that were broadcasting his message across the nation. "I speak now to the rest of America. When your presidential primary rolls around and you find yourself in that voting booth, ask yourself this, "Who do you want to go toe-to-toe with the Republicans this November, a man who has repeatedly shown a complete and total lack of leadership in the executive office, or someone with over 30 years of proven success in the U.S. Senate?" His voice rose to a fever pitch. "Vote Alexander Kirk, for the Democratic presidential candidate in 2012!" Kirk raised his hands high and waved to the pumped-up crowd as he walked off the stage, while hundreds of balloons fell from the rafters and red, white and blue confetti filled the air.

Chapter 2

"Shut that off! Everybody, out of the room, now!" shouted President Emmanuel Bonsam. His staff quickly filed out of the Oval Office. "Not you, Mike," barked Bonsam, so the Vice President returned to his seat

"That fucking redneck," snarled Bonsam once everyone was gone. "How dare he challenge me?" A burning anger had been building within him, anger so deep and so powerful that it threatened to consume him. In the last few months these fits of anger struck Bonsam more frequently and with increasing intensity.

Vice President Michael Holden had always considered Bonsam a self-important upstart, and he could see that the president was about to have one of his notoriously dramatic mood swings. Holden discreetly shook his head. *One minute he's an articulate statesman, the next he's a raving lunatic.*

Bonsam angrily paced the floor while sucking the hell out of a cigarette he had lit once the room had cleared. "It is an unforgivable breach of protocol to challenge the sitting president of your own party. It's not my fault my approval ratings are so low," he yelled as he let out a lungful of smoke. "The extremist enemies of my presidency who plague this country have spent every waking moment since I was elected trying to annihilate me!"

Holden had heard it all before. The president had always been a little high-strung, to say the least, but Holden had begun to seriously worry that Bonsam was ready to go off the deep end once and for all. His behavior became more and more erratic as he continually slipped in the polls to Senator Kirk. Bonsam was obsessed with the polls.

"I was going to lead America along a golden path of prosperity. I was going to usher in a glorious future filled with peace and harmony," he said in a low voice before taking another long drag on his cigarette. "And I could have done it all, but I was sabotaged at every turn by the

Republicans, the racists, the media…they are out to destroy me!"

"*Oy vey*," thought Holden. He fanned the smoke away from his face with his hand. He knew it was senseless to try to reason with the president. Bonsam never listened to anything he said. Holden had long regretted accepting the vice presidential nod from Bonsam. He had swallowed his pride big-time on that decision, considering that he had been in the Senate six times as long as Bonsam.

Vice President Holden was a moderate and a career politician. He became president of the local school board in his hometown in his early twenties and knew then and there that he would never leave politics. His looks were stunning and people often told him that if he ever left politics, he could get a job posing for GQ. He was tall, thin and extremely dapper. His salt and pepper hair was kept in an impeccable style, and his perfect set of teeth gave him a beaming smile.

Holden's only comfort came from the prospect that Kirk would beat Bonsam in the primaries, and one year from now he'd be enjoying his retirement. Holden was actually happy for Kirk. Hell, he and Kirk had always gotten along well when they served together in the Senate. Perhaps instead of retiring, Kirk would give him a nice cushy ambassadorship somewhere in the Mediterranean. How great it would be to sit on a candlelit patio drinking piña coladas, feeling the warm breeze and smelling the salt air from the waterfront below. He smiled at the thought.

"What are you smiling about?" Bonsam yelled as he continued to pace the floor and mutter to himself about the conspiracies against him. "Is this the way it's going to be, come Super Tuesday?"

Holden slowly shook his head no and motioned to the door, indicating his desire to leave. Bonsam flipped his hand and waved Holden out as he continued to pace the room. As Holden got up and turned toward the door, he grimaced at the sight of the most powerful man in the world pouting like a child and ranting to an empty room.

As Holden closed the door behind him, he heard Bonsam explode one last time, "God damn it! Do they realize who they are dealing with? I am Emmanuel Bonsam, President of the United States of America!"

Bonsam walked over to the shelves behind his desk and poured a glass of Johnny Walker Blue as he tried to calm his nerves. He took a big swig and then placed the glass back on the shelf as he felt the warmth of the Scotch work its way down. He leaned forward and placed both hands on the surface of his desk with his head hung low, then took in a large breath of air and slowly released it. "I have got to step up the operations of my agents," he growled to himself.

Bonsam had long been a member of a clandestine brotherhood known as *Enkhtuyaa*. *Enkhtuyaa* had originated in central Asia nearly 800 years ago during the Mongol Empire. It was more powerful than the Illuminati and more far-reaching than the Freemasons. This secret fraternity had members in government agencies throughout the world, and their mission was to protect and serve those with the power to advance the causes of the exploited who for so long had been oppressed by the malevolent ruling classes. By the time Bonsam had become the President of the United States, he had the unlimited support of the *Enkhtuyaa* elders, for he was in the ultimate position to improve the lives of the downtrodden.

Bonsam had a large, loyal following within *Enkhtuyaa*, however, he manipulated many of its members into fulfilling his corrupt desires in his quest for power. From within the brotherhood he had built an extensive secret syndicate of "shadow agents" whose loyalty to Bonsam was greater than their loyalty to the brotherhood. His network of agents conducted a myriad of sinister operations, most of them outside the law. It had taken him years to build the network, and it had high-level moles in almost every federal agency. The only U.S. agency he could not crack was the Secret Service, however, the

Pentagon was crawling with his spies, and he had shadow agents within the FBI, the CIA, and the DEA. Bonsam's spy network touched every facet of the federal government, yet even the most senior members of his presidential administration had no idea that the shadow agency existed.

Bonsam had also cultivated bonds with some of the world's most despotic leaders and warlords. He continually filtered funds to tyrannical governments and criminal organizations, with the understanding that someday he may require their assistance. He had also recruited many of the best computer hackers in the world over the years and placed them in positions that gave them access to the government's most secure network systems, just in case.

Bonsam plopped down in his chair with his head still hung low. The words Senator Kirk had spoken were still playing through his mind. He sat up straight and leaned back in his chair, tilted his head back, and closed his eyes. He could still see Senator Kirk looking straight into the camera as he cheered, "Monumental failure!" The anger he had felt earlier quickly returned.

The rage within Bonsam grew stronger and stronger and his heart pounded furiously. Visions and sounds raced rapidly through his head. It was as if his whole life was flashing before his eyes. He could not control it. Thousands of horrifying images stormed through his mind and he could not make them stop. Faster and faster they flew by.

Bonsam's eyes shook rapidly behind his closed eyelids. He saw visions of his mother crying out for him but he was unable to reach her. He saw the White House crumbling down around him but he was unable to escape from the falling debris. Slowly a glowing, ethereal ancient temple appeared where the White House had once stood. He saw Senator Kirk laughing at him as he struggled to speak. He saw men in hooded robes hiding in the shadows and chanting his name. Their numbers grew until he was completely surrounded. He saw ancient symbols that had been carved in stone tablets. The cryptic carvings possessed a message that he knew was meant for him, but the meaning eluded him. He saw flames all around him as the images continued to spiral uncontrollably through his mind.

As the images became more horrific, he felt his body temperature rise. His skin felt as though it was on fire and his blood seemed to boil. The inferno of pain was excruciating, but he was unable to cry out. The sensations attacking his body and mind were terrifying and he shuddered with thunderous convulsions. He was screaming inside his own mind as his body was racked by spasms and flailed about uncontrollably in his chair.

Suddenly it stopped. There was no more pain. Bonsam felt nothing but peace and serenity. He had escaped the living nightmare, and his consciousness slowly drifted back to reality. Only one vision remained in his mind...flames.

Chapter 3

"Holy shit, Gov," said Brett Mason as he choked back the laughter. "Senator Kirk is doing all the dirty work. That allows us to take the high road during your campaign if someone else points out Bonsam's ineptitude. Even the pinko-lib media that have been drinking Bonsam's Kool Aid for the last three years are really warming up to Kirk. He has replaced Bonsam as the media's darling."

Governor Samuel Clark smiled broadly. "Imagine that," he said as he sarcastically imitated wonderment.

Samuel David Clark became Governor of Michigan in 2008 following 25 distinguished years of service in the US House of Representatives. He gained the respect and admiration of his fellow Republicans from the start, and became more popular as the years passed and his career flourished. His commanding victory in the 2008 gubernatorial race made him the poster boy of the new Republican Party, and Republicans from across the political spectrum were convinced that Samuel Clark was the best candidate to defeat President Bonsam in the 2012 presidential election. So the Republican Party, for once, united early on and chose Governor Clark as its presidential candidate, completely abandoning its typical *modus operandi* of letting a dozen old white guys that most Americans have never even heard of duke it out in the primaries.

Clark watched with respect and admiration as Senator Kirk tormented the president. He was the only person in the Democratic Party with the balls big enough to stand up to Bonsam and point out that their emperor was wearing no clothes. *Bonsam will never survive a full court press from Alexander Kirk.*

"This is almost too good to be true," said Mason. He was right of course. It was Mason's keen political insight and his no-nonsense approach to campaigning that led Clark to select him as his campaign manager.

Brett Mason had been a key player on Clark's campaign team since his early days in Congress. He had a warped sense of humor that Clark found amusing, yet his knowledge of politics and the election process was second to none. He was an unassuming man who stood only five feet eight, and he had a pudgy face and a bit of a paunch. His hairline had receded to the top of his head, but the hair that remained was brown and bushy. He almost always wore a button-down shirt with the collar open, covered by a sleeveless V-neck sweater. He was a devoted family man, and even with his hectic schedule he found ways to spend quality time with his wife and kids and remain active in his church.

Clark silently agreed as he replayed the last lines of Senator Kirk's speech over in his mind. *A man who has repeatedly shown a complete and total lack of leadership in the executive office.* In all his years of public service, Clark had never seen someone disgrace the Presidency the way Bonsam did. Even Jimmy Carter looked like George Washington when compared to Bonsam. It takes a lot more than vanity to be a world leader.

Clark hit the mute button on the remote control and plopped it on his desk. "I never told you this, but Kirk and I served in Vietnam together. He was a meritorious soldier, even though he liked to jump out of perfectly good airplanes." Clark was referring to the fact that Kirk had been in the Airborne Infantry. As a former Infantry sniper, Clark preferred to keep both feet planted on *terra firma.*

"He's the type of guy who would throw himself on a grenade to save others without hesitation. And he was one tough son of a bitch. Everybody thinks he got his nickname A.K. because of his initials. But you know where that came from?" Mason shrugged his shoulders and shook his head no.

"We were outside Khe Sanh during the Tet Offensive. The Viet Cong were all around us, and we were in deep kimchi," said Clark.

"Kimchi is Korean, Gov," said Mason.

"Mason, how long have you been working for me, not counting tomorrow?" Clark asked as he jokingly shot Mason a look that said shut the hell up.

"Sorry, Gov, please continue," Mason said politely.

"Anyway, Kirk managed to sneak through their line, how in the hell he did it we never knew, and kill a VC soldier with his bare hands. He took the recently departed soldier's Kalashnikov rifle and killed another dozen bad guys. A lot of men from our unit are alive today thanks to him, including me," Clark said as he thumbed himself in the chest. "He kept the Kalashnikov AK-47 that he appropriated that day and fought with it the rest of his time in 'Nam. Hence the name, A.K."

"Do you seriously think he can beat Bonsam?" Mason asked, although he already knew the answer.

"Oh hell yeah, Bonsam is washed up. Even after the midterms his future wasn't looking too bright." Clark leaned back in his chair and mocked the president. "I take full responsibility for the results of the election, yadda yadda yadda." He actually had the voice and mannerisms down pretty well. He sat up straight again and said, "Then in his next breath he went on to place the blame on anybody he could." Mason nodded in agreement.

Clark got up from his chair and walked to the window overlooking downtown Lansing. He loved Lansing. To him it was one of the friendliest cities in Michigan. He had always been proud of the city, with its hard work – get it done attitude. "People finally see him for what he really is; an unseasoned senator and an absolute narcissist."

He turned back to face Mason. "The American people just don't buy his line of crap anymore. They expect the President of the United States to man-up, quit making excuses, quit blaming others, and get the damned job done. They want to see results."

Clark resumed looking out the window. "Remember back in 2008 during his campaign when the right-wing nut jobs on conservative radio made fun of him, sarcastically saying that the 'Savior' had arrived? They saw what was going on, but on the other side of the coin, the liberal media seriously believed he could walk on water, and the democratic voters ate it up," he said with a wry grin.

"That's the key block of voters we need to convert to take the White House in November, Gov. We nailed down the independent vote without breaking a sweat. Converting the democratic voters won't be quite so easy," Mason replied.

"Well, that's why I hired you, remember?" Clark said with a smile as he turned back toward Mason.

"I know. I just need to figure out a way to dumb down enough parts of our campaign so they'll be able to understand it," said Mason with laugh.

"Very funny," replied Clark. "By the way, don't you have some campaign manager work you should be doing instead of sitting here cracking jokes?"

Mason looked at Clark for a moment. After a short pause he said, "Oh, I get it, you want me to leave."

"Yes. The sooner the better, Brett."

"Okay, Gov. I'm going back to my office now to do some…" he forgot where he was going with this.

Clark helped him out. Speaking slowly he said, "Campaign manager work."

"That's it! Campaign manager work," said Mason. He turned and walked out of Clark's office saying, "I'll see you tomorrow, Gov."

Clark shook his head and laughed as Mason exited the office. As he returned to his seat he glanced back at the television and noticed that the network was now showing footage of President Bonsam's most recent campaign speech. He picked up the remote and turned the volume back on, just as the network cut back to the anchor desk where three political analysts were comparing Bonsam's last speech to the speech given by Senator Kirk just minutes ago.

The anchorman and two of the analysts were confident that Senator Kirk was on a path to victory in the primaries, however, the other analyst remained silent. When he was finally given a chance to speak, he glanced at the other two analysts and said in a low voice, "President Bonsam is not a man who can easily be beaten. He will prevail."

There was a momentary silence on the set as the anchorman and analysts reflected upon the remark. It sounded more like a threat than an opinion. No one knew what to say, so the anchorman quickly cut to a commercial.

Clark thought about the comment as well. He had always felt in the back of his mind that Bonsam was the type of politician that would go to extraordinary lengths to hold on to power. As the primary season rolled around, Bonsam continually appeared angry, and Clark became more concerned that Bonsam would resort to any desperate political measure necessary to win the election. Clark turned his chair so he was facing the window and said to himself, "Bonsam is dangerous."

It was well past midnight and President Bonsam was completely worn out. He knew that this was a day he would not soon forget. He could not believe that the American people would turn against him after all he had done. *Kirk is inferior! How could they trust and believe in a man like Alexander Kirk?*

He entered the master bedroom thinking ahead to Super Tuesday. He leaned forward toward the fireplace with his hand on the mantle, staring at his reflection in the mirror above. *Kirk's success has been a fluke. How can I possibly lose to him? I am Emmanuel Bonsam, President of the United States!* Then he remembered that the recent polls showed Senator Kirk with a significant lead in most of the Super Tuesday states. *Kirk has to be stopped.* As he looked deeply into his own eyes, he realized that Super Tuesday was the point of no return. He needed to shut down Senator Kirk's campaign once and for all.

Bonsam walked over to the four-post mahogany bed and lay down, still fully dressed, and drifted off to sleep as soon as his head hit the pillow. As he drifted, random images started floating through his mind again, however, with nowhere near the intensity of the episode he experienced earlier this evening. There were no hooded demons, but the mysterious symbols carved in stone appeared once more. Many other non-threatening images passed by, yet he saw the flames again and again. *Why?* One by one the images slowly faded away. The last image to cross his mind before he fell into a deep sleep was an image of his mother.

Chapter 4

Emmanuel Bonsam was actually born Emmanuel Bonsam Durrett. His father, Evan Durrett, had been an E3 in the U.S. Coast Guard. Durrett had been aboard the cutter *Resolute,* which was conducting a humanitarian mission to Africa, when she docked at the Ghanaian Naval Base at the Port of Tema. It was there that he met Ama Bonsam, Emmanuel's mother. She was young and naïve and an easy target for a putz like Durrett to seduce. Durrett promised her he would love her forever and told her anything she wanted to hear, until she finally gave in and gave her body to him. To her shame she became pregnant the first time she made love to Durrett.

Durrett had no intention of taking responsibility, however, that all changed when Ama's father showed up at the port with three heavily armed associates. Asmoah Bonsam was a well-respected businessman in Accra. He owned two major hotels and several other pieces of high-profile commercial property. He was not about to let some white American loser bring disgrace upon the Bonsam family name.

The *Resolute* guards were taken by surprise when Mr. Bonsam and his thugs approached the brow. Mr. Bonsam had a look that showed he meant business, so the Gangway Petty Officer of the Watch quickly placed a frantic call to his skipper, Captain Raymond Strickland, who was on the scene in minutes.

Strickland and Bonsam sized each other up as they shook hands. Strickland admired men like Bonsam, since his own ancestors were of West African descent. Captain Strickland invited Mr. Bonsam aboard to meet with him privately in his quarters, and Mr. Bonsam explained the whole predicament in a matter of minutes. Strickland was furious. He had long considered Durrett a terrible seaman and a constant whiner, and now this. Mr. Bonsam demanded that the man responsible for this dilemma make an honest woman out of his daughter, or else he would take matters into his own hands.

Ghana had always been one of America's closest and most trusted allies in Africa. The last thing anybody needed was an embarrassing international incident that would make the United States look disrespectful toward its African allies. Strickland knew he had to do something and do it quickly so not to further anger Mr. Bonsam.

Captain Strickland and Mr. Bonsam discussed the matter at length, and finally Strickland devised a plan that satisfied Mr. Bonsam's desires. Strickland invited Mr. Bonsam's associates into his quarters and allowed them to stand in the back of the room, and then he called in Durrett. He walked up to Durrett and with his face a mere six inches away, gave him two very simple options. Durrett could marry Ama and return with her to the United States, or he could be left in Ghana to settle this matter on his own. Durrett took one look at Mr. Bonsam and started to shake. The associates shifted their stances, moving their hands closer to their weapons. He looked back at Captain Strickland and realized he wasn't bluffing.

So the following morning Captain Strickland and Mr. Bonsam took Seaman Durrett and young Ama to the U.S. Embassy in Accra, and by the end of the day the two were husband and wife. If it were up to Strickland, he would have had Durrett thrown out of the Coast Guard for good, but that would only have hurt Ama and her unborn child. Captain Strickland knew he would be doing the nation a huge favor by keeping Evan Durrett as far away from Coast Guard cutters as possible, so by the end of the week Strickland had Seaman Durrett transferred to a desk job at the Integrated Support Command in St. Louis, Missouri.

When Durrett arrived in St. Louis, he was surprised to find that no base housing was available. As an E3 with a wife and baby on the way, Durrett's financial situation was poor to say the least. It would be a stretch to afford even the most basic apartments in St. Louis, even with a housing allowance. So across the Mississippi he went to East St. Louis, Illinois.

Apartments there were much more affordable, primarily because they were located in neighborhoods ravaged by violent crime. Durrett, too dense to realize that living there was to put his and his family's lives at risk every day, signed a lease for a two-bedroom apartment located halfway down Old Missouri Avenue.

To Ama, the baby inside her was both a blessing and a curse. She had always dreamed of being a mother some day, but not in a situation like this. Durrett spent little time with her and her days were filled with loneliness. Her sorrow was compounded by the guilt she carried for bringing shame to the Bonsam family.

Ama missed Ghana and her father immensely, but she tried to remain upbeat as her due date approached. She believed the baby would bring her the joy and companionship she had been missing all these months. When she felt the baby inside kick her, she felt happiness like she had never felt since leaving Ghana. She would rub her growing belly every day and talk to her unborn child. Then, just like that, her joy was ripped away and replaced by even more painful sorrow.

On the day before her baby was due, she received word that her father had died of a heart attack. Ama was devastated. She wailed and cried at the news, and then to make a bad situation even worse, her water broke. So on that cold December night, through her tears of sorrow, Ama gave birth to a seven-pound baby boy. Durrett showed up just as the delivery was winding down, reeking of alcohol. Ama chose the name Emmanuel Bonsam Durrett, and her lousy husband was too drunk to object. As Ama looked at the infant son she was holding in her arms, her emotions were tearing her apart. She felt joy and sorrow, a blessing and a curse.

Durrett was eventually kicked out of the Coast Guard, and he abandoned Bonsam and Ama and was never heard from again. Bonsam was only four years old at the time, and he had very little recollection of his father. Ama did the best she could to raise Bonsam on her own, but that was no easy task. She had spent her entire life working in her father's hotels and had only a primary level education, plus her English was not very strong. She cleaned houses and apartments to get by. Ama kept to herself for the most part, since she never really understood the American way of life.

During his childhood Bonsam continually saw his mother being harassed. She could not go to the grocery store or the post office without someone being rude and disrespectful to her. One time when he was young, he saw a convenience store clerk slam change onto the counter and yell, "Go back to Africa, bitch!" because she could not understand what the clerk was saying to her as she tried to make a purchase. These incidents were devastating to Bonsam, and he had come to detest his father and all who were like him. He vowed that one day he would have the power to destroy the lowlife who brought misery to his mother's world. Out of spite, he had his last name legally changed from Durrett to Bonsam when he turned fourteen.

Bonsam's youth was also tough due to growing up without a father, but he got by with his wits and intelligence. He was rebellious and got into trouble a few times while roaming the mean streets of his neighborhood, but he possessed strong determination and sought to get the best education he could. He graduated from high school with honors and was chosen as the most likely to succeed by his classmates.

Bonsam picked up street smarts as well, all the while establishing the connections that made him well known throughout East St. Louis. His charismatic personality drew others to him. He was smooth and well liked, and he learned how to manipulate others to his advantage. He entered politics and quickly learned how the game was played. He saw the corruption in the political world and he embraced it. Bonsam knew that he was destined for greatness. He knew that he would have extraordinary power, fame and wealth one day, and he would have it no matter who stood in his way.

He embodied arrogance, yet he made all the right moves to advance rapidly in the political world. He even married simply to further his career. Although Bonsam was as misogynistic as they come, during his second term in the Illinois State Senate he contemplated the advantages that having a wife and family would bring to his political career. He felt strongly that he could enhance his career, and more importantly pick up votes in future elections, by portraying himself as a loving husband and father. He decided he would do it, even though the thought of it repulsed him. The trick, he thought, was to find a trophy wife that would stand lovingly by his side when necessary, but otherwise keep the fuck away.

As fate would have it, corrupt Illinois politics dropped the perfect woman into his lap. Her name was Raca Viera. Raca was the daughter of a man by the name of Eddomo Viera, who was sitting on death row for crimes he did not commit. He was scheduled for execution by lethal injection for the brutal murders of two little boys from his hometown of Granite City. Raca was doing everything she could to fight this injustice, but was having no success.

Viera and his wife had immigrated to the United States from Antigua many years before and had led a simple life in Granite City. They worked hard, built a small but comfortable home, and brought their lovely daughter Raca into the world. Raca grew to be a strikingly beautiful young woman, who following college enjoyed moderate success as a fashion model. Life in America brought the Vieras many blessings, however, a cruel twist of fate turned the American dream into a living nightmare.

The nightmare began when two young boys who lived next door to the Viera home disappeared. Police officers descended on the neighborhood and went door to door, looking for anyone with information regarding the whereabouts of the boys. Viera, who saw the boys playing in their front yard when he had come home for lunch that day, told the officers everything he had seen. Days went by and the search intensified, but the boys were nowhere to be found.

A week later the boys' bodies were finally discovered in a shallow grave nearly three miles from their home. They had been bludgeoned to death, and signs of sexual assault were present. The community was outraged and demanded that the person responsible for this heinous crime be brought to justice. The media blitz surrounding the murders and the police department's inability to find the killer put intense pressure on City Hall. The mayor insisted an arrest be made, and since Eddomo Viera was the last person to see the children alive, Viera was taken into custody.

The trial that followed was a travesty of epic proportions, due in large part to a hungry new district attorney who was bent on making a name for himself. He knew that prosecuting and convicting the murderer in a high-profile case such as this would surely bring him the fame and recognition he sought, so he went after Viera with a vengeance. He was so determined to win this case that even after evidence was uncovered that would have exonerated Viera, he swept the evidence under the rug. Viera was found guilty on two counts of capital murder, while the real murderer walked freely about, capable of killing again.

As the execution date drew near, Raca traveled to the state capitol to plead for clemency. She provided the governor with information about the mishandling of evidence, overt errors made by the defense during the trial and the appeal, witness tampering, and even sworn statements by people involved in the case who claimed that the DA hid information crucial to proving her father's innocence. The governor, who was a fraternity brother of the DA, listened to her pleas for mercy, but in the end he detached himself from the entire situation and allowed the execution to proceed as scheduled.

Out of desperation, Raca decided to go to the office of her state senator, who at that time was Emmanuel Bonsam, in hopes that there was some way he could help. She tried to remain calm as she explained her plight to Senator Bonsam's secretary, but she was frantic on the inside. The secretary showed sympathy and asked Raca to have a seat while she spoke to Senator Bonsam. Several minutes later the secretary returned and indicated that the senator would see her now, and then she ushered Raca into Bonsam's office.

Bonsam stood as she entered the room and politely welcomed her in. She found Bonsam respectful and exceptionally handsome, but she became slightly disturbed as she shook his hand. His hand felt as cold as ice. Bonsam offered her a seat in front of his desk as he returned to his own seat behind it. He sat with his elbows on the desk and his fingertips pressed together in front of him, occasionally nodding his head, as he appeared to be concentrating on the story Raca was telling him, however, nothing could be further from the truth. He heard the story, yes, but his mind was more focused on Raca herself.

Bonsam secretly glanced admiringly at Raca as she went on. He found her dark smooth skin, long flowing hair, and slender body to be remarkably attractive. In his mind he pictured her holding his hand as they walked across a stage, smiling and waving to voters at a rally. They looked like the perfect couple. He knew that Raca would be perfect for the role of Mrs. Emmanuel Bonsam.

Bonsam snapped out of his daydream just as Raca said to him, "Please, can you help us? I would do anything to save my father."

Bonsam stood and again shook her hand and said with false sincerity, "I'll do everything I can. Make an appointment with my secretary for tomorrow afternoon and I'll share with you what I have found."

"Thank you, Senator," Raca said as she vigorously shook his hand. "Thank you so much." She exited happily through his office doorway, but strangely the disturbing feeling within her still remained.

As the office door closed behind her, Bonsam smiled and said, "Jackpot!" He sat back down and made several phone calls and a few shady deals, and in less than an hour he had found a way to have Eddomo Viera pardoned.

When Raca returned the next day, Bonsam was direct and to the point: He would see that her father was pardoned in return for her hand in marriage. He went on to explain that if she ever mentioned this proposal to anyone, her father would die and there would be no way for her to prove a word of what he had said. Out of love for her father, she grudgingly accepted the offer.

They were soon married. Bonsam was cold and unloving toward Raca and they never even consummated the marriage, but Bonsam kept her in a nice home and provided for her generously. He used his clout to get her a high level job at UNICEF's Midwest Regional Office in Chicago as a development coordinator, which kept her away just as he desired. He constantly arranged photo ops of her standing up for humanitarian causes, and then plastered the photos all over his webpage and newsletters. At public events he would tell the crowds he was deeply proud of her work. His lovely wife brought him the votes he so wanted, but Raca's life was empty, and through it all she knew she was just a pawn in Bonsam's world.

Several years later, Bonsam realized that to the voters, the novelty of his adoring wife had worn off. He insisted that Raca bear him a child, again only for show, which she sorrowfully did in 1996. Bonsam knew that the publicity surrounding his newborn son would capture the attention of the voters in his district, especially senior citizens who were suckers for cute babies. He hoped that the elderly that would vote for him in droves, then go off and die and quit being such a burden on society.

Obimpé Bonsam was the spitting image of his father, but Bonsam spent almost no time with him. By the time Bonsam had become a U.S. Senator, he used his status as an excuse to keep Obimpé out of the public eye, and had him locked down in a private military academy. Bonsam only saw his son once or twice a year, and even when he did, it was staged to create a news event, such as the annual, heartwarming, proudly-welcoming-home-Obimpé-for-Christmas media spectacle.

When Bonsam became president, he wanted to keep Raca further away from him, yet increase her appearance on the world stage for his own selfish motives. He coerced UNICEF into making her a Goodwill Ambassador, which Bonsam used to his advantage. The beautiful first lady was constantly in the news shown in the worst places in the world visiting destitute orphans and children with AIDS and victims of famine and women injured by landmines and on and on as the media spun her up as the next Mother Teresa.

Raca proved to be valuable to Bonsam, especially now as she drew some of the attention away from his failing presidency. However, Raca died just a little bit more inside with every appearance. She prayed that someday she would step on a landmine herself, and escape the misery of being a prisoner of Emmanuel Bonsam.

Chapter 5

The Clark Express had been rolling down the highway since early in the morning. Governor Clark and his campaign team were on the road visiting the Super Tuesday states. Even though he was the only Republican on the ballots, he could not just sit back and wait for the presidential election. It was now critical for him to emphasize his message to the voters in preparation for the showdown with Senator Kirk in November.

Brett Mason joined Clark at the workstation in the center of the bus. "Good afternoon Gov," he said.

"Good afternoon Brett. What do you have for me?" said Clark as he looked over the newspaper he was reading.

"Sir, everything is running according to plan. Your message is getting out and the voters are loving it. Well done, Gov."

Clark lowered the newspaper. "The voters will love any message so long as it's not the same as Bonsam's."

"This is true. However, our polling indicates that we are striking a chord with the disillusioned Democrats, the same voters Senator Kirk is after. We need to keep this momentum because sooner or later these voters will see that Kirk is not just another Bonsam. When that happens, we'll start losing them," Mason bluntly stated.

"I know, Brett. That's why I want to shift attention to selecting my VP running mate. Everywhere we have gone the first question the reporters ask is who will be my running mate. Selecting my running mate early could work to our advantage. Who is on the short list?" Clark asked.

Mason looked puzzled. "You want that already?"

"Yes, Brett, I do. And make sure the Speaker of the House is on that list." Clark knew that demanding the Speaker be on the short list would ruffle Mason's feathers, because Mason had repeatedly stated that he did not think it was such a good idea for Clark to run with a female VP candidate. "I'm going to the back of the bus to grab a nap while you get to work," said Clark as he got up from his seat.

"Right, boss," said Mason, as he contemplated offering the bus driver $50 to slam on the brakes in 10 minutes.

Born and raised in the farm country of Midland County, Michigan, Samuel Clark grew up with a passion for fishing and hunting. His father was an avid outdoorsman who taught Clark and his two older brothers how to cast a line before they could walk.

He also taught them how to shoot. By the time he was seven, Clark was picking off rabbits and squirrels with his brother's pellet gun. Of the three Clark boys, Sam was by far the best shot. He also had the strongest love for guns.

Clark never missed a chance to go hunting with his father. He bagged a 6-point buck at the age of 12. His father continued to teach him about hunting every opportunity he could get. The year he turned 14, his father gave him a brand new .30-06 rifle for Christmas. If it wasn't hunting season, Clark spent every spare minute he could find popping shots into tin cans for target practice.

In high school, Clark was a fairly good running back and even scored the winning touchdown when the team won the state championship. He was easy going, popular, and known for his love of practical jokes. He had a great sense of humor and he enjoyed making other people laugh, and he had a crooked grin and a gleam in his eyes that gave him a look like he was up to some sort of mischief.

Clark was 18 when he graduated from high school and he enlisted in the army the very next day. In basic training, his excellent marksmanship was immediately recognized the first time he went to the rifle range. He always remembered the surprised look on his drill sergeant's face after he shot a perfect score with ease.

Upon completion of basic, he was plucked out of his platoon and sent directly to sniper school. Not only was he a dead-on shot, he possessed a sixth sense that told him where the enemy was. In Vietnam he had taken out plenty of enemy soldiers at distances of over 1,000 yards.

After his tour he returned to Midland County a hometown hero. With his meager savings and a generous no-interest loan from his father, he opened a small sporting goods store on the shores of Wixom Lake in the sleepy little town of Edenville. He sold rods and reels, bait and tackle, camping equipment, hunting rifles and shotguns, and all the goods the local outdoorsmen desired.

Clark's business, Sportsmen's World, did well from the beginning. He took his profits and constructed a log cabin home on 40 acres of land covered with tall red pines. By the time his cabin was completed, he had married his high school sweetheart, Maria. Within four years, Maria had blessed him with two beautiful children, a daughter and a son.

Clark never expected that Sportsmen's World would become so successful. Six years after opening, he had expanded his store to three times the size of the original building. He began selling more and more products, including bass boats in the summer and snowmobiles in the winter. He sponsored one of the most popular bass fishing tournaments in mid-Michigan. The proceeds from the tournament were donated to local schools with the understanding that the funds would only be used to provide education in wilderness conservation. He also established a charitable foundation called Sportsmen Against Hunger, where deer hunters donated venison to local churches to feed the needy during the winter months.

Clark's philanthropy made him very popular in the local community. He received numerous plaques of appreciation from the schools and churches, and was made an honorary member of the local lodges of both the Benevolent and Protective Order of Elks and the Loyal Order of the Moose. He was even knighted by the Knights of Columbus for his generous contributions to Catholic Charities, even though he was Methodist.

Within twelve years of opening the doors to the original Sportsmen's World, he had opened three more stores. The first was in the city of Claire, the second in Mount Pleasant, and the third was located on the shore of Higgins Lake near the town of Roscommon. The Higgins Lake store was enormous, earning the title of Superstore. As the popularity of Sportsmen's World grew, so did the reputation of Samuel Clark. He was a local celebrity in each town that had a Sportsmen's World outlet, and was often featured in local news stories as a successful businessman who always gave back to the community.

In 1981 he broke ground for his next Superstore in Traverse City. Clark had always made friends with the local politicians in the cities in which he built a store, and Traverse City was no exception. Mayor Russ McClellan had long been a fan of Clark and it was he who approached Clark and suggested he build a Sportsmen's World in Traverse City. McClellan saw the benefits in employment and tax revenue that a Sportsmen's World outlet would bring to his city, and with the full support of the city council, he persuaded Clark to research the market potential that Traverse City offered.

Clark quickly became friends with Mayor McClellan, a successful oncologist turned politician. He was a rugged man who loved the outdoors, and he enjoyed hunting as much as Clark. On one of their early hunting trips, McClellan sprang an offer on Clark that was totally unexpected. He promised Clark unlimited support from the Michigan Republican Party if he would run for Congress in the upcoming election.

The congressional seat in Michigan's 4th District had belonged to Eli Swanton for as long as most people could remember. Congressman Swanton was an old school Democrat whose age and deteriorating health prevented him from running for yet another term. All of Clark's stores were within the 4th District, making him well known throughout the area. McClellan explained to Clark that with his popularity, his prior military service, and his image as a clean-cut family man who enjoyed hunting and fishing, he was a shoo-in for the seat being vacated by Swanton.

Clark talked it over with Maria and his children, who enthusiastically encouraged him to go for it. As he stepped into the world of politics, Clark was surprised to find how much he enjoyed campaigning. He loved listening to the concerns of the people in his district, and they in turn found Clark to be a regular guy who wasn't blowing smoke when it came to addressing their concerns. He easily won the election, since the Democrats never found a serious challenger that had the same appeal as Clark.

Clark was a highly respected member of the House for several years. He always supported the causes near and dear to his constituents, such as smaller government, lower taxes, and protection of the environment. Even after his wife Maria died unexpectedly from a rare form of leukemia, he continued to serve admirably.

By the time he had won his 13th term in 2006 he was restless. Congress was challenging of course, but he no longer felt that serving at the federal level was the best way to serve the Michigan residents he so loved. That, added to the fact the Democrats in charge at the state level were a nationwide embarrassment, fueled his desire to leave Washington and return to Michigan.

The current governor of Michigan was in his second and final term, which was turning out to be much worse than his first term. Many people thought that could not be possible. However, when the Detroit Free Press ran a three-part exposé on the corruption that ran rampant throughout the governor's administration, his popularity plummeted and his legal problems skyrocketed. At the same time the governor fought off charges of bribery and kickbacks, the Democratic Mayor of Detroit was on her way to jail on a number of counts of misconduct, including making salacious phone calls to a married staff member on the city payroll.

The people of Michigan had had it with the Democrats, so Clark set his eyes on the governorship. In

2008 he ran a brilliant campaign that captured the attention of the citizens of Michigan, as well as citizens nationwide. For years the media loved to blame all of Michigan's woes on the last Republican president. Clark showed Michigan that it was doing no good to continue to blame Washington for the state's high unemployment. He put the blame squarely where it belonged, on the Democratic governor and the state's political leadership.

Clark's campaign had totally redefined Michigan's political landscape. He was swept into office with high approval in the 2008 election and immediately became the Republicans' superstar. Within days of his election win, the RNC began plotting his run for president in 2012.

Chapter 6

President Bonsam was deeply absorbed in thoughts about his enemies as he sat alone in the White House Theater. His paranoia was becoming stronger every day. He quickly shook the thoughts from his mind and focused on his purpose for being in the theater in the first place.

Since he took office he had been coming here almost every day for one reason and one reason only, to view the projected image of a single PowerPoint slide. He picked up the remote and hit the power button, and within seconds a large image appeared on the theater's screen. It was a photo of the ancient Maya calendar.

The first time Bonsam had seen a picture of the Maya calendar in a textbook, he felt a powerful spiritual attachment to it. He had felt drawn to it and had studied the symbols relentlessly ever since. He was certain there was a message for him within the symbols, a message foretelling what was to come.

A strange feeling came over Bonsam as he viewed the projection on the screen before him. It held him spellbound. During his frequent anger meltdowns, he had repeated visions of ancient carved symbols. He stared at the calendar hoping to find the connection between the symbols on the calendar and the symbols in his dreams. *What am I missing?*

When Bonsam was elected in 2008, his interest in discovering this mysterious message became an obsession. As soon as he took office he put his shadow agents on alert to report on anything they saw or heard involving ancient Maya artifacts. The agents recruited spies wherever Maya culture was being studied or archaeological digs were taking place.

He read the Maya Prophecies Report that his shadow agents provided first thing each morning. He read it even before the National Security Report. Unfortunately, the information in the reports had not changed much over the past several months; the Maya calendar was set to run out and ancient prophecies suggested that when it did, it would bring about the end of the world.

Bonsam continued to stare at the projection of the ancient calendar, desperately trying to unravel the mystery of the prophecy. He was certain that he was part of the prophecy, whatever it turned out to be. Bonsam knew that once he was reelected, the calendar's prophetic event would take place during his watch. If something marvelous were to happen, it would be of his doing. If the world were to end, well then, it would end on his terms.

Chapter 7

The D.C. campaign headquarters of Senator Alexander Kirk was bustling with activity. Kirk's staff and supporters were busily preparing for the last big push before Super Tuesday. Kirk's campaign manager, Bobby Davis, was running the show. Davis, a moderate Democrat himself, had spent his entire career inside the beltway and had known Kirk for years. When Kirk offered him the job as campaign manager, he jumped on it with both feet. Davis's views mirrored Kirk's in every way and he, too, saw that the Bonsam administration was driving the country into the ground.

Davis was in high spirits tonight. In four more days his boss could wipe out any chance of Bonsam getting the Party's nomination. An incumbent president losing in the primaries would be an event of historic proportions, and the thought of that made Davis want to pop the champagne. He walked around the headquarters giving handshakes and words of thanks to his staff. One of his staff members whispered something in his ear, so he made his way back to his private office.

Senator Kirk had been waiting for Davis in his office. As Davis walked in and saw Kirk sitting behind his desk, a big grin crossed his face. "A.K.!"

Kirk rocked the desk chair and looked down at it on both sides and said, "Mighty comfy chair you got here, Bobby." Both men laughed as Kirk got out of the chair and came out from behind the desk. They shook hands firmly and stepped back to look at each other, both filled with enthusiasm.

Davis said, "Come on A.K., let's go out and greet the staff. They would be thrilled to see you tonight."

"Not now, Bobby, I have something I want to talk to you about." Kirk's demeanor became serious, "About Bonsam." Kirk slowly walked behind the desk and sat back down.

Davis immediately knew where this was going. Kirk was a down-to-earth man and a straightforward politician. He was a man of honorable character who treated his friends and foes alike with respect, but Davis knew that Kirk was extremely suspicious of President Bonsam and didn't trust him a bit. Kirk had always said that he felt an indescribable eerie vibe every time he was near the president.

"One last time, Bobby. Tell me what you think is going on in Bonsam's mind right now. You know he isn't just sitting in the White House ignoring the polls, yet he acts like he has the nomination in the bag. What do you think he is up to?"

"I don't know, A.K.," replied Davis. "He has always been notoriously sly and devious in his campaigns. Since he first ran for public office in Illinois he has found ways to ruin his opponents. And if he couldn't ruin his opponents he would play the race card and he would deal it from the bottom of the deck. Think of all the times in the last three years that he has done that. Each time he did he put his political opponents on the defensive and directed attention away from his own crooked machinations."

Kirk sat in silence as Davis's words sunk in. Finally he said, "There is no way Bonsam can attack my record when it comes to introducing legislation that supports minorities. There has to be something else. But what?"

"I wish I knew, A.K."

The two men looked at each other, not knowing what to say next. Davis took a seat in a plush office chair facing the desk, and waited for Kirk to speak. He could sense that Kirk had something to say but was having difficulty saying it. He gave Kirk all the time he needed to collect his thoughts. Minutes later Kirk asked, "Do you really believe the 'urban legends' about Bonsam?"

"A.K., you know I do," said Davis.

Kirk stood up and began rubbing his clasped hands together. "I just cannot fathom the thought that Bonsam, the leader of the free world, has his whacko disciples secretly placed in every corner of the government, willing to do his evil bidding. Yet, for Pete's sake Bobby, the thought of it keeps me awake at night," said Kirk.

"A.K., the rumors have been floating around Washington since the day Bonsam took office," replied Davis. "Remember his followers during the 2008 campaign? They were borderline cult members. They were like the Manson family and Bonsam was Charles." Kirk cringed at that remark.

Davis continued. "Seriously, A.K., I'm not just talking about supporters who went door to door to get out the vote. I'm talking about high level people throughout the federal government and powerful business leaders. It's rumored that he has ties to organized crime. I really believe that Bonsam has the connections and resources to allow his followers to set up hidden cells everywhere. And not just in the government and private companies but in foreign nations as well. Rumors persist that they are just waiting for their marching orders from Bonsam. Heaven only knows what havoc they would wreak if Bonsam turned them loose."

Kirk paused for several seconds. He had been in the Senate for years and found it hard to comprehend that this could be going on right under everyone's noses and not be detected. Still, he had an ominous feeling about Bonsam and the things he was willing and capable of doing to stay in power. Finally he replied, "Ok, thanks," and headed toward the door

As Kirk walked past Davis, Davis said, "Do you believe it?"

Kirk paused when he reached the door, then slowly turned and looked back over his shoulder at Davis and said, "Yeah, I do."

Chapter 8

President Bonsam got up from his desk in the Oval Office and stretched his arms high in the air as he let out a long, loud yawn. He walked over to the couch where Vice President Michael Holden was sitting and plopped down beside him.

"I want to thank you for all your hard work over the last few days, Mike," he said. "You campaigned hard and you did it with class. Together we have ensured ourselves certain victory in tomorrow's primaries, and we will continue to be victorious all the way to the nomination."

Holden looked at Bonsam. *What planet is he on? We are behind in almost every poll!* "You're welcome, Mr. President."

"I know what you are thinking," Bonsam continued, "that we are behind in the polls."

The hair on the back of Holden's neck stood up. *That was creepy.*

Bonsam's voice deepened. "But my people will not let me down. My people know that I alone am the chosen one to lead this nation. They will rise up tomorrow, and see that I remain the one true leader of the United States."

Holden could not believe what he was hearing. *My people? Chosen one?* He decided that now would be a good time to leave the office. "Yes, sir. Is there anything else you need before I go?" he asked.

"No, Mike," Bonsam replied. "Go get some rest. Tomorrow is going to be a momentous day."

Holden did not like the sound of that. He got up and exited the office as quickly as he could. Once Holden had closed the door, Bonsam smiled and said, "Tomorrow will be very momentous indeed."

Chapter 9

The Super Tuesday results were in. President Bonsam had a few insignificant wins, but the day belonged to Senator Alexander Kirk. It was still mathematically possible for Bonsam to win the primaries, but he would need a miracle.

In Governor Clark's view, President Bonsam's demise was inevitable. Bonsam had to be the biggest idiot ever to hold the presidency. He bungled everything he touched. The economy, the war, even the fiasco surrounding his selection of personal friends to be federal district judges was just too stupid to be believed.

Clark also found Bonsam extremely weak. He repeatedly capitulated to the whims of every world leader he met. Clark hated that. Not once did he take a strong stand against any anti-American world leader. China, North Korea, and Venezuela all got a free pass and it got worse and worse as his term wore on. The *coup de grâce* was when Iran lobbed a few Fateh-110 missiles into Tel Aviv.

Bonsam's initial reaction was a pathetic display of his weakness. He was touring an automobile plant and shaking hands with the union workers when some hack from MSNBC shoved a microphone in his face and announced that Iran had just attacked Israel. His deer-in-the-headlights expression, followed by three consecutive "umms" and a "daherr," was seen on televisions around the world about, oh, a billion times over the next two or three days.

President Bonsam pontificated about doing something while doing absolutely nothing. Heaven forbid that he do anything that might upset the Iranians. He simply looked the other way, leaving Israel to fight it out alone. What little manhood he still possessed was sliced away as Israel pounded the Iranians into an unconditional surrender, while the members of his administration curled up into the fetal position and wet themselves. To Clark, that was the final nail in the coffin of his failed presidency.

"Well, there it is, Bonsam is finished," Clark said to Brett Mason as they stood in Clark's campaign headquarters watching the final results roll in on CNN. Clark turned to his secretary and said, "Thanks for working late tonight, Emily. You can have Friday off if you'd like, give yourself a nice three-day weekend."

"I had already planned on it," Emily replied with a smile.

Emily Kates had been a part of Clark's team for the last eight years. She was cute, perky, and had a bubbly personality. She was a petite young woman, who had curly dishwater blonde hair and a tiny cluster of freckles on her nose. She had lived in Saginaw County all her life and had received an administrative assistant degree from Delta Community College. As she was completing her studies, she became old enough to vote and took an interest in politics. At that time she found that she shared many of the same political ideals and values of Congressman Sam Clark, so she volunteered to work on one of his reelection campaigns.

The head of Congressman Clark's Saginaw campaign office was blown away by Emily's skills and professionalism. He was a good friend of Clark's, and he told Clark that he had to meet her when he campaigned in Saginaw. Clark took a liking to her right away. He was impressed by her administrative skills, and he liked her wit and her spunk. He offered her a job on his congressional staff, which she excitedly accepted. Years later when Clark became governor, he made Emily his top administrative assistant.

"Good night, Governor," said Emily as she headed toward the door.

"Good night, Emily," he replied.

Clark and Mason returned their attention to CNN. Reporters around the country were being shown interviewing voters as they left the polling places. The overwhelming majority of the interviews showed enthusiastic support and praise for Senator Kirk.

"Looks like I'll be running against the good senator from South Carolina," Clark said contentedly.

"Well hallelujah for that," Mason replied. "Really, Gov, it would be a cakewalk to win the presidency if you ran against Bonsam, but it is better for everyone, and I mean everyone, now that Senator Kirk has won the primaries and Bonsam is history. Balance has returned to the force."

"Thanks for your input Obi-Wan," Clark replied sarcastically. "Now go get your lightsaber and start preparing for our press conference tomorrow. Everyone will want to know our reaction to Kirk's victory."

"Let me rephrase that, Gov; our reaction to Bonsam's defeat," Mason replied. He pointed to the television and said, "Check it out."

Three men wearing black leather jackets and black berets were shown scuffling with a team of security guards outside a polling place in Cleveland. The reporter at the scene of the disturbance described the chaos and stated that the air was filled with tension. The cameraman zoomed in on the apparent leader of the trio, who was shouting, "Don't be a traitor! Don't vote for Kirk!"

Chapter 10

The media had swarmed to Reagan National Airport the morning after Super Tuesday. They all wanted to speak to Senator Alexander Kirk now that he was the heir apparent to the Democratic Party throne. Kirk was due to arrive at any minute and the reporters were bustling with anticipation.

The White House had issued a press release that morning as well that stated that President Bonsam was happy with the results of yesterday's primaries and that he looked forward to the primaries to come. It also stated that for personal reasons, the president would not be speaking to the media until tomorrow. Everyone just assumed that Bonsam needed the time to lick his wounds and regroup after yesterday's blowout.

Senator Kirk, however, was riding high. Super Tuesday was in the books and he was now ready to sprint to the party nomination finish line. As Kirk's limo pulled onto the tarmac and headed toward his Learjet, the crowd awaiting him pushed forward, but the security personnel on duty held the excited supporters safely behind the barrier ropes.

Cheers rang out as Kirk exited his vehicle and made his way to the jet. So many reporters shouted so many questions at once that it was impossible to make any sense of it. Kirk laughed at the spectacle as he stopped and motioned to the crowd to quiet down. A moment later he took a megaphone from an aide and said, "Thank you! Thank you all. Last night's victories are yet again a clear signal that America is looking for a new direction. I promise to keep on fighting for you all the way to the nomination!"

He was going to say more, but the cheers from the crowd were loud and continuous. Kirk handed the megaphone back to the aide who patted him on the back and smiled. Kirk climbed the few stairs of the Learjet, stopping at the top to turn and give the media and the cheering crowd a final wave before heading off to South Carolina.

As he entered the cabin he gave a big smile to his entourage. They had worked so hard for him. "I am very, very proud of you all," he said as he made his way to his seat.

His steward handed him a cold bottle of water as he made himself comfortable. He glanced over at his PR advisor, Celia Young, who was talking away on her cell phone. Celia was one of the best in her business and she had worked around the clock during Kirk's campaign. She looked over and saw Kirk looking at her. She said, "Hold on," into her phone, and extended her arm offering the phone to Kirk.

"Not now, Celia," he said as he stretched out his legs.

"Sir, you're going to want to take this call," she replied. Her smile let him know that this was no ordinary phone call.

He took the phone from her and returned the smile. "Senator Kirk," he said.

"Senator, Sam Clark here."

"Why you dirty rotten leg! This call comes as quite a surprise!" Kirk laughed out loud. He was not at all expecting to receive a call from his old war buddy Sam Clark. For a moment he felt bad that he had called Clark a "leg," a derogatory term for Infantry soldiers who are not Airborne qualified, but the feeling quickly passed. He was about to say more, but was temporarily distracted by the steward who was motioning to him to fasten his seatbelt.

Nearby on the tarmac, three men sat in an aircraft refueling tanker truck watching as Kirk's plane taxied by on its way to the end of the runway. They wore the uniforms of airplane refuelers, uniforms they had stolen a week before. The man in the middle turned to the driver and said, "There he is, Jorge."

"*Vaya con Dios*, Senator," whispered Jorge, and he and his two partners snickered.

Chapter 11

"Congratulations on the big win, A.K. I've got to hand it to you, your campaign has been superb," said Clark.

"Thanks, Sam. That means a lot coming from you. You know a large part of my success came from the ideas I borrowed from your gubernatorial campaign in '08," Kirk replied, placing special emphasis on the word 'borrowed.'

"Yeah, about that..." said Clark, as both he and Kirk laughed.

"No, seriously, Sam, there is no one in the government I respect more than you."

"The feeling is mutual, my friend. Remember, I owe you my life."

"Did you ever think while we were fighting our way through the jungles of Vietnam that someday we'd be running against each other for the Presidency?"

"No way, I was just thinking about staying alive."

"Yeah, I know what you mean." Kirk said with a smile. Then he switched gears and said, "Sam, the country has never been in worse shape. This election will be the most important election in a hundred years. The American people have been through so much hardship. We owe them the opportunity to regain respect for the presidency."

Clark agreed. "You're absolutely right. I give you my word A.K., there will be no mudslinging during my campaign."

"I already knew that," said Kirk. "Rest assured there will be no dirty tricks coming out of my campaign, either."

Kirk's plane was now number one for takeoff. The engines whined as the pilot hit the throttle, and the plane sped down the runway. As the plane approached the end of the runway the pilot pulled back on the yoke and the plane climbed into the morning sky.

"We're taking off, Sam," said Kirk. "Thanks again for the call. I'll see you in..." Alexander Kirk, U.S. Senator and presidential hopeful, didn't get to finish his sentence.

His plane was no more than 100 feet off the ground when it exploded in an enormous ball of flames.

Chapter 12

"I'll see you in…" was the last thing Clark heard before the line went dead. *That was weird, it didn't sound like a lost connection. Too much other noise.*

"Hello? Hello?" said Clark as he fiddled with his phone. *What in the world happened?*

He was about to get up when his secretary unexpectedly burst into the room. "Sir, sir, you've got to see this!" Emily was visibly shaken and her hands trembled as she pointed the remote control toward the television in Clark's office.

"Emily, are you okay?"

"Oh my God, sir, this was on Fox News Live. It just happened," she cried as she flipped the channel to Fox News. She turned and looked at Clark with tears flowing down her cheeks. "They are reporting that Senator Kirk's plane crashed on takeoff."

Clark stared at the television in utter disbelief. *This cannot be happening!* He felt as though the wind had been knocked out of him. As he watched a news clip showing the accident, he felt tears welling up in his eyes. Another clip was shown immediately after the first but this time in slow motion. Clark was stunned. *I was just talking to him!*

"That was not a crash! Look at it! It just exploded. That was not a crash!" yelled Emily as they watched the footage play over and over. Clark walked over to Emily and put his arms around her. She was sobbing terribly, and her hands were still shaking. She buried her head into his chest, still sobbing, "That was not a crash."

Brett Mason had sprinted down the hall and into Clark's office. Together they watched the reports coming in live now from the site of the plane's wreckage. The first reporter on the scene said what everybody already knew, "There is no way anyone could have survived this crash."

Clark was floored. He wanted to speak but no words would come out. Fox replayed the footage again and again of the plane lifting off and then bursting into flames. Mason turned to Clark and said, "That didn't look like an accident to me. My gut feeling tells me someone brought down that plane intentionally."

"Duh!" sobbed Emily as she held her palm toward the television. Clark remained speechless.

Dozens of ambulances and fire trucks were now being shown racing toward the wreckage. Far off in the distance, a tanker truck could be seen heading in the other direction.

Clark was finally able to speak. He said just one word, "Bonsam."

Chapter 13

The death of Senator Alexander Kirk shocked the entire nation. Across the country people were glued to their television sets. There was around-the-clock coverage on every cable news network. Even the broadcast networks cut into regularly scheduled programming to cover the event non-stop. Stories poured in showing people's reaction to the horrible news. Everyone who was anyone in Washington, D.C. was being interviewed about the tragedy surrounding Kirk's death. Baffled experts tried to explain what might have gone wrong in the air.

Governor Sam Clark watched the news reports, still in disbelief. Brett Mason and Emily Kates watched with him. Emily's grief had not let up since yesterday's disaster and every report showing someone devastated by Kirk's death made her cry even more. Even Clark and Mason got choked up while watching the footage of hundreds of citizens converging on Columbia, South Carolina, to lay flowers at the door of Kirk's campaign headquarters.

Much of the coverage was still focusing on the plane crash. National Transportation Safety Board investigators were being shown on the scene. The NTSB spokesman repeatedly reported that the official investigation had just begun and it would take some time to complete. He added that in all his years of experience, crashes of this nature were typically due to mechanical failure, but at this point it was only speculation.

Mechanical failure or not, conspiracy theories abounded throughout the media. They listened to the reports as people described their suspicions that there was foul play involved in the plane crash. "If they determine that the explosion was from a bomb, I can't wait until they find out who was responsible. I hope they string 'em up." Emily said angrily. "I was going to vote for Senator Kirk."

Clark and Mason simultaneously raised their eyebrows and exchanged glances with one another after that remark.

Just then, the coverage of the crash site was interrupted and the scene switched to the station's news desk. The banner across the bottom screen displayed Breaking News in big bold letters. The lead anchor announced, "Ladies and gentlemen, this just in. President Emmanuel Bonsam will be making a statement to the nation regarding the horrible tragedy that claimed the life of Senator Alexander Kirk. We now take you live to the White House Briefing Room."

Clark and Mason glanced at each other again. "This should be interesting," said Mason.

The scene flashed to the Briefing Room. Pete Stratton, the president's Press Secretary was already fielding questions. "At this time we have nothing more to report on the cause of the crash. The National Transportation Safety Board investigators are still sifting through the wreckage, which is strewn across an area over half a mile long. The NTSB spokesman has stated that it will take several weeks to determine the exact cause of an incident of this magnitude."

The pool of reporters simultaneously fired off a barrage of questions so loudly that Stratton could barely be heard over the din. "Ladies and gentlemen, ladies and gentlemen, please hold all further questions," he said. Stratton looked to his right and signaled to someone off screen, then returned his attention to the press corps and said, "Ladies and gentlemen, the President of the United States."

Clark's eyes narrowed as he watched President Bonsam step up to the podium. He frowned as he watched Bonsam stand before the press pool with a smug air of superiority.

"My fellow Americans," he said solemnly. "Yesterday our nation suffered a tragic loss with the death of Senator Alexander Kirk. Our thoughts and prayers go out to his family and the families of the other passengers and crew members who were aboard the ill-fated flight. I am ordering that the flag be lowered to half-staff for the next ten days in memory of Senator Kirk." Bonsam then paused and bowed his head.

Clark was shocked. Bonsam came across as sincere in both his voice and mannerisms, and he kept the message brief and to the point. Even Mason noticed and said, "Wow, that wasn't half bad."

Bonsam raised his head and continued. "Senator Kirk was the longest serving member of the United States Senate and a close personal friend of mine."

"Uh-oh, here it comes," said Mason under his breath.

"I assure you, his death will not be in vain." Bonsam's demeanor slowly changed, and his voice became deeper and louder. "I, as your president, will continue to boldly lead this nation into a glorious, prosperous future!"

Clark stared at the television as he watched Bonsam arrogantly babble on about his amazing leadership. He could not believe that the president would take a somber moment such as a tribute to Senator Kirk and turn it into a self-aggrandizing spectacle. "That bastard," he said as he turned and walked away in disgust.

As Clark walked off, Mason said, "Oh by the way Gov, the Secret Service is doubling your detail. They don't want to see another candidate involved in any 'accidents' like Senator Kirk's."

Chapter 14

Jorge Delgado had barely slept since he left Reagan National Airport two days before. He was still so full of adrenalin that he could barely sit still. He always felt a surge of energy after a hit, but the Kirk assassination was the mother of all hits. He was ready to climb the walls. He looked out the windows of the SUV as it made its way through the Maryland countryside. *I need to be calm, I am about to meet with my boss.*

As the miles rolled by, Delgado's mind wandered. He thought about his life as a boy growing up in Oakland. He never knew his father and his mother had raised him alone. Consuelo Delgado spent years working in a factory to provide for her son, a factory that was more like a sweatshop. She was just another lowly *señorita* in the unending rows of illegal Mexican immigrant women who sat at their sewing machines stitching garments fourteen hours a day.

Delgado's life in the barrio was rough, but he was headstrong and he didn't let anyone push him around. He did the gang thing, but he had seen too many of his friends die in gang violence. He knew that staying in a gang was a certain death warrant, and he was smart enough to find a way out. He enlisted in the Navy, and soon thereafter became a member of a Sea Air and Land Team. He excelled as a SEAL and participated in several black operations that were so sensitive that there were no records of the operations' existence.

He smiled as he thought back on the many exhilarating adventures he had had as a SEAL. He was smart, tough, physically fit, and good with a gun or a knife. His specialty was demolitions. He could place an explosive anywhere. "Just ask Senator Kirk," he thought to himself.

He loved being in the Navy; however, there was a dark side. The Navy denied its existence but it was there – racism. There was discrete but persistent discrimination against Hispanic and Black SEALs. His commitment to the Navy had always been tempered by his utter disdain for those, who in spite of their shared passion for defending the nation, believed that they were somehow superior to minorities. Even though it ate away at his soul, Delgado was able to suppress his anger toward the prejudiced dickheads who tried to make his life miserable.

Although Delgado was very adept at keeping his emotions regarding race relations in check, his inability to deal with the inept authority that he sometimes encountered led to his downfall in the military. He was on a covert mission in Afghanistan when a cracker lieutenant gave an order that would have gotten their entire team killed. When Delgado objected, the lieutenant called him a wetback. The lieutenant received a broken jaw and Delgado received a dishonorable discharge.

The discharge had closed the doors on his military career, so Delgado returned to Oakland and soon found himself drawn back into the gang world that he had so desperately hoped to avoid. The drug trade had become very profitable for his old gang and a man with his combat skills was extremely valuable. By the time he was 26, he had taken out so many rival gang members with car bombs that his enemies started taking the bus.

Delgado became notorious in the drug wars and it was that notoriety that caught the attention of a high-ranking official in the DEA by the name of Mario Aguilar. Aguilar was also a member of *Enkhtuyaa* and one of its first members to ally himself with Bonsam. He offered Delgado the opportunity to become a member of the "shadow agency" within the secret brotherhood, and Delgado was all too eager to join. When he was assigned to a rising politician from the slums of East St. Louis, he never imagined that one day he would be the lead shadow agent for the most powerful man in the world.

After passing through a series of security checkpoints, the agent driving the SUV turned onto the final stretch of road leading to Camp David. Soon the SUV parked directly in front of Laurel Lodge. The agents hopped out of the vehicle and led Delgado inside. He was ushered into the main conference room, and there at the center of the conference table sat President Emmanuel Bonsam.

Even though Delgado was a former Oakland gang member and a former Navy SEAL with a number of kills under his belt, he could not explain the feelings of fear that swelled through his mind when in the presence of Emmanuel Bonsam. Bonsam had always intimidated him. As Delgado cautiously entered the conference room, Bonsam powered off the large flat screen television that hung on the wall across from the conference table. Delgado only got a quick glance at the screen before it went dark, and he saw an image of the ancient Maya calendar.

Bonsam motioned Delgado forward. Delgado swallowed hard as he walked toward Bonsam. As he got nearer, he saw that the president was looking down at a newspaper. He stopped in front of Bonsam, who finally looked up and stared, his eyes so devoid of emotion that Delgado's blood ran cold. Just as quickly, Bonsam snapped out of it and his appearance instantly became relaxed. He picked up the paper and turned it around so Delgado could see the front page. The headline read, "Senator Alexander Kirk Killed in Plane Crash."

Bonsam stood and said, "Well done, Jorge. Well done."

Chapter 15

Delgado beamed with pride. "Thank you, Mr. President," he said as he bowed slightly. Bonsam sat back down and motioned to Delgado to have a seat at the table across from him.

"You have done your country a great service. Kirk was a miscreant who posed a great threat to our nation," Bonsam said in a matter-of-fact tone. "He was a piss-ant that needed to be crushed." He leaned in toward the table and said, "We must crush all of my enemies, Jorge."

Delgado stared at Bonsam and nodded affirmatively. He could tell that the president had more plans for his services. Bonsam had a distant look in his eyes now. "I have a vision, Jorge. I see a future where the entire nation praises my name and bows before me."

Suddenly Bonsam snapped his attention back to Delgado. His voice became angry. "But I also have visions of people who are out to stop me. They are evil. They hope to destroy the destiny of this nation. Demons wearing hooded robes come to me in my dreams night after night, haunting me. They need to be stopped, Jorge. We must stop them. We must destroy them!"

Delgado was frozen in fear. He did not know what to say. Bonsam stood up quickly, causing Delgado to jump to attention. Bonsam plopped a folder onto the table in front of Delgado. "This is your next assignment. You are dismissed," said Bonsam as he sat back down.

Delgado hurriedly grabbed the folder as he turned toward the door. He was more than ready to get out of there. The agents were waiting for him outside the door and they quickly escorted him back to the SUV. As he climbed into the vehicle, Delgado glanced down at the folder. Across the cover only three letters were written: KKK.

PART 2
Seven months later

Chapter 16

Clay Jackson scanned the room. Never before had he seen so many illiterate, inbred, tobacco-chewing, banjo-playing, country-fucks in one place. It was as if he had stepped down a rung on the evolutionary ladder. Even though the filth of those present made his skin crawl, he was happy to be here. It had taken some time, but he had finally breached the Militia's inner circle.

The Michigan Militia was a paramilitary organization established years ago by a bunch of paranoid crackpots who feared the Federal Government. Its membership had declined over the years and many people considered the Militia defunct, but splinter groups had emerged. Some of the splinter groups had such close ties to the Ku Klux Klan that the line between Militia and KKK had become severely blurred.

Clay was about to meet Colonel William Seward Lane. He was the leader of the Washtenaw County Chapter of the Michigan Militia, the largest and most renowned militia group in Michigan. His compound was located just outside the city of Ypsilanti on an isolated plot of land on the shores of Ford Lake. It was well guarded and heavily fortified. "Colonel" was a title that Lane had bestowed upon himself, even though he had never served in the military. The colonel was notorious for his hatred of the federal government, and all people who were not white Protestant Americans.

Colonel Lane came into the room and sat across from Clay. "Clayton Jackson," Lane stated as a gruesome smile revealed his tobacco-stained teeth. "Any relation to Stonewall Jackson?"

"Not sure, but I hope so," replied Clay. *I'll bet the Colonel would shit himself if I told him I was actually related to Jesse Jackson.*

Clay was mixed race, with a black mother and a white-trash father. Sadly for him, he resembled his father, light skin and all. Wade Jackson, a whiskey-drinking son of a bitch who could never hold a job, smacked Clay's mother around regularly and often when Clay was a child. A pain shot deep through Clay's heart every time he remembered all the nights of abuse, crying and pleading with his father to stop as he beat the hell out of his mom. Sometimes he would try to pull his father off her, which only got him slapped upside the head. If his dear old dad wasn't beating her, he was screaming every racial slur he knew directly in her face.

Clay's mother Miriam was a saint. She was a shy woman, devout, with the face of an angel. She never left the house. She would sing Clay to sleep at night, even after suffering at the hands of her no good husband. Clay never had the chance to ask her why she married his father. He never understood why she didn't just leave the abusive prick. But the day came when Clay finally realized that *he* was the reason she stayed. All the suffering she endured by staying was so she could to be there to keep him safe.

"Well, welcome boy!" Lane shouted with a hearty laugh.

Boy? I hope he said Roy. Normally a remark like that would have immediately brought he who said it severe and painful knife wounds, but Clay kept his cool. He would have his chance to strangle the life out of this cretin all in good time.

Chapter 17

Sam Clark had been campaigning all day under the clear blue skies of South Florida. He had been shaking hands and kissing babies all across the greater Miami area. Clark loved being on the campaign trail. He was a politician who was truly at home among the citizens of this great country, unlike so many other politicians who only gave lip service when it came to their connection with constituents.

He was happy to be at the final rally of the day. The crowd was buzzing with energy, but Clark knew that at this particular event the excitement of the crowd wasn't due to his presence. The supporters were here to hear the first major campaign speech by Kenna Martineau, Clark's VP running mate.

Congresswoman Kenna Martineau had become the first female Republican Speaker of the House of Representatives back in 2010 following the voter onslaught against incumbent representatives of the Democratic Party. When the Republicans took control of the House, Martineau was the unanimous choice to be their Speaker.

Martineau had broken all kinds of barriers on her way to becoming Speaker of the House. Her fortitude during her years in Congress was admired across the board. Martineau was a staunch conservative who demonstrated that the GOP was no longer just a good old boy network. The Democrats in the House considered her a formidable opponent and secretly credited her mettle while serving as the minority leader as one of the reasons the Democrats got slaughtered in the midterms. As House Speaker, her leadership had been a key to slamming the Bonsam machine into reverse.

Miami Congressman Alberto Ochoa stood at the lectern as the crowd simmered with anticipation. "Ladies and gentlemen, please help me welcome the next Vice President of the Unites States, Kenna Martineau!"

Clark gave Martineau a discrete wink as she strode across the podium to join him and Congressman Ochoa at the lectern. Cheers erupted followed by thunderous applause. Ochoa gave her a brief hug, then she and Clark joined hands and raised them above their heads as they waved to the cheering crowd. Clark felt the enthusiasm emanating from the crowd, which reaffirmed his conviction that Kenna Martineau had been the perfect choice to round out the Republican ticket.

Martineau was born and raised in a French Creole community near Lafayette, Louisiana. She was French-African on her father's side and Spanish-Native American on her mother's. The blend of ethnicities made her a gorgeous woman. She was tall and slender with piercing brown eyes and full black hair that hung past her shoulders. Her caramel complexion was smooth and flawless. Martineau was extremely proud of her multiethnic heritage, and she was known to politely but firmly correct anyone who referred to her as an African-American. She was an American, period.

Martineau was an only child, but she had a large extended family in the area and had plenty of cousins to play with while growing up. She loved the outdoors and spent many days hunting and fishing with her cousins, but her greatest love was books. She was a voracious reader who found interest in almost any topic. Her parents, relatives, and teachers all recognized her intelligence and unlimited potential while she was still very young.

When she was 12 her family moved to New York due to her father's promotion at his company. The raise in salary her father received along with his promotion allowed him to enroll Martineau in a private school that was well respected throughout New York. The school was much more challenging than those in Lafayette, and she met the challenge head on. She excelled in every subject at each grade level, and graduated high school a year early while she was only 17.

Shortly after entering Columbia University's School for International and Public Affairs, Martineau met a classmate named Marc Fortier. He, too, had a French Creole ancestry and the chemistry between them was evident from the start. Fortier shared many of the same goals as Martineau, and showed the same tenacity in achieving those goals. The relationship became passionate just a few weeks after they met, and together they enjoyed a level of love and happiness that very few couples experience. He was her soul mate, she was certain.

Martineau and Fortier married the day after she received her doctorate degree. Martineau had made numerous contacts in her field and had several papers published while at the university, so for professional reasons she chose to keep her maiden name. She began her career with the United Nations as an International Consultant advising new members of the international justice system, as Fortier continued to rise in the ranks of a Political Action Committee devoted to human rights. Fortier was on the fast track and was considering a run for city council, when in an instant his life was snuffed out on the 95th floor of the World Trade Center.

Martineau was devastated by the death of her husband. New York City now held nothing but painful memories for her, so she left the U.N. and moved back to Louisiana where her family welcomed her home. To honor her husband's legacy, she dove straight into a career in politics. Remarkably, she was elected to be the Republican congresswoman from Louisiana's third district less than a year later. Soon after that, she became famous for her courageous actions that saved many lives during the Hurricane Katrina disaster, and her determination in quickly securing government assistance for the rebuilding of homes that had been destroyed.

Martineau had worked with Clark often during their time in the House together. She considered Clark her mentor. Clark admired her spirit and determination and her ability to get the job done. From afar he watched with pride as she spent the last two years whipping the Republican House members into shape so they could stop Bonsam's legislation dead in its tracks.

Martineau took a deep breath as she stepped up to the lectern. She was surprised at calm she felt as the hundreds of Floridians who had come to this rally waited to hear her speech. She gave Clark one last look, then turned to the crowd with a delightful smile on her face. She leaned forward slightly as she prepared to speak into the microphone. "The Bonsam presidency," she said, "is coming to an end. The time for bold new leadership is at hand. So move over Bonsam-Holden, 'cause Clark-Martineau are coming to Washington to restore faith in the government!"

The crowd loved her straightforward message as she continually lambasted the Bonsam administration. Her speech ended to even more thunderous applause. Clark stepped up to join Martineau and they again clasped hands and raised them in the air to the delight of the crowd. "Great speech, Kenna!" Clark yelled as they walked offstage. She gave Clark a wink and high-five. The crowd in the stadium was still cheering wildly. "You're a natural!" he said.

"Whew, that was fun," she said. "But I had no idea that campaigning at this level would be so exhausting."

"Well, that's one of the reasons I chose you as my running mate. Campaigning is tough. Many people can't hang, but I knew you could, Kenna. You have been doing a great job."

"Sam, you know how hesitant I was to accept your offer, but once I did I have never looked back. I have zero regrets. We have the opportunity to turn the country around," she said with a smile.

"I know Kenna, I know! And that is how I knew with complete certainty that you were the ideal choice for VP," said Clark. "Your work in the House as Speaker over the last two years has been phenomenal. I'm sure you have given the president a migraine or two!" Clark laughed and patted Martineau on the back as they walked off the stadium grounds toward the campaign bus.

Chapter 18

In the Oval Office, President Bonsam flipped off his television. "I cannot stand to watch one more minute of that bitch Kenna Martineau singing the praises of Governor Clark," he said to himself. He sat there alone, remembering how miserable she had made things for him after she became the Speaker of the House. She made sure that the Republican House members toed the party line when it came to voting on legislation, which killed over a dozen tax-and-spend programs Bonsam had been trying to ramrod through congress. She had vehemently spoken out against his stand on the second amendment, which caused a gun-restriction bill that he had so proudly brought before congress to get tabled in committee, where it died. That embarrassed Bonsam, and he did not like to be embarrassed. He always had spies watching her, but since she was selected as Clark's VP running mate, he cranked up the surveillance on her several notches. He knew her every move and he knew where she was going to be even before she did.

Bonsam felt his temperature rise, so he got up from his chair and walked around the room. He desperately wanted to avoid yet another bout with the demons that came to him in the visions. "She is starting to get to me," he said. "I have to stop her." He walked to the thermostat on the wall and cranked up the air conditioning to help himself cool down. His mind felt cluttered. As he sat back down at his desk, the clutter in his mind was quickly wiped away and was replaced by absolute clarity. He knew what had to be done.

He picked up his phone and punched in a number. A moment later he heard, "Yes, sir!" in the receiver.

"Jorge, contact your team leader in Manhattan. I have another mission for you," said the president.

Chapter 19

Clay was extremely happy to be leaving Ypsilanti. *Ypsitucky is more like it.* He headed up South Huron Street with his windows down. The air was refreshing, especially after sitting in Colonel Lane's hovel half the night. He pulled his truck into a Speedway gas station to top off the tank for the ride back down I-94 to his apartment.

Clay knew that Jorge Delgado would be interested in hearing the report on his meeting with Lane. Delgado had instructed Clay to contact him as soon as the meeting broke. Clay thought about Delgado for a minute. He couldn't explain it, but something about Delgado had always rubbed him the wrong way. Sure, Delgado was the person who made him a member of the team that would carry out a dream assignment. Still, he never fully trusted Delgado.

Fuck George! Delgado hated it when Clay called him George. He decided he would contact Delgado when he was damned good and ready. He finished filling his tank and screwed the gas cap back into place, then made his way into the store. He paid the old coot behind the counter for the gas, and since he was feeling lucky for finally getting to meet Lane, he bought a Mega Millions lottery ticket.

Clay felt the need to wash the funk off his skin from shaking hands with an untold number of rednecks that evening, so he headed for the restroom. He washed his hands vigorously. He seriously considered checking himself for ticks when he got home. Once he felt that his hands were adequately sanitized, he cupped them together and pulled a big splash of water to his face. He did it again and then looked into the mirror. For a moment he was taken aback when he saw his own reflection.

Clay felt that he looked very different since he got his hair cut in preparation for tonight's meeting. His dark black hair had been shaved close to his head so that only stubble remained. That was Jorge's idea. Delgado said that it made his appearance more convincing because it made him look like a skinhead. "Plus," Delgado added, "you can't go in to meet Colonel Lane looking all nappy." Clay shook his head. *Jorge is such an asshole.*

As he continued looking into the mirror, he felt a strong pang of sorrow deep in the pit of his stomach. He found it hard to look at himself in the mirror sometimes, because he looked just like his father. This always took him back to the painful memories of his childhood.

Suddenly his mind flashed back to one of the typical nights when his father's friends would come over and hang out in the garage, drinking Jack Daniel's and behaving like bullies on a playground. On these nights, his father would always break out his guitar. Wade Jackson, in his own mind, was an equal to the legends of country western music. He often bragged that he was related to Alan Jackson, but once you heard him butcher *It's Five O'clock Somewhere*, it was quite evident that he and Alan were not of the same bloodline.

Clay's hands trembled. He tried to block the memory that came racing into his mind. This one was the worst of all. He could see his father stumbling in from the garage after yet another drinking binge, steaming with anger because his friends had had the nerve to make howling dog noises while he tried to play and sing. Clay remembered the ominous feeling that shook his nerves when he saw the look in his father's eyes that night. Clay, who was just a few weeks past his tenth birthday, immediately felt tremendous fear flush throughout his body. He quickly jumped to his feet and went racing down the hall. He screamed to his mother, hoping to warn her as to what was about to come. He only made it halfway down the hall when his father grabbed his shirt collar and threw him backward. Clay hit his head on the wall and fell to the floor. He was in pain, but he had to warn his mother. He cried out for her, but he knew it was too late.

His enraged father viciously kicked the bedroom door right off the hinges. Clay remembered the look of horror in his mother's eyes. She wasn't looking at his father, though — she was looking at him. Clay saw tears streaking down her cheeks. She looked as if she knew that she would never see him again.

His father grabbed his mother by the hair and dragged her off the bed, kicking her hard in the ribs as she hit the floor. He still had a firm grip on her hair as he pulled her down the hall to the front room. She screamed Clay's name over and over. Clay could still hear it in his mind. He looked back into the mirror, and he hated what he saw. He buried his face in his hands and sobbed.

After a while, Clay pulled himself together and left the restroom. He kept reminding himself that it was his looks that had secured his place on this assignment. He got back into his truck, but paused before he started the engine. As much as he didn't want to, he looked at himself again in the rear-view mirror. God, he hated looking like his father. He always wished he looked more like his Uncle Matthias, the man who raised him after his mother was killed and his father incarcerated.

Chapter 20

Following his mother's death, Clay was placed in the Ypsilanti, Michigan, foster care program. John and Denise Parks, the couple that took him in, were fine Christian people. Mr. Parks was a deacon at St. John the Baptist Catholic Church and Mrs. Parks was a part-time nurse at St. Joseph's Mercy Hospital. They were kind to Clay in every way, but all he could remember of that time was crying himself to sleep every night.

About a month after he had joined his foster family, Mr. Parks told Clay that a man was coming to meet him. He wondered who it was and became frightened, but Mr. Parks assured him it was a person who would help him. That still didn't shake his feelings of fear.

On the day of the meeting, Clay was a bundle of nerves. *Who is this person and why does he want to meet me?* When the doorbell rang, Clay nearly leaped out of his socks. Mr. Parks took him by the hand and led him to the door. Clay could hardly contain his feelings of dread.

Mr. Parks opened the door, and there stood the largest black man he had ever seen. He was a tall, broad, imposing figure. He had steely eyes and a rock-solid expression on his face. His hands were placed on his hips, and he stood there motionless, looking down on Clay.

Clay gasped and stepped back as the man leaned down toward him, but the man's eyes softened. He smiled and gently said, "Hello Clay, I am your Uncle Matthias."

"But, but," Clay stammered, "I don't have any uncles."

"Yes, you do, Clay," Matthias replied. "I am your mother's brother."

"Please come in Mr. Grant," said Mr. Parks. "Let's move to the kitchen, shall we?"

Mr. Parks led Matthias and Clay to the kitchen. Clay was still in shock from the news he had just received and could not think of anything to say. Mrs. Parks poured Matthias a mug of coffee, which he politely accepted. Clay could not take his eyes off Matthias. He had never known that he had any relatives on his mother's side. She had never talked about her family. After thanking Mrs. Parks for the coffee, Matthias told a story that held Clay spellbound.

Matthias Grant was the older brother of Clay's mother. Matthias and Miriam had been born and raised in Jackson, Michigan, only 45 miles away. They were raised in a loving family by wonderful parents. Matthias described Miriam as a girl who was always full of life. Matthias and Miriam were very close and Matthias watched over her in a very protective way. Miriam knew in her heart that as long as Matthias was around, things would be all right, and Matthias always made sure his little sister was kept safe from the lowlife that never stopped trying to get at her.

Matthias took a big swig of his coffee and then paused for a moment. He wanted to remain upbeat as he continued to tell Miriam's story, but her life had its share of problems as well.

Miriam had been born prematurely and she had suffered from mild intellectual disabilities all her life. She was easily confused and had attention deficit problems. She struggled in school year after year, but managed to pass each grade due to the love and support of her teachers and the school system's special education director. Her decision-making abilities were often hindered by her disability, and she frequently had difficulties interacting with others.

Matthias realized that it would do no good to mention Miriam's mental ailments at this point, so he continued on with his story.

Matthias left home and joined the US Marine Corps when Miriam was only 16, and was just completing boot camp at Parris Island when he received a frantic call from his father. Miriam had run away. Miriam had left a note saying she had been very depressed since Matthias had gone off to join the Marines. She felt alone and scared, and no longer felt safe in her neighborhood and school. She concluded her note by saying that she loved her parents dearly, but she could no longer stay in Jackson.

Miriam vanished without a trace. Police searched for weeks but came up empty. Since there was no sign of foul play, they eventually stopped the search. Miriam became nothing more than a sad statistic, another teenage runaway. Her parents were devastated, and Matthias was never able to stop blaming himself for what had happened.

Matthias then told Mr. Parks and Clay about his service in the Marine Corps, and how he had embarked on a career in law enforcement. It was then that he learned of his sister's fate. The murder of Miriam Jackson had been splashed across the headlines of every major paper in Southeastern Michigan. When Matthias saw the name Miriam he feared the worst, and with a little help from his friends in the law enforcement community he sadly discovered that the murdered Miriam Jackson was indeed his long lost sister. Matthias also learned of Miriam's orphaned son, and without hesitation set out to bring Clay into his family. Matthias's wife and children gave him their total support.

Matthias looked at Clay and said, "Clay, you are part of my family and I've come to take you home."

Mr. Parks and Matthias made arrangements so that Clay could have one more day at the Park residence to gather his belongings, and Matthias would pick him up the following afternoon. "See you tomorrow, Clay," said Matthias as he walked to the door.

"See you tomorrow," Clay replied. After a few seconds he added, "Uncle Matthias." Matthias smiled and shook his head up and down, knowing that he had made a connection with his nephew.

At first Clay was nervous about leaving the Parks' home to live with Matthias, but he soon became very excited about the move. He could feel his mother's love in Uncle Matthias. He admired his uncle and was eager to meet the rest of the Grant family, especially his two male cousins. Also, he thought it was funny that he was moving to a town with the same name as his last name...Clay Jackson from Jackson.

Clay never really knew what had happened to his father after his arrest. He asked Uncle Matthias soon after arriving in Jackson, but Matthias simply said that his father had been put in jail and was never coming back. Clay was glad about that.

Unbeknownst to Clay, Wade Jackson just so happened to be residing in Jackson as well, locked up in the state penitentiary. Even more coincidentally, Matthias Grant just so happened to be an officer in the Michigan Department of Corrections. Matthias's career in the prison system had made him a firm believer in the "what goes around comes around" principle. Therefore, he personally arranged to have Wade Jackson placed in the worst cellblock of the prison. It was the cellblock specially reserved for the most uncontrollably violent murderers, rapists, and thieves within the Michigan penal system. It was poetic justice, Matthias thought, that Wade Jackson now spent his days and nights on the receiving end of a brutal sexual relationship with his African-American cellmate, a very large and rather psychotic inmate with a horrific violent streak, who was serving 10-20 for the aggravated assault and attempted murder of a female police officer who had pulled him over for speeding. The police officer was still in a coma.

Clay's cousins turned out to be identical twins that were four years older than Clay. Isaac and Isaiah Grant were big like their father. They were only 14 but they stood nearly six feet tall. They were built like Matthias, strong and solid.

Isaac and Isaiah were the best cousins a boy could have. They looked out for Clay each and every day. One time soon after Clay had arrived at their home in Jackson, a neighborhood punk tried to pick on Clay, making fun of his light skin. Isaiah jacked the punk up against a building wall, holding the punk two feet off the ground with his forearm pressed firmly against his throat. Isaiah had a look in his eyes as if he were criminally insane, and he spit in the punk's face with every other word he said while describing in graphic detail what would happen to him if he ever fucked with Clay again. Word soon got around the 'hood that there would be no messing with the kid with light skin.

Isaac and Isaiah loved Clay like a brother. Even when they went off to Western Michigan University, they always made a point of coming back to Jackson to spend time with him. Isaac and Isaiah were all-state high school football players and each received a four-year free ride to Western, and sometimes they would invite Clay out to Kalamazoo to watch one of their games.

The Grant brothers were brutal. They were fan favorites of the Broncos' football team, notorious for their ferocious tackles and sacks. During the season opener of their junior year, Western took on their conference rivals from Bowling Green State University. They fired up the crowd with their devastating defensive play, and the poor quarterback of the BGSU Falcons ended up spending eight weeks in traction after the brothers blindsided him, one high and one low.

They were good, solid players, but unfortunately the Broncos finished toward the bottom of the Middle Atlantic Conference every year the brothers played. Pro scouts never gave them a second look. So when graduation day arrived and they left WMU with worthless degrees in Psychology, they knew that gainful employment was not in the cards. They realized then and there that it hadn't been such a good idea to let football groupies do all their homework and write all their papers for four consecutive years.

Matthias, who loved his sons dearly, wanted to kill them. Instead, he threatened to take them to the local Marine recruiting office the day after graduation. Isaac and Isaiah, who had no strong desire to spend the next several years in Afghanistan, promised their father that they would find employment and find it soon. Their job hunt took off at a glacial pace, which angered Matthias even more.

One morning shortly thereafter, the twins awoke to find themselves in headlocks that were bordering on chokeholds. Matthias dragged them into the living room and simultaneously sent them airborne and onto the sofa. With his wife at his side, Matthias informed his sons that they were going to attend an upcoming State and Federal Law Enforcement job fair that was coming to his Corrections Department facility. He went on to emphasize that they were going to find jobs before they left, and if they didn't, they could just go ahead and shave their heads and start learning the lyrics to *The Halls of Montezuma.*

With that incentive, Isaac and Isaiah got up at the break of dawn on the morning of the job fair and put on their Sunday best suits. That was probably the first time Isaac and Isaiah had worn ties in a decade. Clay chuckled as he watched Uncle Matthias tie the knots around his own neck before transferring the ties to his sons' necks. Uncle Matthias made sure that he pulled the Windsor knot good and tight against their throats as he reminded them once again in no uncertain terms that they were going to find employment that day. He also told them that Clay was allowed to tag along.

Isaac, Isaiah and Clay arrived at the job fair before the doors opened. Once they were let inside, the twins bolted straight to the recruiting tables while Clay aimlessly wandered through the aisles, ignoring the men at the booths trying to get his attention. He was getting quite a laugh out of watching Isaac and Isaiah going up to each booth, standing there in their pressed shirts and new ties, saying, "Yes sir, yes sir," repeatedly to the recruiters. It sounded as though they were about to recite *Baa, Baa, Black Sheep*, and Clay had to fight back the urge to walk up behind them and say, "Three bags full!"

Clay was looking at some State Police brochures that were sitting on an unattended table, when a well-dressed man approached him. He greeted Clay and shook his hand,

and introduced himself as Special Agent Martinez. Clay looked him over but could not quite figure out what made him so special. He was cool and smooth though, with his jet black hair slicked back and his perfect pronunciation of every word he spoke, but with a thick Spanish accent.

He asked Clay questions about his career goals, but Clay told the man he was only there waiting for his cousins. Special Agent Martinez was professional and polite, and asked Clay to fill out a contact form anyway. Clay had no intention whatsoever of working in law enforcement, but he figured he'd never hear from the man again so he completed the form and left.

After Clay had walked away, Special Agent "Martinez" removed his nametag and tossed it in the trash. Special Agent Delgado was very pleased that he had made contact with one Clayton Jackson with relative ease. Clay was the perfect dupe for an upcoming mission, a mission of supreme importance to the president. Delgado smiled as he left the room, thinking about how much fun it was going to be to use and abuse young Mr. Jackson.

Chapter 21

Kenna Martineau had quickly become an even bigger political sensation and had more than proven her value to the Republican ticket. She had been hitting the talk shows all weekend long and performing in spectacular form. The political pundits wanted to talk to her more than they wanted to talk to Governor Clark, and that was just the way Clark liked it. He could focus full-force on the job at hand, which was now more than just winning the presidential election. He could continue to consult experts and develop a comprehensive game plan for his presidency without being constantly inundated by the media. He had full faith in Martineau to get his message out.

This particular morning, Martineau had just finished wiping the floor with the tenacious crew from *Good Morning America* that had tried in vain to trip her up. She had the crew so flustered with her straight-forward answers and her relentless criticism of President Bonsam's policies that they were reduced to taking long, slow pulls from their coffee cups and straightening out stacks of paper as they looked at one another with the dire hope that someone among them would come up with a way to prevent her from making them look even more foolish. Unfortunately for them, it was way too late for that. Even before the interview had ended, Drudge, Slate and many other political websites pounced mercilessly on the GMA team for letting Speaker Martineau get the best of them.

Martineau left the studio with her entourage and proceeded toward the elevators. As they rounded a hall corner, she stopped to look out a large window. The view of New York from Times Square Studios was impressive, but it brought back the painful memories of her husband's death, which had occurred only a few short miles away.

She stepped into the elevator and let out a deep breath. It was exhausting to fire off criticism against the president with the whole world watching. The elevator doors closed and the lift started descending. Moments later, the elevator came to an abrupt stop, catching its passengers off-guard. Everyone onboard let out a "whoa" and looked around at each other. Seconds later a loud pop was heard followed by a small spray of sparks falling from the ceiling.

The lead Secret Service agent was closest to the door and reacted quickly. He ripped the small metal door of the box containing the emergency phone off its hinges and drove the edge through the crack of the elevator doors, and then he and the other two agents managed to pry the doors apart. They were over halfway down a floor, and the only way out was to climb up.

The sizzling sound of an electrical short could still be heard above them, and the smell of burning wires filled the elevator. The agents pulled Martineau forward and one yelled, "You're first, ma'am," as he and his partner grabbed Martineau by the shins and raised her upward onto the open floor above.

Martineau was momentarily dazed, but she quickly regained her composure. She laid flat on the floor and extended her hand into the elevator and shouted, "Come on!" One by one, she helped pull up her colleagues, who each dropped down beside her and helped her pull the remaining trapped passengers out of the elevator.

Suddenly, Martineau's world slipped into slow motion. She screamed to the three agents still inside the elevator. The lead agent grabbed one of his fellow agents by the waist and hoisted him upward, and Martineau and the two staff members beside her lifted him up to the floor. He immediately pulled the staff members away from the opening and jumped down beside Martineau, throwing his hand down toward the agent that the leader was trying to hoist up next. In less than a second there was another loud pop followed by a much bigger spray of sparks.

Martineau yelled, "No!" but she couldn't stop what was about to come. The agent beside her pulled her away from the opening just as the elevator gave way, plunging the two remaining agents to their deaths. As the sound of a terrible crashing and crunching of metal reached Martineau's ears, she rolled onto her back and cried in sorrow.

Within minutes, a rescue crew arrived on the floor and attentively treated those fortunate enough to escape with their lives. A paramedic wrapped a blanket around Martineau and carefully examined her for injuries and shock. Another paramedic was tending to her assistant, however, as he went through the procedures, his eyes were totally fixated on Kenna Martineau. A minute later he slipped off down the hallway, pulling out a cell phone as he walked. He was not looking forward to this call at all. He punched the speed dial button that took him straight to his boss.

"Yeah?" said the voice on the other end.

"Sir, the mission failed, the target survived," said the shadow agent who was posing as a paramedic.

"Go back and kill her!" screamed Agent Jorge Delgado.

Chapter 22

Clay Jackson found himself at yet another gun show with his militia brethren. He was certain that it was at an event much like this that the hillbilly roles for *Deliverance* were cast. Clay had traveled all the way to Martinsburg, West Virginia, for this event with Lane's top two lieutenants, Spencer Boyd and Bud Kenner. Their collective IQ was only slightly higher than that of your average primate, making them the most intelligent members of the chapter and the natural choice for Lane's assistants, Clay surmised.

The three men wandered the aisles of the auditorium, thumbing AK-47s, Mausers, World War Two vintage M-1 Garnands, and any and every kind of pistol you could name. Kenner had a laundry list of ammo to purchase for Lane, so he and Boyd wandered off to the ammo aisle. Clay decided to stop off at the souvenir stand, where he purchased two "Impeach Bonsam" bumper stickers as gifts for Kenner and Boyd.

Over the last few weeks, he had slowly begun to earn Colonel Lane's trust. That was no small feat, seeing that Lane was the most paranoid person he had ever met. Every vehicle that entered his compound was searched for hidden weapons or explosives, and the drivers were patted down, even if they were active members of the branch. Lane never traveled without bodyguards, and his routes were planned in advance with contingency routes identified should something go wrong.

Clay made his way back to the rifle aisle and saw Kenner and Boyd heading his way, each pulling a hand truck loaded to the top with boxes of ammo. "Looks like y'all found what you were looking for. Oh, and here, these are for you," Clay said as he handed a bumper sticker to each of them.

"Thanks, Clay," said Kenner as he took the sticker. He looked at it and said, "What does 'impeach' mean? Is that some way to kill somebody?" Clay just nodded his head yes.

Boyd tapped on the box on the top of his stack and said, "We did pretty good, but they ain't got no 12-gauge shells."

Clay cringed on the inside. *Ain't-got-no.* Clay found it mentally taxing to be around these gomers. He could feel his ability to hold an intelligent conversation slowly deteriorate with every passing minute he spent with Kenner and Boyd. It was going to be an unadulterated joy to wax them and every other member of Lane's group. This was a dream assignment. *And to think it came from the president himself...*

Clay was just like all the other recruits that Delgado deceived. Delgado lured his recruits with wild tales about covert government operations of national importance that his agency was ordered to carry out, and he could only do that with the help of local spies. Delgado enjoyed telling his recruits that they were on a secret mission for the president. It amplified the perverse thrill he got while disposing of them once their services were no longer needed.

Chapter 23

Agent Delgado was surprised when he received a message from a White House staff member by the name of Craig Dolan, stating that President Bonsam wanted to speak to him. Dolan was merely a low-level presidential aide who worked in the Communications Office in the West Wing, however, he was also the lead shadow agent stationed at the White House and one of President Bonsam's most trusted spies. Delgado and Dolan had come up through the ranks together as agents for Bonsam and had known each other for several years. Dolan, one of the few white agents in Bonsam's spy network, possessed a strong backbone when it came to covert operations and had proven himself time and again. Delgado liked Dolan and considered him a first-rate agent, even though he found Dolan's alternative lifestyle extremely distasteful. Gay or not, Delgado respected Dolan, for he understood what it was like to be lumped into a category of society that the majority of Americans looked down on.

Delgado was still smarting from the ass-chewing he had received from Bonsam a week earlier following the botched hit on Kenna Martineau. Bonsam's outrage had been scathing, and Delgado dreaded the thought of experiencing more of that outrage at tonight's meeting. He once again found himself on the grounds of Camp David, only this time he was being escorted into the Aspen Lodge. He was led into the main sitting room, where he saw President Bonsam sitting in an armchair near the fireplace. Delgado froze. The image of Bonsam sitting beside a roaring fire was strangely unnerving.

Delgado tried to remain calm as he took a seat in the armchair next to Bonsam, but he could feel beads of sweat forming on his forehead. Bonsam was in comfortable clothes, leaning back and looking relaxed. He held a glass of Scotch in one hand, and a cigarette in the other. Bonsam stared into the crackling fireplace. Delgado held his breath as he looked at Bonsam. He was fearful that yet another torrid outburst was about to come.

However President Bonsam spoke calmly. "Jorge, last night a vision came to me while I slept. It was awe inspiring."

Delgado remained speechless. The only sounds came from the popping of the logs in the fireplace as they rapidly burned. Another uncomfortable minute passed before the president spoke again.

"Jorge, this vision brought to me a magnificent plan, a plan that will eliminate any chance that Governor Clark has of stealing the election." For the first time since Delgado arrived Bonsam took his eyes off the fireplace. He looked at Delgado, but Delgado avoided direct eye contact.

"I need your help to bring this plan to fruition, Jorge," Bonsam continued, "but first you will need to make some drastic changes to your mission to eliminate the KKK in Michigan."

Chapter 24

"Hey, Moon Goddess! The oceans are rising, Jupiter has aligned with Mars, cats and dogs are living together! My God, they were right, it's the end of the world as we know it!"

Ixchel Cobán gave her classmate Patrick a blank stare and thought, "Does he really think his stupid remarks about the Maya prophecies are still funny?"

Ixchel was a kind and likable young woman who was normally polite and professional, but when people like Patrick became irritating, she never hesitated to put them in their place. "Shouldn't you be concerned with more pressing matters, Patrick, such as, say, the fact that you haven't gotten laid since your freshman year?"

Patrick's face turned red with embarrassment as everyone in the University of Virginia's archaeology lab let out a collective "Phhffft!"

"Really Patrick, you are starting to exhibit all sorts of homosexual tendencies these days," she said in jest. "You should get some help. Or perhaps, a boyfriend."

"Go back to Guatemala, Moon Goddess!"

Daniel Adan jumped in and sarcastically said, "Whoa, nice comeback, Patrick. You should do stand-up." Daniel was the top grad student on the Ancient Maya Civilization Studies team at the university.

"Don't waste your breath on him, Daniel, he is nothing more than an insignificant annoyance, kind of like a piece of gum stuck to the bottom of your shoe that you just can't get rid of," Ixchel said with a smile, flipping back her long black hair.

Oh God, did I really just flip back my hair? Could I be more obvious? Ixchel had been attracted to Daniel since the first time she saw him lecture on the ancient temple of Chichén Itzá. He had a head of thick black hair, and the strong facial features and deep dark eyes of his Moroccan ancestors. He worked out every day and it showed. More than once Ixchel had caught herself checking out his buff body, but to Ixchel, Daniel was more than just your ordinary hunk. Daniel was the consummate gentleman and treated Ixchel with kindness and respect, which she found quite alluring.

"Really? Because I was thinking he was more along the lines of a mosquito that buzzes in your ear when you're trying to sleep," replied Daniel as he gazed at Ixchel.

For Daniel, the attraction was mutual. Ixchel was a total package, with flawless olive skin, brilliant white teeth, dark sultry eyes, and long, straight, silky black hair. Daniel often found himself imagining holding her voluptuous body in his arms and feeling her luscious breasts pressed against his chest. What made Ixchel even more attractive to Daniel was that she was by far the preeminent undergrad in the entire Anthropology Department. She was a fabulous archaeologist, and her insights into ancient Maya civilizations were unmatched by anyone he had ever encountered.

Ixchel was a direct descendant of the Maya and she felt an inexplicable connection to her Maya heritage. Her ancestors might have been the people who carved the Maya calendar themselves. With all the hoopla surrounding the impending "end of the world" predictions associated with the Maya calendar, she avoided the cosmic nonsense that was running rampant through Hollywood, television, and poorly written novels. There were no comets, no black holes, and no phantom planets on a collision course with Earth. NASA had long ago proven that absolutely nothing was going to happen when the Earth passed through the Milky Way's galactic plane. That event would be about as sensational as Y2K.

Even the calendar's predicted end date of December 21, 2012, was just an arbitrary date that scientists studying Maya archaeology came up with to impress others in the scientific community. They found the Maya calendar to be consistently precise, however, it was the Gregorian calendar that had so many lapses and gaps over the years that it was impossible to synch the two. In reality, no one knew an exact date. The best estimate that scientists had ever developed had the calendar ending some time during a span of over several months before or several months after the twenty-first of December.

She was certain that there would be no world-ending calamity from the stars. For as long as she could remember, she had possessed an indescribable feeling that the prophecy's true meaning was beyond comprehension. She could still remember as a child, intently listening to the stories of the ancient Maya civilization as told by her great-grandmother, Ixazaluoh. Ixazaluoh had lived to be 107. Her stories had nothing to do with cosmic catastrophes. Her stories warned of evil. Ixazaluoh was one of the chosen few who understood that the ancient Maya prophecies foretold of a monstrous evil more powerful than the world had ever seen, an evil that came from the depths of humanity itself.

Chapter 25

The next morning Daniel walked into the lab with a noticeable spring in his step. "What's up, Dan-o?" Ixchel asked, looking up from an impressed sheet of Maya pictographs she was translating.

"I just got some interesting news. Great news. Once-in-a-lifetime news," he said, grinning from ear to ear. He was enjoying teasing her.

"Well? Give it up already," Ixchel said with a mock impatient tone. She scowled, crossed her arms over her chest, and began tapping her foot. She was holding back the urge to flip her hair.

"I was just on the webcam with Professor Sean Jameson. The team conducting the dig at Chacchoben found something old, really, really old. Chacchoben is the site of a well-known Maya temple on the Yucatan Peninsula of Mexico."

She saw in his eyes that this was something big. "What is it?"

"Pack your bags. We're heading to Chacchoben to find out!"

Ixchel and Daniel discussed their plans to travel to Chacchoben, playfully flirting the entire time. Finally, they left the lab. Patrick, who had been standing just inside the lab's equipment storage room the whole time, walked into the lab towards the phone. "Those two lovebirds make me want to puke," he said under his breath as he picked up the receiver.

He paused for a minute, and placed the receiver back on the hook. He needed to think this through carefully before he made the call. All this time watching and waiting had finally paid off. *This phone call is going to bring me a nice chunk of change!* Finally he dialed the number he had been given months ago but had yet to use.

"Yeah," said the voice on the other end.

"Sir, this is Patrick Jones, from the Ancient Maya Studies Department at UVA," he said with a slight gulp. "I have some information that you will find very useful." He went on to recount the conversation he had just overheard. After a long pause, Patrick finally received a reply.

"*Gracias, amigo.*" Click.

Chapter 26

Jorge Delgado raised his eyebrows in surprise as he hung up the phone. It had been several months since he had received any tips about Maya relics, and he certainly hadn't expected a call from that UVA geek Patrick. He had been so busy taking out KKK groups that he had almost forgotten about Bonsam's directive to report the discovery of Maya artifacts. Delgado found the Maya assignment boring. He was never a believer in ancient prophecies, but the president sure was, and if something was important to the president, it was important to him as well.

Delgado plopped his cell phone onto the passenger's seat as he continued heading up I-40 through North Carolina. He was riding high from yesterday's extermination of 11 members of the Aryan Nations who had a compound set up in the backwoods south of Raleigh and he didn't want to be bothered with Maya artifacts at this time. He was having much too much fun killing white supremacists. He smiled as he reminisced about his operations over the last few months. He started out with simple plans, shooting a prominent Klansman here and a notable Klansman there. He even lynched a few in Texas and Florida, which he felt was only fair.

Word spread fast through the Klan community that Klansmen were being killed and others had disappeared under suspicious circumstances. This reduced Klan activity across the country; however, the onesie-twosie killings weren't having quite the impact that Bonsam desired. So Delgado became a little more creative. He started taking out Klansmen *en masse,* such as the time he and his team took the Wizard of the Knights of the KKK and several of his goons and tossed them into a murky pond in the middle of Arkansas, bound and gagged with cinder blocks chained to their feet. He had carried out a few similar operations that removed groups of KKK members from the face of the Earth, but by far his favorite mission was when he orchestrated an air assault attack on the Imperial Klans of America compound in western Kentucky. He and his gang of storm troopers got to blow up several buildings that night, sending dozens of Klansmen straight to their graves.

Delgado was very eager to get to his next mission in Michigan. Few people realized the extent of the Klan infestation in the rural areas of Michigan. Most people thought that the Klan was confined to the southern states, but the KKK was alive and well and thriving up north in the Wolverine State. This mission was unlike any of the others, for this was the one that President Bonsam himself had planned. It was going to go down in history.

When he reached Raleigh, he grudgingly hopped over to I-95 and headed north to Charlottesville. He called Agent Dolan and gave him instructions to meet him in Charlottesville and then briefly went over his plan to pay a short visit to Mr. Patrick Jones. "This better be worth it," he said to himself.

Chapter 27

Long ago, a mysterious man who claimed to be very interested in obtaining Maya artifacts had approached Patrick Jones. The man told him that he was willing to pay great sums of money for quality artifacts, and he asked Patrick if he would be willing to assist. All Patrick had to do was contact the man if any new artifacts were discovered. He told Patrick that if the information led him to valuable artifacts, Patrick would be richly rewarded.

Patrick was well aware that there was a huge black market for Maya artifacts in Mexico and Central America, and this *hombre* looked and sounded like he was from that region. The man would not reveal his name, but he gave Patrick $100 and a card containing a phone number. Patrick took the card and the money, thanked the man and left. "Freaking bandito," Patrick thought as he walked away.

Now it was time to cash in. Patrick left the campus around 7:00 p.m. and drove south into rural Albemarle County. He wound his way down the Thomas Jefferson Parkway, and then turned onto a curvy country road that led to a secluded bluff overlooking the Rivanna River. Patrick parked his car and approached the meeting point with trepidation. He saw that *Señor Bandito* was already there, holding a brief case. *My money!*

Patrick told the man everything he knew about the find. He gave the location of the dig and explained that this particular Maya artifact had to be a significant discovery since the best archaeologist from UVA had been invited to examine the relic.

"Tell me, Mr. Jones," Delgado said while over-exaggerating his Spanish accent, "tell me about this archaeologist of whom you speak?"

"Her name is Ixchel Cobán," Patrick replied. "She's a Guatemalan of Maya descent, and because of that she has brainwashed the entire faculty into believing that she is some kind of archaeology genius. She's the first person they consult whenever an unusual artifact is discovered. Personally, I think she's a big ol' lesbian."

"This is very interesting, Mr. Jones," Delgado said. "I appreciate the work you have done for me." Delgado extended his arm and held the briefcase in front of Patrick. "This is for you," he said.

Patrick smiled. *Mine all mine!* As he reached for the briefcase, he saw a shadow move on the ground before him. That was the last thing he ever saw. Agent Dolan, who had sneaked up behind Patrick as he talked to Delgado, had a good follow-through as he crashed his billy club across the back of Patrick's skull. Patrick's body became slack and hit the ground with a thud.

Delgado looked at the crumpled body at his feet and smiled. He looked up at his friend and said, "Toss him in. Be sure you put lots of his blood on one of the rocks down there."

As Dolan grabbed Patrick's ankles and dragged his unconscious body down to the riverbank, Delgado said aloud, "I'm sure the president will be thrilled when I tell him about this artifact."

Chapter 28

Late the next morning Ixchel and Daniel headed out to the airport. It was a two-hour haul to Dulles International from Charlottesville, but Ixchel didn't mind since it gave her plenty of alone time sitting close to Daniel in the back seat of the airport shuttle. When they first entered the vehicle, she noticed that Daniel seemed to be deep in thought. Once they were on the highway, she turned to him and asked, "What are you thinking about?"

"I have known Professor Jameson for a long time," he replied. "I get a sense that he is somehow agitated by the discovery of this artifact. I can't explain it. The more I think about the webcam conversation we had, the more I realize he seemed nervous or something."

"What do you think could be bothering him?" asked Ixchel.

"I don't know. He's normally a down-to-earth guy, but I know he doesn't write off ancient Maya legends as mere myths. And I think he believes that there is a spiritual connection between the ancient world and the present world. He's been studying archaeology for years and has been on dozens of digs. He lives and breathes Maya culture and history. Daniel paused then said, "Something about this artifact has spooked him." Ixchel took Daniel's hand and squeezed it tightly, and for the rest of the journey they rode in silence.

Once they arrived at their gate, Daniel decided to check back in with the lab to let them know their status. He left Ixchel in the waiting area and stepped away to a more quiet location to place the call. Daniel's long-time friend, Thomas Gordon, answered the phone at the UVA archaeology lab. Daniel and Thomas had met in Archaeology 101 during their freshman year, and the two had been best friends ever since. He gave Thomas the details of their status, and asked him to let Professor Jameson know that they'd soon be wheels up. Thomas was very helpful as always, and promised to pass on the message to the professor.

Daniel's spirits had been lifted as the conversation with Thomas wound down. Thomas was very reliable and that always put Daniel at ease, however his mood quickly changed when, just as he was about to hang up, Thomas asked a question that caught Daniel completely off guard. "Daniel, did you see Patrick today? He never showed up at the lab and no one has been able to find him."

Daniel was so surprised he was unsure of what to say. "Dan, you still there?" asked Thomas.

"Yeah Thomas, I'm still here," he replied. "Did you try to reach him by phone?"

"We've been calling him all morning," said Thomas. "He's not answering his cell and his voice mailbox is full. One of the undergrads just left to go see if he is at his apartment."

Daniel paused. "I'm sure Patrick has a good explanation," he said with uncertainly. "Let me know when you get in touch with him."

"Will do," replied Thomas. "Have a safe trip. Talk to you later."

"Later," replied Daniel and he hung up his phone.

Daniel walked slowly as he returned to the waiting area outside their gate. As he approached, Ixchel could sense that something was wrong. "Is everything okay, Daniel?" she asked.

Daniel sat down and Ixchel joined him. Daniel still felt uneasy as he told Ixchel about the conversation with Thomas. "Say what you will about Patrick, at least he's dependable when it comes to covering his shifts at the lab," said Daniel. "And he's never missed a class since I met him, as far as I know."

Ixchel was worried, too. *Patrick didn't show up at the lab?* The more she thought about it the more it bothered her. Something about this just didn't feel right. She couldn't explain why, but she sensed danger. A chill ran down her spine, and from out of nowhere, in the back of her mind she heard a voice softly cry out, "I am here."

Later that same evening, Agent Delgado received a call from President Bonsam. He had been waiting for this call for hours, cleaning his favorite pistol to calm his nerves. He was anxious to hear what the president would have to say about his latest report.

"Jorge, I found your report about the discovery of the Maya artifact most intriguing," the president said. "I need you to find out everything you can about this artifact. Place one of your agents as a mole at the excavation site, or recruit someone that is already at the site to feed you information. Let me know immediately if there are any further developments or any more artifacts discovered. "

"Yes, sir. I will."

"Oh and Jorge, find out everything you can about this Ixchel Cobán," Bonsam added, and as his thoughts of Ixchel intensified, the image of the Maya calendar appeared in his mind. "I may want to meet with her someday."

Bonsam hung up before Delgado had a chance to reply, but he continued speaking. "Perhaps she can provide the answers to the questions that plague my soul."

Chapter 29

Professor Sean Jameson was busily supervising the archaeological studies students under his tutelage at the excavation site near the Chacchoben ruins. Since the recent discovery of the ancient Maya artifact, his students were filled with excitement and working harder than they had ever worked before. Jameson didn't want anyone passing out under the hot Mexican sun. "Slow down, drink some water," he called out as he walked toward the students. "These ruins have been here thousands of years, no need to be in such a big hurry."

The students laughed out loud. They loved working for Professor Jameson. He was an expert in the Maya prophecies and serious about his studies, but he was also a kind, grandfatherly figure and a pleasure to work with. He was a portly man who had a snow-white beard that he kept neatly trimmed. His hair was silky white as well but there was very little on top, so most of the time while he was at the excavation site he wore his trusty pith helmet, which made him look like he was on an African safari preparing to go big-game hunting. He wore a bandana around his neck that gave him a rugged look, but he also wore round wire rimmed glasses that gave him a scholarly look.

"There's nothing to see here, please keep moving," said one of the students as he imitated a police officer at a crime scene. "Keep moving," he said again, waving a small shovel at Professor Jameson like he was managing crowd control.

"Very funny, Jesse," laughed Jameson. "Don't forget who has the ticket for your return flight. Keep that up and you'll find yourself with a long walk home." Jesse Wilson was the unofficial student leader of the dig. He was Jameson's prized student, a young man filled with intellectual curiosity and a born leader. His classmates all looked up to him, even if he was the class clown.

"Hey Professor, looks like we got some company," Jesse said as he pointed his spade toward their main camp.

Jameson turned around and saw a dusty truck bouncing down the rough dirt road that led to their camp. He smiled and said, "Excellent!"

Moments later Jameson was standing next to the truck with his two visitors. "Daniel, it is great to see you again, my friend!" he said as he vigorously shook Daniel's hand. He turned to Ixchel and said, "And Ms. Cobán, what a pleasure it is to finally meet you. Come in, come in," he said as he motioned toward the door of the dig-site cabin where the artifact was being stored.

Once they were inside Jameson said, "Make yourselves comfortable, as comfortable as you can in these conditions," he chuckled. "There is bottled water in that cooler, help yourselves."

Jameson spun the dial on his safe as Daniel and Ixchel retrieved some water. Once Jameson had the artifact and Daniel and Ixchel had their water, the three met at the table in the center of the room. The relic that Jameson brought to the table was wrapped in cloth. As he removed the cloth, he revealed a stone tablet covered with ancient Maya symbols carved into the surface. Daniel and Ixchel were amazed by what they saw.

"I studied the typology of this tablet and have reason to believe that it is over 5,000 years old," said Jameson. "That's as old as the Maya Calendar, maybe even older. I wanted your team to look at it because it is well known that the lovely Ms. Cobán here is the best when it comes to deciphering the symbols on Maya relics." Jameson gave Ixchel a wink, which caused her to blush. His tone became more serious as he looked at Daniel and said, "And I have never seen symbols such as these."

Jameson slowly removed the cloth that was wrapped around the tablet. The instant Ixchel saw the tablet in its entirety, there was a burst of white light before her eyes. She became lightheaded, as the world around her seemed to go into a spin. She gasped as she reached for the table to steady herself.

Daniel quickly grabbed her by the shoulders and held her up. "Ixchel, are you all right?" He looked her in the eyes, but it was as if they had rolled back into her head. "Ixchel!" Daniel gently shook her shoulders.

Ixchel could barely see Daniel through her blurred vision and the sound of his voice was muffled and distant. In her mind she again heard a soft voice call out, "I am here." She looked down at the tablet again and suddenly felt as though a blast of wind blew right through her. She was shaking as her world returned to normal, and she found herself breathing heavily as she looked into Daniel's eyes.

Professor Jameson looked on in surprise. Daniel once again asked, "Are you all right?"

Ixchel was still shaken, but she tried to laugh it off. "Whoa, I'm sorry about that. I think this heat is getting to me," she said as she fanned her face with her hand.

Jameson was shocked by what he had just witnessed, but he also tried to laugh it off. "Yes and I'm sure the jet lag is catching up to you, too. It happened to all of us when we first arrived," he said. He had been feeling strange ever since the discovery of the tablet and now Ixchel had experienced an obvious reaction to it as well. He started to feel uneasy again.

Daniel had been shocked as well and still looked at Ixchel with concern. Ixchel could tell he was worried about her. "I'm fine, really, I'm fine now," she said. "Let's take a look at that tablet, that's what we're here for, right?"

The tablet was indeed worth the trip. Neither Ixchel nor Daniel had ever seen anything like it. Jameson gave a full account of its discovery, and concluded by saying, "Unfortunately, it looks as though a piece of the tablet has been broken off at the bottom. Or maybe this edge is the top. I'm not sure." He pointed to the jagged edge of the relic. "But my team is continuing the dig and we hope to find the missing piece soon."

Ixchel studied the tablet closely with a magnifying glass. "The markings along the left and right sides are minor symbols found on the Maya calendar, indicating that the two may somehow be related," she said.

She was intrigued by what she saw. "Look at these four symbols running down the center. Most Maya symbols were carved to keep a historical record of people and events." She pointed at the symbols on the tablet, starting from the top and moving her hand downward. "But this layout suggests that together they form an announcement of some kind."

"What do you mean?" asked Daniel.

"The Maya were strong believers in omens, and there have been several findings of artifacts whose symbols were prognostic in nature."

Jameson shook his head as he listened to Ixchel. "What do you make of these symbols?"

"The first two symbols contain markings that seem to indicate some kind of fire."

"Fire," said Jameson. He was staring at the tablet intently. Daniel looked up at him and noticed his brow was furrowed.

"I can't be certain without further research, but the first symbol appears to represent sky-fire. I know there are similar Maya symbols used in ancient carvings to illustrate comets and meteor showers." As she said this, Jameson moved his face closer to the tablet. "I think I have some of those in my database," Ixchel said as she pointed to her flash drive sitting on the table, "I'll look for them tonight."

"Yes, please do," replied Jameson, never taking his eyes off the tablet.

"The second symbol is definitely the symbol for a temple. This symbol appears in carvings within many of the ancient Maya temples themselves," Ixchel said. She paused for a moment and added, "But I don't get the connection between temple and fire."

Jameson's eyes were fixed on the tablet. "Please continue, Ms. Cobán," he said quietly. Ixchel and Daniel exchanged glances. Daniel had never seen Professor Jameson this serious before.

"I have no idea what the third symbol represents," she said as she held the magnifying glass over the symbol. It was basically just a circle. "But by its nature it appears to suggest something large, extremely large. I know of several other Maya symbols that were used to indicate size. I'm pretty sure I don't have any images of those on my flash drive, but when I get back to UVA I'll go through our main database and examine the images closely to see if I can determine any similarities with this symbol."

She then took a long close look at the fourth symbol. Something about it was eerie to Ixchel. "I have never seen anything in Maya carvings that remotely resembles the fourth figure," she said hesitantly. The symbol was indeed unusual. It was a wide, flat oval shape, with two arched lines protruding from the top of the oval. The lines were mirror images of each other.

Ixchel and Daniel stood up straight but Jameson continued to lean over the tablet, his eyes running up and down the symbols. Finally Daniel asked, "What do you think, Professor?"

Jameson slowly stood up straight. "I have spent my entire life studying the ancient Maya civilization," he said, "and I am convinced that Ms. Cobán has done a superb job of deciphering the symbols thus far. However, she did make one mistake."

"What was that?" asked Daniel.

Jameson looked directly into Ixchel's eyes and said, "The tablet does not contain an announcement. It contains a warning."

Chapter 30

Jameson removed his glasses and wiped his eyes. "I think I'll get some fresh air," he said as he slowly made his way toward the cabin door.

"I'm going with him," Daniel whispered to Ixchel.

Once Jameson and Daniel had left, Ixchel picked up the magnifying glass and reexamined the fourth symbol. The longer she looked at it, the more confused she felt. She was certain that she had never seen the symbol before in any Maya carvings, but somehow it was familiar to her nonetheless. Somewhere deep in her mind she knew she had seen it before. She ran her fingertips lightly over the symbol, and a rush of wind once again shook her entire body. She quickly removed her fingertips from the tablet and headed toward the door.

Just then Daniel opened the door and reentered the cabin. Ixchel stopped in her tracks. "Is everything okay with the professor?" she asked.

"I don't know, I've never seen him act like this before," Daniel replied. "Anyway, he said he was going back to his tent to get some rest. He told me to put the tablet back in the safe and spin the dial. How are you doing?"

Ixchel lowered her eyes and said, "I'm okay, it's just been a long day."

"Speaking of long days, I totally forgot to touch base with the lab. I told Thomas yesterday that we would report back via webcam once we made contact with Professor Jameson."

Daniel sat down at Jameson's computer and logged into UVA's network. As he waited for the network to connect, Ixchel came and sat beside him. She smiled as he reached over and playfully patted her on the shoulder.

When the connection went through, Daniel saw that Thomas was still online. He sent Thomas an invitation to join him on the webcam, and Thomas immediately accepted. When his image came up, Daniel quickly saw that something was wrong. Thomas was one of those guys who are always smiling, however now it was obvious that he was quite upset. Before Daniel could even say hello, Thomas cut him off. "Dan, you're not going to believe this. The police just found Patrick." Thomas paused then said, "Face down in the Rivanna River. He's been murdered."

Chapter 31

Clay lay in bed and went through the next phase of the plan over and over in his mind. Soon he would get his vengeance on the band of degenerate swine who shared his father's hostile prejudices, prejudices that caused his mother's suffering and ultimately her death. Clay hated those militia jerk-offs, and he was sickened knowing that his own father had been one of them. As he stared toward the ceiling in the darkness of his bedroom, his memories slowly wandered back to the day when he learned of his father's involvement in the KKK.

Clay went through the school of hard knocks while growing up in Jackson. He was clever and cunning, and he quickly learned how to protect himself in a hostile urban community. He always carried a knife and he knew how to use it. Another skill he acquired along the way was the ability to pick locks. There were very few he could not pick. He loved to pop locks of every type, just to see if he could do it.

He could get into just about any car made in less than five seconds, but he never stole a car for money. Sure he went on a joyride or two, but he always returned the car to where he found it and the owner probably never even knew the car had been moved.

One day when he was just 16, he found himself home alone and very bored. For want of anything better to do, he decided to poke around Uncle Matthias's room. This was a cardinal sin, he knew, but Matthias was out of town and he was just going to take a look around out of curiosity's sake.

He popped the bedroom door lock with ease. Matthias kept his room Marine-quality organized. Clay briefly looked through the closet and then moved on to the dresser. The bottom drawer had a lock on it, and he picked it as well. Inside the drawer he found pictures from Matthias's

Marine days, military service medals and plaques, and even a box of bullets.

There was also a box, plain and simple with no markings. He paused for a minute to examine it. Finally he opened it and immediately tears came to his eyes, for it contained photographs of his mother. For the first time in his life he saw pictures of his mother when she was just a girl. She had a big bright smile in every picture. He laughed and cried simultaneously as he looked at picture after picture of his mother enjoying life with her mother, father and Uncle Matthias.

Clay set the pictures aside to see what else was in the box. There were several newspaper clippings about his mother's murder. He looked at the headlines but he didn't read the articles. He didn't have to, he had been there when it happened.

He set the clippings next to the pictures and saw one last item in the box. It appeared to be a notebook of some kind. He lifted it out of the box and turned it over. He nearly lost his breath when he saw what was written on the cover. In big black letters was written, "Wade's Journal."

He slowly opened it and was immediately disgusted by what he had discovered. He skimmed through the pages and saw entries written by his father that told of his hatred of blacks, his love of the KKK, and his involvement in the Michigan Militia.

His disgust turned to outrage as he read further. His father described how he always felt like a loser when it came to women, and how he came to resent them deeply. Clay felt a wave of nausea run through his stomach as he saw his mother's name for the first time. He squeezed his eyes tightly hoping he could make it go away, but he knew he had to look. There only a few short entries involving his mother, but Clay read enough to fully understand just how sadistically his father had treated her.

His father had found his mother hitchhiking along a long stretch of open highway east of Jackson, and he offered her a ride. She was tired, cold, hungry and thankful for the chance to rest her legs and warm her hands. At last, his father wrote, he could finally take out the frustration and anger he held against women on this poor little runaway he had lured to his home. His next few entries described how he essentially held her in captivity, and violently raped her repeatedly. They were never even married. To his father, Clay's mother was nothing more than his slave.

Clay breathed deeply as he rolled to his side to look out his bedroom window. He thought about how ironic it was to be discovered by Delgado and recruited to be on a mission that would give him the perfect chance to exact his revenge. Little did he know that Jorge Delgado had not "discovered" him, Delgado had been studying him for a long, long time.

Chapter 32

Daniel and Ixchel stayed up late into the night talking about Patrick's death. They were in a state of disbelief. Patrick wasn't the most likeable guy in the world, but neither Daniel nor Ixchel could imagine why anyone would want to kill him.

"The police told Thomas that whoever did it tried to make it look like an accident, but they are convinced it was murder," said Daniel grievously. "I feel so bad. I was never very nice to him. Now he's gone."

Ixchel was feeling the exact same way. Patrick could be irritating at times, but for the most part he was a pretty decent guy. She recalled how she felt a deep sense of foreboding when she first heard of Patrick's disappearance yesterday. Then her thoughts turned to the strange feelings she had had when she first saw the Maya tablet today. These incidents were totally unrelated, but somehow the strange feelings she felt both times seemed to be interwoven in some mysterious way. She stared off into space. *What is the matter with me?*

Daniel stood up and said, "I'm going to hit the sack."

Ixchel snapped out of her daydream. "I can't sleep," she said. "I'm going to look through my databases to see if I can find anything about sky-fire."

"Okay, but don't stay up too late," Daniel said. "Good night, Ixchel."

"Good night, Daniel," she replied. Their eyes met for a moment, and they both smiled.

Once Daniel was gone Ixchel plugged her flash drive into Professor Jameson's computer and uploaded everything she had on Maya symbols. Next she ran a search through all her databases looking for Maya symbols related to sky-fire. She found several symbols that were vaguely similar, but the sky-fire symbol on the tablet had a quality of uniqueness about it.

She sat there staring at the screen, trying to decide what to do next. Finally she did what any serious scientist does in times of doubt; she turned to Google. She googled SKY + FIRE and briefly glanced through the list as it popped up, but then went straight to images. The first several images showed pictures of Senator Alexander Kirk's plane as it exploded back in February. *This does me no good.*

She was about to scroll down the page to see if there was anything relating to Maya relics, when she became mesmerized by one of the pictures of the plane explosion. She could not take her eyes off it. She downloaded the image, then used the zoom feature to examine it in more detail. After two or three clicks, all that was left showing was the ball of flames. Ixchel's mouth fell open and she gasped. Hidden within the picture of the flames was the exact image of the tablet's sky-fire symbol.

Every time she looked at photos of Kirk's plane exploding, she saw the sky-fire symbol. She pulled up video footage on YouTube, and again she saw the symbol within the flames as the videos played. She could not think of any sane reason to explain why this was happening, yet now she could not escape the feeling that the symbol and the explosion were connected. *This is crazy.*

She continued to flip through picture after picture of Kirk's plane exploding and every time she saw the sky-fire symbol buried within the flames. She racked her brain to come up with an explanation as to why an ancient Maya symbol could be connected to a modern day tragedy, but she came up blank.

Unexpectedly, Daniel entered the cabin, so Ixchel quickly closed the Google window. "I can't sleep," he said.

"Are you doing okay?" Ixchel asked.

Daniel wiped his hand over his mouth and replied, "Yeah, I'm ok." He was still distraught over Patrick's death, but he didn't feel like talking about it. He looked at the computer and said, "Did you find anything?"

"No, nothing yet," she replied. "I'll need to do more thorough research when we get back to UVA." The mention of UVA reminded them both of Patrick, and they sat in silence for several minutes.

"Well, since neither of us can sleep, why don't we start preparing for the trip back to Charlottesville," said Daniel. "We need to be sure that we have copies of all of Professor Jameson's information on the tablet and that we take plenty of pictures of it before we leave."

"Good idea," Ixchel replied. She paused several seconds, then looked at Daniel and said, "Dan, this is completely off the subject, but what do you know about the plane crash that killed Senator Alexander Kirk?"

Daniel took in a deep breath and let it out slowly. "Well, one thing I know is that many people believe that President Bonsam had something to do with it."

As Ixchel heard those words, foreboding images stormed into her mind. *Kirk, sky-fire, Bonsam.* She could not comprehend their relationship, yet still she sensed an ominous connection. As the images faded away, she once again heard a soft voice call out in her mind, "I am here."

Chapter 33

Tonight would be the beginning of the end for Colonel Lane. Clay would see to that. The time spent with Lane and his ilk taught him well about the ways of the militia. He now knew the best way to get their undivided attention. Weapons. Lots and lots of weapons.

The overarching belief of Lane and his followers was that the best way to stop a tyrannical government from taking over their God-given white-American way of life was to arm the nation's citizens and arm them well.

Clay backed his car alongside Lane's, put it in park, and switched off the engine. Lane slowly walked over with Kenner and Boyd in tow. Clay could sense Kenner and Boyd's excitement. They could hardly contain themselves as they peered over Lane's shoulders. Lane, on the other hand was smooth as ice. "You got them, Clay?" he asked.

"Right here," Clay replied as he moved toward the trunk. He took his time sliding the key into the lock. He was playing this to the hilt. Slowly he popped the lock, lifted the trunk lid, and took a step back. Boyd nearly tripped over his own two feet as he tried to move forward, but Lane held out his arm and stopped him. Clay felt the tension in the air rising.

Lane remained standing in place, looking straight at Clay through squinted eyes. He pulled a pack of Marlboros from his jacket and slowly removed a cigarette. He never took his eyes off Clay as he tapped the cigarette against the pack before placing it between his lips. He lit a match and used it to light the cigarette, and for the first time in several minutes he took his eyes off Clay.

Lane took a long drag on his cigarette, and then slowly let out a lung full of smoke. He looked back at Clay and said, "So tell me again how it is that you know this arms dealer and I don't." Lane tilted his head to the side as he waited for his answer.

"He's new to the arms trade, I'm telling you. He is very secretive, and all I know is that he was born and raised in the Upper Peninsula and has been importing drugs from all over the world for years. He hates coons as much as you do and he steers some of his profits to several small Klan groups in the U.P. That's how I learned about him. He's got large estates on both the American side and the Canadian side of Sault Ste. Marie and has everybody in Customs on his payroll. He moves everything through Canada because it is much less dangerous that way. Back when the drawdown began in Iraq, he found creative ways to get his hands on military weapons and he imports them through the same pipelines that he uses for his drugs." Clay remained calm on the outside, but he was a complete wreck on the inside. *I sure hope that was a convincing performance.*

Lane took another long drag on his cigarette. Finally he said, "Let's take a look."

Clay took another small step back as Lane stepped forward and peered into the trunk. "Hoo," Lane gasped.

Inside the trunk lay over a dozen firearms. Not your standard hunting rifles and shotguns, but heavy-duty military weapons; M-4 Carbines, M-16 Assault Rifles, including four that were equipped with M-203 grenade launchers. There was even an M-202 rocket launcher. Lane reached into the trunk and pulled out an M-4. As he examined it, he let out a long whistle and said, "You say this guy can get us lots of these, Clay?"

"Truckloads," Clay lied.

Chapter 34

"So the president is going to make a last ditch effort to win the Michigan delegates? He knows he can't win Michigan, yet he's coming to Detroit and holding a rally at the Palace of Auburn Hills this late in the game. Doesn't that seem a little unorthodox to you?" Kenna Martineau asked Governor Clark.

"No, I heard it is open to people of all religions," Brett Mason said with a grin.

Clark, Martineau, and Mason had gathered in Clark's office to discuss the unexpected announcement that President Bonsam wanted to make a last minute change to his campaign schedule and hold a rally in Detroit.

Martineau turned and shot Mason a dirty look. She turned back to Clark and said, "I'm serious, Sam. Bonsam has never had a chance in Michigan. He has many more places that he should be spending his time and money right now. There are still a few states that are too close to call, and some of them have lots of delegates." Martineau was speaking very emphatically. "This doesn't feel right."

"Please relax Kenna, he's desperate. He's grasping at straws. I am quite sure the Detroit Pistons won't mind loaning out their arena for President Bonsam's swan song," Mason said facetiously.

That was it. Martineau got out of her chair and marched straight over to Mason and got in his face. "Am I talking to you, Brett?" Martineau said angrily. "Of all people you should be the most concerned over this, you are the campaign manager!" Martineau said, putting strong emphasis on both 'campaign' and 'manager.'

Mason's eyes widened but other than that he remained perfectly still.

"Kenna is right, Brett," Clark said. "We need to take this seriously."

Mason was still a little concerned about the look Martineau was giving him. "What do you think we should do, Gov?" he asked.

Clark straightened up in his chair and placed his elbows on the desk, his hands clasped together. "Call MDOT and have them shut down I-75 from College Drive to Baldwin Road. Have the sanitation guys create a water main break the entire length of Lapeer Road until the street is underwater. Get a couple of tanker trucks full of chlorine to overturn on Championship Drive."

Mason stared at Clark in disbelief. Clark stared back.

"I'm kidding Brett. Jeez."

Mason let out a sigh of relief. Martineau threw her head back in frustration, sighed heavily, and returned to her chair.

Clark looked at Martineau, "Sorry! Sorry, Kenna. I couldn't resist."

"Well, I'm glad you boys think this is funny, because I sure don't," she replied with anger in her voice. "You weren't on the elevator with me at ABC studios. You weren't on the Learjet with Alexander Kirk." She glared at Clark. "You and I both know that Bonsam was involved! It may never be proven, but that doesn't mean it isn't true. Now Bonsam is unexpectedly coming to Detroit and you boys want to make jokes?"

Clark and Mason both sat in silence. Finally Clark said, "Kenna, you are absolutely right. The word going around is that Bonsam has become completely irrational with his own campaign team. Anything that Bonsam does at this point should arouse suspicion."

Mason offered a suggestion. "Can we just prevent him from holding his rally? He's giving us pretty short notice and you know the enormous security complexities involved when a president visits a location. Let's just tell the Bonsam team that it would be impossible to support them at this late date."

"Maybe that's just what Bonsam wants," replied Martineau. "He could get on TV and lambast Governor

Clark for playing dirty politics by keeping him away from the Michigan voters."

"You are right," Clark said to Martineau. "If the president wants to speak to the good people of Michigan, then by all means we will welcome him. Let him have his moment." He paused as he waited to see Martineau's reaction. "What we need to do," Clark continued, "is just be far away from Detroit. We do nothing to steal his thunder. We give him nothing that he in his warped mind could use against us."

"Where do we go? Should we campaign in another state?" asked Martineau.

"I need a break from campaigning, Kenna," said Clark. "It's supposed to be unseasonably warm this weekend. Let's go to the summer residence. After all, this may be the last time we get to go there."

"All right, Sam. That sounds like a good plan," Martineau said. "But just tell me I'm not alone in thinking that Bonsam's visit just doesn't feel right?"

Clark folded his arms across his chest and slowly shook his head, "No, you're not alone."

Chapter 35

The trip back to Charlottesville from Mexico seemed like it was never going to end for Ixchel, but now that she was finally back she felt that she could start to unwind. It was early Friday night and she looked forward to a long, relaxing weekend that would allow her time to catch up on her sleep.

Sleep. Peaceful sleep had eluded her since she first learned of the Maya tablet that had been discovered by Professor Jameson. Her nights since had been restless. Each night she tossed and turned, her mind preoccupied with vivid recollections of the strange sensations she had experienced when she examined the tablet and studied the sky-fire symbol. If she wasn't thinking about that, she was unable to get the thoughts of Patrick's murder out of her head.

Daniel had gone straight home, but Ixchel wanted to stop by the archaeology lab and spend just enough time to organize the information she had brought back from Chacchoben. By this time everyone else had cut out for the weekend, and she found herself alone in the lab. With the news of Patrick's murder and the strange things that she had recently experienced in Mexico, she was surprised at how comfortable she felt in the lab this evening.

As she unpacked the items she had brought back from Chacchoben, she felt the urge to take one more look at the pictures of the sky-fire symbol. She popped her flash drive into her computer and pulled them up. As she looked at them, her thoughts went back to seeing the image of the sky-fire symbol embedded in the flames of the explosion that had brought down Senator Kirk's plane.

"I know I shouldn't do this," she thought, but she pulled up a picture of the explosion and placed it next to the picture of the sky-fire symbol on her computer screen. She still saw a definite connection between the two, however, she was thankful that she wasn't hit with any unusual feelings this time. She continued to stare at the pictures for a long time.

As she looked at the picture of the explosion, the words Daniel had spoken while they were in Chacchoben echoed through her head, 'Well, one thing I know is that many people believe that President Bonsam had something to do with it.'

"I know I *really* shouldn't do this," she thought, as she went to Google images to find a picture of President Bonsam. She selected a high-resolution portrait of Bonsam, copied it, and then placed it on the screen between a picture of the symbol and a picture of the explosion that destroyed Senator Kirk's plane. Her eyes darted between the three pictures. What she was looking for she did not know. She stopped to focus solely on the portrait of Bonsam. She enlarged the image and looked directly into Bonsam's eyes.

Oh God no! Another flash of brilliant white light burst before her eyes. The image of Bonsam pulsated as if it were coming right off the screen. With horror she watched as Bonsam's eyes became filled with flames. The pulsations grew stronger and the flames gave off such an intense heat that she felt as though her skin was going to burn. Her screams echoed through the halls of the building, but there was no one there to hear them. A blast of wind struck her yet again, even harder than the time before, knocking her to the floor.

On the screen of the computer on the table above Ixchel, the portrait of Emmanuel Bonsam continued to pulsate. Even though she was unconscious, a voice from within her mind called out, "I am here."

Chapter 36

Colonel William Seward Lane took a long slow pull on a cigarette as he looked out the van window. He stared straight ahead, deep in thought, as the van sped down the long country road.

Clay caught a glimpse of Lane out of the corner of his eye as he drove to the rendezvous point. *He has no idea what's coming.*

Clay certainly hated Lane and everything he stood for, but in a strange way he admired him. Lane was a painfully misguided individual, but he possessed powerful leadership genius. He was smooth, definitely, and he ran his operation with extreme finesse. Lane had the charisma of a televangelist, and he captivated his audiences with his dynamic speeches. Even though most of his followers were a bunch of dimwits, their loyalty to Lane was unequivocal. Lane made sure that no one in his branch became too powerful. His previous second-in-command foolishly made a power play to usurp control of the branch, and shortly thereafter was found hanging by his neck in the woods behind the compound. Clay knew it would be a serious mistake to take Lane lightly.

Lane didn't know what was coming, but he sensed danger. He always sensed danger. His paranoia was what kept him in power. He trusted no one. He treated everyone as if they were set to betray him. Clay was within Lane's comfort zone, but still...

Lane looked over at Clay. He really liked Clay, but if Clay made the smallest false move, Kenner and Boyd were there to take him out.

Clay could sense that Lane's eyes were on him. *I wonder what's going through his mind right now.*

Clay pulled off the main road and headed down a dirt road that went through a heavily wooded area. Lane sat up straight, took one last pull on his cigarette, and flicked the butt out the window. Kenner and Boyd put their hands on their weapons.

"We pull up, my contact will show you the weapons, we give him the money, transaction complete. Shouldn't take more than 10 minutes, depending on how fast we transfer the weapons to our van," said Clay.

Lane gave Clay an, "Uh huh," and pulled the duffle bag with the money off the floor and onto his lap. Clay glanced at the duffle bag. It was packed. That was another tribute to Lane's leadership. He could raise funds. Oh, could he raise funds. Lane knew plenty of powerful like-minded people with deep pockets who discreetly supported him and his cause.

Clay shot another quick glance toward the duffle bag. Soon it would be his. It was his reward for delivering Lane, Kenner and Boyd to Delgado. Delgado had assured him that the death of Lane would send shockwaves throughout the white supremacy world. Just the kind of revenge Clay was looking for.

Clay slowed the van down to a crawl and put his parking lights on as they approached a clearing. There was a full moon in the sky so Clay could easily see where he was going. A few seconds later, what appeared to be a large delivery truck came into view. It was a UPS-style truck, with a roll-up back door. Lane leaned forward, squinting to get a better view. Clay looked into his rear-view mirror, only to see Kenner and Boyd smiling like children on Christmas morning.

They stopped about ten yards from the truck. Clay left the engine running and stepped out of the van. Kenner and Boyd slid open the side door and piled out, taking their sawed-off double barrel shotguns with them. Lane stepped out last, making sure Boyd and Kenner were in front of him before moving toward the truck.

Lane could see a man standing in the shadow beside the truck, so he continued forward cautiously. When they were about 10 feet away, Lane saw the man raise his hands, indicating that he was unarmed. Lane relaxed a little, but only a little. The trio approached the man, stopping near the rear of the truck. Lane was uneasy that the man stood in the shadows, but he figured he'd be doing the exact same thing if he were in the man's position and making a transaction like this.

Lane paused, then said, "Can we take a look?"

Delgado lifted his hand toward the rear of the truck and replied, "Be my guest."

Lane heard the Spanish accent and immediately realized he had been set up. He grabbed Boyd by the collar and flung him over so that Boyd was between him and the man in the shadows. "Shoot! Shoot! Shoot!" he screamed.

In an instant the back door of the SWAT truck flew up and Delgado's agents jumped forward with their custom-made rifles. Boyd was startled by being unexpectedly yanked by Lane and Kenner just looked on in surprise. The agents fired three quick shots, and down went Lane, Kenner and Boyd.

The rounds the agents had fired were not bullets—they were tranquillizer darts. Boyd and Kenner were out cold instantly, but Lane faded more slowly. As he rolled onto his back, he saw Clay standing off to the side. *God damn you.*

Delgado walked over to Lane and squatted near his head. He leaned over and looked directly into Lane's eyes. He slapped Lane on the side of his face with two soft slaps, smiled and said, "*Buenas noches.*"

As Lane drifted toward unconsciousness, he summoned up one last breath and said, "You fuckin' spic."

Chapter 37

Clay walked over to where the duffle bag had landed after Lane was shot. He was impressed by the weight of the bag as he picked it up. *This is it!* But Clay was anxious to get out of there. He knew that Delgado had been lying all along. Delgado had repeatedly said that the objective of the mission was to kill Lane. So why the tranquilizers?

Clay turned to head back toward the van. Delgado, who was supervising the agents as they loaded Lane and his partners into the back of the SWAT truck, called out to Clay, "Hey, wait up."

Oh fuck. He had to play it cool. Clay stopped and turned toward Delgado. As Delgado got close, Clay asked, "What's with the tranquilizers, Jorge?"

"Just a last minute change in plans, *muchacho*," Delgado replied as he closed in on Clay. "Your service to the nation is greatly appreciated. The president sends his thanks." Delgado took another step forward, drew his M9 pistol and pumped three rounds into Clay's chest at point blank range.

Clay was blown back six feet and landed flat on his back, his arms out to his sides. Before Delgado even lowered his weapon he was hit by high-beam lights coming from a vehicle that was hidden behind the tree line a mere fifty yards away. A Jeep Wrangler roared its engine as it raced from the woods directly toward Delgado. *The operation has been compromised!* Delgado grabbed the duffle bag full of money and bolted toward the truck. "Go!" he shouted.

The agents looked up. They had just finished closing and locking the back of the truck as Delgado ran past them on his way to the driver's seat, still shouting, "Go! Go!"

"Jorge, we need to get Clay's body first!" yelled one of the agents.

Delgado was on the verge of panic. He did NOT want to screw up again, especially on the mission that had been planned by Bonsam. "No! Let's get the hell out of here," he screamed as he started the truck. He stomped on the accelerator just as the agents climbed in, and sped toward the dirt road leading out of the woods.

The Jeep bounded across the clearing toward the site of the ambush. Isaiah pointed toward the van and shouted to Isaac, "Over there! Over there!" Isaac did a hard right turn and gunned the Jeep forward. As they reached the van, Isaac slammed on the breaks, sending the Jeep into a short skid.

The Grant brothers leapt from the Jeep and ran to Clay. Isaac reached Clay first, dropping to his knees beside him. He slid his arm under Clay's neck and lifted his head off the ground. "Clay! Clay! Oh man. Clay, come on. Come on Clay! Come on," Isaac pleaded as tears formed in his eyes. He shook Clay gently, but Clay remained unresponsive. He pulled Clay to his chest and hugged him, rocking him back and forth. "Please don't die brother, please don't die."

Isaiah had run a few yards down the dirt road in a futile pursuit of the truck as its taillights disappeared into the night. He stopped and stared into the darkness as the sound of the truck faded away. He turned and walked back toward Clay and Isaac, his pistol still in hand. He stopped after only a few steps. He looked ahead and saw Isaac hugging Clay's limp body, sobbing and calling out Clay's name. Isaiah felt fury like he had never felt before. He clenched his teeth and spun around. Pointing his weapon down the dirt road, he screamed at the top of his lungs, "We're gonna kill you, motherfucker!"

Chapter 38

The head of the Secret Service Presidential Protection Detail was not happy with the news he had just received from President Bonsam. There was nothing more unnerving for the Secret Service than to have the president make a last minute change to the travel arrangements. He could not believe that Bonsam had decided to travel by motorcade in lieu of helicopter from the Detroit Metropolitan Airport to Auburn Hills, which was located almost an hour away from the airport. A helicopter could get him there in less than ten minutes.

Bonsam had made the call to the Secret Service as soon as he had rolled out of bed. He indicated that he felt obliged to drive through downtown Detroit as a sign of gratitude to the many faithful supporters of his reelection. Regardless of the reason, the Secret Service was now forced to scramble together Michigan law enforcement teams to provide security along the route with less than four hours notice. The head of the Presidential Detail had been on the phone all morning to make this happen. It was an excruciating task. Once he felt that he finally had the situation under control, he leaned back in his chair, rubbed his temples in an effort to relieve his headache pain, and said to himself, "I hate Mondays."

President Bonsam arrived at Detroit Metro Airport shortly after noon, and minutes later, he and the top two managers of his reelection campaign team climbed into the presidential limo. Soon the motorcade was racing down I-94 East toward downtown Detroit.

"Sir, when we get to the Palace we will start rehearsing your speech," said one of the managers. "We'll have plenty of time before the rally begins, but it behooves us to rehearse early so we can tweak the speech if necessary."

"We want to be sure your message resonates with concern for the issues that most affect the people of Detroit," said the other manager, "like unemployment, crime, et cetera."

Bonsam sat in the back of the limo with his hands on his knees, staring straight ahead. He was oblivious to the conversation that was going on around him. The managers looked at one another, and quietly closed their folders. It was clear that Bonsam's mind was elsewhere, and they knew that it was in their best interests to remain reticent for the rest of the trip.

Bonsam was burning with anger, but he had come to control the anger that encompassed his thoughts and feelings. In the back of his mind, visions of fire were swirling about and trying to consume his thoughts, but he was able to keep the visions at bay. He focused solely on the view out the windshield in front of him as the limo merged onto I-75 and made its way toward downtown. Minutes later the limo merged onto the John C. Lodge Freeway and headed straight toward Cobo Center.

Cobo Center is an enormous convention center that has hosted numerous concerts and sporting events, and each January it is the venue for the world famous North American International Auto Show. It is located next to the Detroit River and is one of the city's most famous landmarks. The freeway actually goes directly under the mammoth building complex.

Bonsam smiled as the limo approached the underpass. As it sped beneath the building, he imagined what was to take place above later in the evening. As the limo emerged from the other side of the underpass, *the* most famous Detroit landmark came into view, the Renaissance Center.

The Renaissance Center is the world headquarters for General Motors, and like Cobo Center is located on the shore of the Detroit River. It is an amazing complex containing interconnected skyscrapers that together form the pinnacle of the Detroit skyline. The RenCen is practically its own city within the city of Detroit.

Bonsam pushed the intercom button connected to the driver and said, "I want you to pull over and stop directly in front of the Renaissance Center." The shocked driver instantly contacted the head of the motorcade and informed him of the unexpected stop. Within five minutes, Bonsam was standing before the RenCen as Secret Service agents swarmed the area.

Bonsam looked upward and stared steadily at the central tower, the Detroit Marriott Hotel. It was over 70 stories high, and surrounded by four 40-story office towers. Neither his campaign managers nor his aides had any idea what Bonsam was doing, and soon most of them found themselves staring at the tower as well, trying to discern what the president was looking for.

Auburn Hills was another 30 miles north of downtown Detroit, and to have the president stop and expose himself to the public at large with no warning was a Secret Service nightmare. As nearby citizens realized what was going on and moved toward the motorcade, the agents hastily cordoned off the area to keep the onlookers a safe distance from the president.

Bonsam knew that by making this stop, his plan would be bolstered even more. He snapped out of his trance and looked at the people who had gathered. He quickly dropped into his charismatic mode and started waving and shouting to the crowd that was forming. He even winked at a group of elderly ladies, which made them cheer with excitement. A minute later he climbed back into his limo and ordered the driver to continue to Auburn Hills.

Chapter 39

The Palace of Auburn Hills was packed with fans and supporters of President Bonsam from across the Detroit Metropolitan area. The Palace is the home of the Detroit Pistons, the "Bad Boys" of the NBA. Many people consider Detroit's entire male population to be bad boys, and a good chunk of the female population as well. Detroit is consistently rated as one of the worst cities in America due to its astronomical crime rate. Detroit was also home to one of the worst race riots the country had ever seen. The Twelfth Street Riot of 1967 left forty-three dead and hundreds injured. During the five days of violence, more than 2,000 buildings were burned to the ground. President Bonsam knew all of this when he selected Detroit for his "October Surprise." It was perfect.

He sat alone in the Pistons' locker room mentally preparing for what was about to come. He closed his eyes and smiled to himself. He had struggled to gain control over the visions that had been haunting him, and he had begun to succeed. In his mind he saw himself hovering high above the men in the white hooded robes, only this time they were screaming in agony as their bodies went up in flames.

Clark, Martineau, Mason, and Clark's closest friends and supporters were celebrating their final visit to the Governor's summer residence on Mackinac Island. The island, located in Lake Huron between Michigan's upper and lower peninsulas, is a scenic natural wonderland. The residence had been built in 1902 and used as the Governor's summer residence for over 60 years. It is located high on a bluff overlooking the crystal blue waters of the Straits of Mackinac.

People mingled about on the large porch of the residence and the mood was festive. Martineau stood at the center of the porch with her elbows resting against the top of the railing. The vista before her was spectacular. Clark approached Martineau and he, too, placed his elbows on the railing next to her. He leaned over and bumped his shoulder against Martineau's shoulder causing her to laugh. "Beautiful, isn't it," he said as he gestured toward the Straits.

"Unbelievable," she replied. "This has been the best three-day weekend ever."

Clark stood up straight. "Yeah, only a week and a day to go, Kenna. It should be smooth sailing for us from now until then," he said.

Martineau flopped her head forward and shook it back and forth. She stood up straight and knocked her knuckles against the wooden railing twice. "Sam, I can be very superstitious at times," she said jokingly, "I'm Creole, remember? Don't say things like that. You're going to bring us bad luck."

As they both laughed, they heard Brett Mason call out from the porch door, "President Bonsam is about to give his speech!" Everyone made their way back into the residence and gathered around the large television in the main room.

Cheers erupted in the Palace as President Emmanuel Bonsam stepped onto the stage. He was so full of himself. He arrogantly strode to the front of the stage, waving to the crowd. He continued waving while doing a slow 360-degree spin, acting like he was the supreme pontiff himself. He scanned the crowd, absorbing the energy in the room, while making sure that everyone and everything was in place. Kirk's death had assured him the party nomination. Tonight's events would secure the presidency. His presidency. His Providence.

Clark, Mason, and nearly everyone else in the room burst into laughter watching Bonsam's *pirouette* on the stage. Mason dropped into a news reporter voice and announced, "Ladies and gentlemen, Caesar has entered the Coliseum." More laughter followed.

Bonsam walked up to the podium waving and smiling. As the crowd's applause died down, his expression changed. He glowered sternly toward the audience as he spoke. "My fellow Americans, the problems our country faces are many."

"Oh God, here we go again," Clark told the room. The laughter rolled on. He looked over at Martineau, who smiled and gave the television a halfhearted salute.

"Problems that are brought about by our enemies who have vowed to prevent the manifestation of our glorious future!" Bonsam yelled into the microphone as his hand pounded the podium.

"Whoa, wasn't expecting anything like that," said Clark, as he and the others stared on in disbelief. The laughter in the room had stopped. Even the crowd at the Palace had fallen silent.

"There is a well-organized, well-financed network of racist hate mongers that has repeatedly tried to destroy us, to destroy our divine Providence!" yelled Bonsam as he waved his hands with palms upward toward the Palace crowd. Low murmuring had begun as the overwhelmingly African-American crowd focused nervously on President Bonsam. The crowd was extremely uneasy about the way this was going. Many people started making their way toward the exits.

Mason looked toward Clark and quietly said, "What in the hell is he doing?" Clark was incredulous; he didn't know what to say.

Bonsam was pounding the podium and shrieking like a third-world dictator. "I stand here before you tonight on the eve of history's last election..." and as he said the word election, he flinched ever so slightly.

A second later the sound of rapid gunfire split the air. The podium in front of Bonsam began to disintegrate as bullets sent splinters of wood spraying into the air. Bonsam did a hard dive to his right and landed behind the row of seats that held local dignitaries and supporters of his campaign. As he hit the floor, the lights of the Palace went out, and gunshots and screams were all that could be heard.

Chapter 40

Clark quickly turned to Mason and yelled, "Go find Stryker and tell him to fire up the helicopter, now!" Mason grabbed the closest Secret Service agent by the arm, rushed out the door and headed toward the landing pad in search of Stephen Stryker, the pilot of the governor's helicopter.

Martineau turned to the nearest aide and said, "Contact Lansing. Find out what is going on!"

The staff members present became frantic. Soon every member was on a cell phone trying to ascertain what had happened at the Palace. The network signal from the Palace went down when the power went out and the network anchors were desperately trying to reach their reporters on the scene, all the while reporting to their audience that an assassination attempt had just been made on the president's life.

Amid the chaos in the darkness of the Palace, Jorge Delgado and his two-man team donned their night vision goggles and went to work. Bud Kenner and Spencer Boyd's drugged, unconscious bodies were dragged along the catwalks high above the arena floor by Delgado's agents. Since last night's ambush Delgado had kept the rednecks on ice, figuratively speaking, so their blood would be nice and fresh when the authorities found their bullet-riddled bodies. Once they were in place Delgado checked their pulses one last time, then picked up an automatic rifle and riddled their bodies with bullets.

"Who could have done this, Sam?" asked Martineau as they raced toward the helicopter.

"I don't know, Kenna, but we have to get to Detroit," Clark said.

A moment later they reached the helicopter, which was already prepared for take off. The noise caused by the rotor wash was almost deafening. Mason and two Secret Service agents were standing at the pad with their hands covering their ears.

Clark grabbed Mason by his jacket's lapel and shouted, "This is going to be a nightmare. Make contact with the Lieutenant Governor. We need to call out the National Guard, the State Troopers, and every law enforcement agency within 200 miles and have them converge on Detroit. I'm sure he has already started doing that, but contact him anyway and tell him that I'm on the way."

Mason gave a thumbs-up and raced back to the residence. The two Secret Service agents pushed down on the shoulders of Clark and Martineau as they escorted them under the spinning blades of the helicopter. All four quickly piled into the helicopter and fastened their safety belts. Martineau looked up at Clark and said, "You're right. This is going to be a nightmare."

Delgado crouched down low on the catwalk while his agents dashed off to get the chief redneck, Colonel William Seward Lane. The sounds of the screams and gunshots below were music to his ears. In an instant his men had returned with Lane. There was an agent under each of Lane's arms as they carried him forward, Lane's toes dragging along the surface of the catwalk. The agents stopped when they reached Delgado, turning Lane so his back was against the railing of the catwalk.

Delgado stood up and grabbed Lane by the front of his shirt. He raised Lane's head upward and slapped him a couple of times while saying, "Time to wake up!"

He had given Lane a dosage of drugs smaller than the dosage he had given Kenner and Boyd, giving Lane just enough so that he would regain consciousness this evening. Lane was starting to come around and his eyes slowly opened. He blinked rapidly trying to get his eyes to focus. A moment later he was looking straight into the glowing green eyes of some kind of a monster.

"Remember me?" Delgado said. "I'm the fuckin' spic who ambushed your ass!" Lane's eyes grew wide in horror. Delgado smiled as he pushed both of his hands hard into Lane's chest. Lane did a back flip over the railing and plunged face first toward the arena floor below.

As soon as they were airborne, Clark turned to the Secret Service agent sitting next to him and said, "See if you can pick up a satellite feed on the onboard television and find us some news. We need to know what is going on."

He looked at the other agent and said, "Are you getting anything on the cell phones?"

"No, sir. Reception this far north can be ridiculous," he replied. "I'm going up front with the pilot to see what I can get over his radio."

"Good idea, thanks," said Clark.

Clark turned to Martineau with a depressed look on his face. "You were right. Bonsam's sudden schedule change to campaign in Detroit never felt legit. I should have listened to you."

Martineau leaned over and placed her hand on top of Clark's. With a look of deep concern on her face, she replied, "Don't let it happen again."

Delgado and his agents raced down the catwalk and made their way to the arena floor. Through their night vision goggles they could see people stumbling around helplessly in the pitch-black darkness of the Palace. Just for fun Delgado let out a bloodcurdling scream and fired several rounds into the air, causing more screams as the people around him crashed into one another as they dove for the floor.

Delgado raced over to the spot where the bloody body of a Secret Service Quick Reaction Force agent lay. The weapon that Delgado had used on Kenner and Boyd moments ago had been the QRF agent's automatic assault rifle. Delgado unslung the rifle from his shoulder and placed it next to the agent. He rested his hand on the chest of the corpse and said, "Thanks for letting me borrow your rifle. You're a hero, really, dying in action like that. By the way, great job taking out those assassins before your demise."

Delgado got up and laughed sadistically as he and the agents made their escape from the Palace. The three men went out a service door and disappeared into the Detroit night. They were just warming up.

Chapter 41

Ixchel, Daniel, and Thomas had gathered at Thomas's apartment for a night of pizza eating and rally watching. Neither Daniel nor Thomas were big Bonsam fans, and like millions of other Americans of the same mind they had decided to tune in to the president's rally out of sheer curiosity. One could never know what the president would do next these days.

Ixchel had never told Daniel that she had passed out in the lab after viewing Bonsam's image next to the sky-fire symbol. She seriously worried that she was losing her grip on reality, and she was too embarrassed to let anyone know. Now even the mention of President Bonsam's name made her shudder.

Ixchel had been studying the symbols on the tablet for two straight days and Daniel had felt that she needed a break. She had told Daniel that she didn't want to go to Thomas's with him, but he eventually persuaded her to go. Ixchel's stomach was a bundle of nerves and she barely even touched her pizza. When Thomas announced that the rally was about to start, her nerves kicked into overdrive. As she heard the CNN anchor introduce the arrival of the president, her entire body trembled.

From the moment she saw President Bonsam step onto the stage, Ixchel's world slipped into slow motion. A feeling of dread overwhelmed her. Her senses were telling her that something terrible was about to happen.

Ixchel stared at the TV, frozen in fear. Daniel and Thomas were sitting together on the couch, too busy drinking beer and ridiculing Bonsam to even notice Ixchel's condition. Ixchel's eyes widened as Bonsam approached the podium. As the camera slowly zoomed in on the president's face, her hands started shaking. Ixchel looked into his eyes with horror. The burning evil had returned as his image pulsated before her eyes.

Finally Thomas glanced Ixchel's way and noticed she was not looking well. He elbowed Daniel and nodded toward Ixchel. "Hey, is she okay?"

Daniel looked over at Ixchel and was about to ask her if she was all right, but before he could he saw her raise both of her hands to her mouth as she let out a scream. Daniel and Thomas stopped what they were doing and looked at Ixchel, noticing that her eyes were fixed on the television. The men quickly turned their attention back to the TV, just in time to see Bonsam scream, "To destroy our divine Providence!"

In unison they looked back at Ixchel, who was now standing there with tears pouring down her cheeks. "Whoa!" said Thomas.

Daniel stood and was about to approach Ixchel when the sound of gunfire erupted from the television, startling the hell out of all three of them. As they watched the podium shatter and the lights in the Palace go out, Ixchel collapsed to the floor.

Chapter 42

Clark's helicopter was over halfway to Detroit. "Sir, we're getting something," said the Secret Service agent as he backed away from the television. "I've picked up DMBC. The news out of Detroit is not looking good."

Clark and Martineau watched as the news reports jumped from one reporter to the next. People had poured into the streets and riots were breaking out across the city. At each location, the violence and destruction were getting out of control. There were scenes showing mobs of people looting stores and other scenes of homes and cars on fire. In almost every scene, police cars and ambulances were shown racing through the streets of downtown Detroit with their lights flashing and sirens blaring. The only bright side was that no deaths had been reported so far.

Clark was deep in thought. He knew that he would have to act fast to prevent lawlessness from overtaking Detroit. "This is a tinder keg that could ignite at any second," he said. "I wish I could get a hold of the Lieutenant Governor."

They sat in silence for a few minutes, watching more of the reports as they came in. Martineau then turned to Clark and said, "I wonder what happened to Bonsam?"

"I was wondering the same thing," Clark replied.

As if the news network had been reading their minds, the scene jumped to a hastily prepared press conference room. The president's press secretary was shown motioning with his hands for the crowd to be quiet. "I know you must have a million questions," Press Secretary Stratton told the crowd of reporters. "However, I am only going to take two or three after I read this announcement."

You could hear a pin drop in the press conference room as the press secretary read his prepared news release. "President Emmanuel Bonsam is alive," Stratton announced.

The crowd erupted as shouts came from the reporters. The press secretary waved down the crowd again. "Let me finish," he said loudly.

As the crowd quieted down, Stratton continued. "Miraculously, the president received no bullet wounds. He did, however, injure the elbow and shoulder of his right arm when he selflessly risked his own life to protect those seated near the podium, but the injuries are minor. The president is aboard Air Force One as we speak and is heading back to Washington. I have nothing further."

Again the reporters shouted out all at once. Stratton pointed to a reporter, who stood and asked, "Do you know who is responsible for this attempt to assassinate President Bonsam?"

"The Secret Service killed three of the assassins inside the Palace. Their identities have been uncovered, however we are not releasing any names at this time. The Secret Service and the FBI are conducting an extensive search for any accomplices," replied Stratton.

Stratton turned and pointed to a reporter on the other side of the room, who quickly blurted out, "Were they terrorists?"

Stratton paused for a moment. He placed his hands on the side of the podium, took a deep breath and replied, "Yes, they were terrorists, the worst kind of terrorists. Homegrown terrorists." Stratton then looked directly into the camera and delivered the line that Bonsam had instructed him to deliver, "And President Bonsam has vowed that every terrorist in the Michigan Militia will be brought to justice!"

Clark was shocked beyond belief. "Oh my God, no!" he yelled. "How in the world could they make an announcement like that at a time like this? We are going to have a full-fledged race war in Detroit!"

Back at the press conference, Stratton had left the podium and the reporters filed out of the conference room. The two reporters who had asked the questions smiled to one another as they pushed their way through the crowd.

Once they had exited the conference room, they made their way together to the parking lot and climbed into their DMBC news van.

Chapter 43

In Charlottesville, Daniel and Thomas were trying to revive Ixchel. They had moved her onto the couch and laid her down. Thomas had gone into the kitchen and put some cool water on a cloth and was now pressing it gently to Ixchel's forehead. "Dan, she is burning up," he said.

Daniel was rubbing Ixchel's arm with his hands. He gently called out, "Ixchel? Ixchel, are you okay?" Daniel looked at Thomas and said, "Did you see what happened? When she saw the shots fired at Bonsam she totally lost it. My God, did you hear that scream? I mean, hell yeah, it was a traumatic event, but not enough to make a person pass out."

"Dude, she screamed before the shots were fired," said Thomas, as he looked Daniel straight in the eyes.

"What?" said Daniel. He was about to ask Thomas what he meant by that remark, when he realized what Thomas was saying was true. In his mind, Daniel saw Ixchel's hands come to her mouth as she screamed in horror, moments before the shots were fired. He paused and looked at Ixchel, then up at Thomas and said in almost a whisper, "You're right." Daniel was stunned.

Daniel began rubbing Ixchel harder, almost to the point of shaking her. His voice grew louder, "Ixchel, Ixchel!"

Ixchel started to come around, so Thomas stopped dabbing her forehead and stepped back. He looked down at Daniel and Ixchel for a moment, then turned his attention back to the television. He watched in absolute disbelief as the news reports showed Detroit falling into total pandemonium.

As Air Force One began its descent, President Bonsam watched with exultant joy as reports came in showing the violence in Detroit surge toward critical mass. He knew that Delgado's planned actions would soon push the city over the edge. Clark would be blamed for the rioting that was sure to come, and he would never be able to live down tonight's catastrophe.

Bonsam looked out the window next to his seat and saw the reflection of his face. He could see fire in his eyes. He touched his fingertips to the glass as he continued to stare at his own reflection and said, "My Providence."

Chapter 44

Like most other parts of Detroit, violence and destruction raged through the Cass Corridor section of town. Cass Corridor is one of the most violent parts of Detroit on the best of days, but with tonight's announcement that some white-trash KKK scum had tried to kill the first African-American president, total mayhem ensued.

Joseph Franklin Jr. had lived in the Corridor all his life. As a boy he grew up in one of the many rundown apartment buildings filled with drug dealers, pimps, and hookers. Joseph's father had very little education, but he was a hard worker and he kept his family safe. Joseph Sr. had worked his entire adult life in a small hardware store on Cass Avenue that had been owned by his uncle. Since his uncle had no children of his own, he left the hardware store to Joseph Sr. when he died. Joseph Jr. then inherited the store from his father, and had been eking out a living there ever since.

Joseph ran down the street past the vacant storefronts until he had reached his hardware store. He saw roving packs of hoodlums in every direction as he slowly turned in a circle. He saw windows being smashed and cars being torn apart, yet his hardware had not been touched. "Thank you, God," he said to himself as he moved to unlock the metal bars barricading the entrance to his store.

As he turned the key, he looked over his shoulder to see if the coast was clear. To his dismay he saw his eleven-year-old son running toward him yelling, "Dad! Dad!"

Joseph grabbed his son and yanked him into the store. He pulled down the metal bars rapidly and closed the lock. He spun around and grabbed his son by the shoulders and shouted, "My God, Danté, what are you doing here?"

"I was worried about you, Dad," Danté replied. He was breathing rapidly and there was fright in his eyes.

The sound of a windshield being smashed echoed through the store. Joseph pulled Danté to the floor and together they crawled behind the counter. Joseph slowly peered over the top of the counter. The noises outside were getting closer now. He looked down at Danté and said, "We're going to be all right," but he was so frightened he wasn't sure if he really believed it.

Up the street less than a half-mile away from the hardware store sat an abandoned service station. Inside the garage were two large, heavily souped-up 4X4 pickups. Inside the trucks were the only white men who dared to be in this part of town tonight. The driver of the first truck punched a number into his phone and placed it to his ear. When the person on the other end answered, he spoke in a mockingly southern drawl. "Howdy boss, we're in place and we have our costumes on." The man laughed as he looked down at his Tony Lama cowboy boots, Mack truck belt buckle, and the Dickies flannel shirt that was covering his Kevlar body armor. "We just saw two men enter the target. We're ready to move out on your word."

"Ok, you are a go. Stick to the plan, and don't get caught, you stupid gringos," Jorge Delgado said with a laugh. He turned to his agents and said, "Phase One is underway!"

The members of this team were ex-special forces warriors from each branch of the military who, like Delgado, had become disillusioned by the ignorance that ran rampant throughout the military's leadership. They were young, white reprobates with a soldier of fortune attitude. They had no agenda, political or otherwise, and offered their services to the highest bidder. In this particular case, however, they had no idea that the bidder actually despised them.

Even though they were working freelance, Delgado referred to them as "agents," which they found, in their words, "extremely cool." Agent Erik Torgersen set down his cell phone and raised his hand into the air with his index finger pointing upward, and shook it in circles indicating to the rest of the good old boys that they were moving out. One of Torgersen's fellow agents, Keith Dixon, flung open the garage door. He hopped into the back seat of the second truck and gave two hard taps to the back of the seat in front of him. Torgersen let out a loud, "Whoooooo eeeee!" and gunned the truck out of the garage with the second truck right behind.

The trucks sped down Cass Avenue with their engines roaring. Torgersen and the other driver swerved back and forth recklessly, causing the rioters to flee the streets for the safety of the sidewalks. The rioting came to a complete stop as onlookers watched two trucks loaded with white guys come screeching to a halt in front of Franklin's Hardware Store.

The agents exited the vehicles and started hollering, "Yee Haw!" like they were at a hootenanny in the middle of Appalachia. The rioters and onlookers in the area stared in disbelief. Several of the hoodlums present huddled and started to cross the street with every intention of totally fucking up whitey. The agents just joked and laughed as they watched some high school punks approach. They were carrying metal pipes, baseball bats, bricks, and various other rioting implements.

The biggest kid in the group stepped forward and unsheathed a Samurai sword that he had just looted from a pawnshop a few blocks over. Upon seeing this, the agents pulled their automatic rifles from the beds of the trucks and began spraying bullets into the air. Screams could be heard from the crowd as the hoodlums scattered in every direction. When the shooting stopped, Agent Torgersen tipped up the brim of his cowboy hat and yelled out, "Never bring a knife to a gunfight, Sambo!"

Inside the store, Joseph and Danté hit the floor as the sound of gunfire ripped through the air. Joseph slid closer to Danté and said, "Son, you have got to get out of here. There are no bars on the bathroom window. I know you can fit through it. Go! Go now! Run as far away from here as you can!"

"Dad, I need to stay with you! I need to stay with you," cried out Danté.

The roar of trucks' engines could be heard getting closer, and a moment later, a loud bang of metal crashing against metal rang out. Joseph grabbed Danté by the shirt and yelled, "Go, now!" With tears in his eyes, Danté got up and ran to the back of the store.

Out front the trucks had been backed up to the front of the store, and Dixon and another agent were feverishly wrapping chains that were already hooked to the trucks' tow bars to the metal bars barricading the front of the store. Other agents continued to shout out and fire shots into the air to keep the hoodlums at bay. The entire crowd of onlookers peering from their places of cover was in shock.

Once the chains were secure the agents stepped beside the trucks and banged twice on the side of the beds. Both Torgersen and the driver of the second truck simultaneously revved their engines and lurched forward, ripping the metal barricades completely off of the storefront and crashing open the store's front windows. There was more hollering, and the agents fired more bullets into the air. The trucks dragged the barricades into the middle of the street and stopped. The agents who had secured the chains to the barricades quickly unhooked the chains from the barricades and tow bars and threw them next to a footlocker into the bed of the first truck. Then Torgersen and Dixon each pulled a large bottle from the footlocker and made their way back to the storefront.

Joseph cringed at the sound of the barricades crashing down. He slowly inched his way up and peered over the counter. His eyes widened in horror as he saw two men walking toward his store, each holding a bottle with a lit rag dangling out of the top. He stood up quickly and began waving his hands over his head while shouting, "Please don't! Please don't!"

The men with the Molotov cocktails laughed as they saw a man in the store waving his arms in sheer terror. They took their time, making sure everyone who was watching got a good look at what they were doing. Finally Torgersen looked at Dixon and said, "On three." They each took three shuffle steps forward and launched the bottles toward the store.

As Joseph watched the bottles sail through the air, his last thought was of his son Danté. He whispered, "Please God, don't let him die," just as the firebombs hit the floor before him. Within seconds Joseph Franklin and his family hardware store went up in flames.

The trucks sped away from the scene with Agent Torgersen's truck in the lead. He slowed down as they approached the service station from which their mission began. He smiled once he saw a white DMBC van in the parking lot in front of the station. Torgersen honked the horn a few times as he passed the van, while Dixon and the other agents in the trucks whooped it up and gave the occupants of the van the thumbs-up. Police cars heading toward the fire raced past the trucks as they drove off in the other direction. As the police cars sped past the service station, the DMBC van pulled onto the street and took off following them.

Chapter 45

The Detroit Metro Broadcasting Company was busy this evening. Reports were pouring in from the field showing violence and destruction throughout Detroit. Darius Robinson was the DMBC Newscast Producer who was trying to bring order to the disorder in the studio control room as the reports flooded into the station. It was he who decided what breaking news stories were broadcast and when.

The control room was filled with commotion. When Robinson stepped away to answer a call he had received on his personal hand held radio, no one even noticed. He answered by saying, "Lion One."

"Lion One, this is Lion Three. The hardware store fire was just started. We will be pulling up any second," replied the voice on the other end.

"Good job, Three. Give me a live shot of the fire. Interview as many witnesses as possible." Robinson smiled as he stuck his radio in his pocket and made his way back into the control room. He couldn't wait to broadcast the story of a poor black businessman whose business was set on fire by a bunch of white hooligans. That would make the president very happy.

Darius Robinson had known President Bonsam his entire life. They had grown up in the same apartment building and spent much of their adolescence gallivanting the mean streets of East St. Louis. They were the textbook examples of juvenile delinquents, who over the years together shoplifted from stores, vandalized public property, and even made healthy profits fencing stolen car stereos.

They developed a strong and loyal friendship. Once when they were in junior high, they decided to torch an abandoned house just for kicks. As they fled the scene of the crime, the police caught Bonsam, but Robinson managed to get away. Bonsam spent eight hours at the

Salem Police Station under intense pressure to give up the name of his accomplice, but he refused to sell out his good friend.

Robinson was grateful and made a stringent pact promising to support Bonsam in the future should the need arise. When Robinson entered the news business, Bonsam cashed in on the promise. Robinson became Bonsam's best mole in the broadcast news industry, and over the years he skillfully recruited many reporters across the nation to support and ensure Bonsam's rise to power. Robinson's actions tonight at DMBC Studios would be the zenith of his career as an operative in Bonsam's deceptive schemes.

"Darius, we are getting spectacular video of a business fire in the Cass Corridor," called out one of the assignment editors. "It was definitely arson and it appears that there may have been people inside the building."

Robinson was smiling on the inside but serious on the outside. "Good God, that is horrible! Tell the reporter to stand by and keep the video running. I'll feed the information to the anchors. I'll have Reaves cut to the reporter right away."

Chapter 46

Clark and Martineau continued to watch in disbelief as the reports showed the rioting taking place across Detroit. Every report showed the downtown streets in the midst of bedlam and chaos. "My God, will you look at that? It's total anarchy," said Clark.

"Heaven help us," said Martineau.

The lead DMBC anchor, Dean Reaves, was now beginning to report confirmed deaths. The number was low at this time, but Clark knew that at any moment the number could start to climb.

"We need to get a close look at downtown," Clark yelled to cockpit.

"We'll be there in ten minutes sir," Stryker yelled back.

"This is going to be a long ten minutes," Clark said to Martineau.

"Didn't the timing of the press secretary's announcement seem to be more than just a matter of bad timing?" asked Martineau. "It was as if he were intentionally trying to stir up a hornets' nest."

"Well, he succeeded," Clark replied. He paused for a moment. "This has Bonsam written all over it."

Chapter 47

The Canadian Customs officials at the Ambassador Bridge had their hands full tonight. The Ontario-bound traffic was backing up for miles as people desperately tried to get out of downtown Detroit by crossing the border to the safety of Windsor. Plus, Canadian police officers weren't letting any Michigan-bound traffic cross over into Detroit for obvious reasons, which was causing an unbelievable amount of gridlock on the Windsor side of the bridge.

Owen McGraw was standing in the main lobby of the Customs headquarters with several of his fellow Customs agents who were waiting for their shifts to begin. They had gathered around the lobby television and were watching the reports coming out of Detroit. As he was about to leave for his post, a news report came on that stopped the agents dead in their tracks.

An elderly man was in tears as he told the reporter what he had witnessed. "They drove their pickup trucks right up to Joe's hardware store then ripped off the entire storefront. Poor old Joe was standing there pleading for mercy, but them cowboys just up and firebombed the store with Joe still in it."

"Can you describe the men who did this?" asked the reporter from DMBC.

"Yeah, they was some white country boys. Five or six of them. They was driving great big pickup trucks, two of them. Brand new ones with a back seat with their own doors. They was all jacked up, the body way up high over the wheels," said the man. He paused for a minute and then the tears returned. "Oh, them farm boys killed Joe Franklin in cold blood. Ol' Joe would never hurt nobody."

McGraw shook his head in disgust. "It's going to be a long night," he said as he left the headquarters building and made his way to his booth. The Customs agent he was relieving stepped out of the booth to allow McGraw to enter. As McGraw took his seat, his colleague patted him on the back as he peered at the never-ending line of cars that were honking their horns and said, "It sucks to be you, eh."

As his colleague walked off, McGraw settled into his position and called the next car forward. As the car was pulling up he looked further down the row of cars heading his way. Much to his surprise he saw a couple of decked-out Ford F250 pickups only four cars away, loudly revving their engines.

The driver who had pulled forward was waving his passport at McGraw and calling out, "Hello?" McGraw ignored the driver as he picked up his phone and placed an urgent to call his boss.

Chapter 48

Stanley Kaczmarek was confused as he drove through the downtown streets that were quickly becoming a war zone. *What is going on? It is early on a Monday night!* He looked over at his wife Lidia and could see she was frightened. In their 38 years together, he had never seen her so scared.

Stanley just wanted to get out of the city and back to Hamtramck, but that was proving difficult. Every street he turned onto had people on it yelling and fighting. He was about to make a right turn when he saw someone bash out the windshield of a car on that street. He looked to his left and saw a car on fire. He gunned his engine and drove straight on, not really sure where he was going.

Stanley drove fast but cautiously, and after traveling less than a mile the street seemed clear of rioting. He allowed himself to relax a little. He took Lidia's hand and squeezed it gently. She turned and gave him a smile. To Stanley she was just as beautiful today as she was when they first met all those years ago.

Without any warning a car bolted out of a side street and stopped perpendicularly directly in front of the Kaczmareks' car. Stanley slammed on the brakes. He looked at Lidia and saw that the fear in her eyes had returned.

The driver of the other car climbed out and walked toward Stanley's door. As the driver closed in, Stanley saw that it was a woman, and she was wearing a jumpsuit that had a badge pinned to it. She motioned to Stanley to roll down his window, which he did.

"Sorry about that sir, but I had to stop you. It's not safe to continue up this road. The rioting has gotten out of control and the police are blocking off the area."

Stanley relaxed once again. "Thank you, ma'am," he said. "Which way should I go?"

She pointed to the side street from which she had come. "Just turn down there, there is someone at the end directing traffic to safe streets."

Stanley smiled and said, "Thanks."

She smiled back and said, "You're welcome. Please be careful."

Stanley made the turn and entered the side street. He had only driven a short way when it appeared that the street was blocked off only a few yards ahead. "What's going on?" he said as he gazed into the darkness of the street ahead.

He looked in the rearview mirror and saw headlights coming up fast behind him. He looked at Lidia and said, "Everything is going to be all right."

The car behind him stopped close to his rear bumper and the driver got out. It was the woman again. As she approached, Stanley rolled down his window to ask her what was going on. When she reached the window, she drew a handgun and pumped a bullet into the heads of Stanley and Lidia Kaczmarek.

Chapter 49

Agent Gisela Schroeder looked through Stanley Kaczmarek's wallet as she walked back to her car. She pulled out her radio and clicked the button. "Lion One, this is Lion Four, over."

"Go ahead Lion Four."

"Couple. Two elderly Caucasians," she said as she looked at Mr. Kaczmarek's driver's license.

"Oooh, a couple of Polacks. *Opa* would have been so proud," Schroeder said to herself. Her grandfather had been a prominent member of the Third Reich back in the old country. Her father had always said that little Gisela would someday grow up to be just like her grandfather, and he was right.

"Perfect. DMBC van is on the way. You know what to do."

"Roger, out." Schroeder smiled as she put down her weapon and radio. The kills exhilarated her. She couldn't wait to tell Erik Torgersen all about them. She knew that her longtime lover would be most impressed.

Schroeder unzipped her jumpsuit and stepped out of it, revealing that she was dressed like a $20 hooker. She had on a skintight white blouse that was only buttoned half way up, her large pearly white breasts nearly spilling out of the top. She wore a short leather skirt that also left little to the imagination. She caked on some bright red lipstick and then shook her head from side to side as she let down her long blonde hair. She slipped on a pair of black Stiletto shoes that perfectly matched the full-length fishnet stockings that were stretched tightly up over her long, supple legs. Finally, she removed the necklace with a swastika pendant that she had been wearing and went to the end of the street to wait for the DMBC van.

The broadcast van was right behind the first two police cars that arrived at the scene of the Kaczmarek murders. As the officers stepped cautiously out of their vehicles, the first thing they saw was a bleached blonde prostitute running erratically toward them and screaming hysterically.

"It was the Black Family Mafia! I know them gang punks anywhere! The Black Family Mafia!" Agent Schroeder yelled using her best bimbo voice. "They shot that poor old white man and that poor old lady straight in the head. I saw the whole thing!"

As the police officers approached the Kaczmarek vehicle, Agent Schroeder kept on frantically screaming about the two dead white people while the DMBC crew captured it all on tape. At the DMBC studio, Darius Robinson watched the event unfold on the control room monitors. He knew that a report of black gang members killing an old white couple from Hamtramck would certainly piss off the white viewers, which is just what he wanted. He looked at the nearest assignment editor and said, "Get this ready for air, this story is up next." He pushed the microphone button that connected to Reaves's earpiece. "Dean, we got another racial incident. It's coming your way." Robinson released the button and chuckled, knowing that Reaves would over-sensationalize the story just like he always did when there was breaking news.

McGraw had switched to speakerphone and was now listening intently to the directions being given to him by the Ontario Provincial Police superintendent on the other end of the line. "Take plenty of extra time checking passports before the trucks reach you. We need you to stall them to give us enough time to set up," said the superintendent. McGraw followed the order as he anxiously awaited the arrival of the first truck.

Agent Torgersen's front seat companion Keith Dixon turned to Torgersen and asked, "What if they decide to search us, Erik?"

"Don't worry about it," he replied calmly. "Since we stashed all the weapons back at the safe house near the train tracks, there is no reason for them to hold us even if they search us. We just play it cool." Torgersen pulled forward to the booth, ecstatic that he had finally gotten there. "Took you long enough, Canuck," he yelled sarcastically at the booth. McGraw made no eye contact with Torgersen as he examined the passports and handed them back, then waved for him to proceed.

As the truck pulled forward, Dixon exclaimed, "What the hell was that? I thought you said play it cool?"

"I was just playing the obnoxious American. It would have aroused suspicion if I had been polite," Torgersen laughed.

Torgersen impatiently tapped his hands on the steering wheel as the traffic inched its way through the gridlock at the base of the bridge. His cell phone beeped, so he pulled it from his shirt pocket to see who had sent him a message. An unusual look came over his face as he read the message. Dixon asked, "What is it?"

Torgersen looked at Dixon and smiled. "Gisela had two kills tonight! She says she's almost to the bridge."

"Way to go, G!" exclaimed Dixon.

"Oh man, Gisela gets really horned up after a kill," Torgersen said. "I'm gonna get my lobster boiled tonight!"

His truck continued to inch along, but as he looked ahead he saw a row of Customs agents standing where the traffic pattern bottlenecked, rerouting vehicles in several different directions in an effort to alleviate the congestion. "Thank God," he whispered.

When Torgersen reached the chokepoint, a Customs agent gave his whistle a loud sharp blow and pointed his flashlight toward the far right lane. Torgersen checked his rear-view mirror and was relieved to see that his second truck was directed to the far right lane as well. For the first time in hours, Torgersen was able to drive faster than five miles per hour. He pulled ahead, but traveled only a couple hundred feet before he came to another checkpoint. A Royal Canadian Mounted Police officer stepped between the roadblock barrier and the front of the truck and raised his hand until Torgersen pulled to a stop. Torgersen nearly barfed as he viewed the officer's bright scarlet tunic, round tan hat, and knee-high leather boots. He rolled his eyes in exasperation and said, "For the love of God." Dixon laughed as he watched Torgersen become frustrated, and then Torgersen started to laugh as well. He beeped his horn twice and yelled, "Get out of the road, Dudley, or I'll run your ass over!" causing Dixon to laugh even harder.

The Mountie lowered his head so his eyes were hidden behind the brim of his hat as he approached the driver's side door. When he reached the open window, he looked up quickly and in an instant placed the barrel of his 9mm Smith & Wesson against Torgersen's left temple. Before Torgersen even realized what was happening, twenty Ontario T.R.U. members stormed the trucks with their sub-machine guns drawn and ready. The Mountie cocked the hammer of his weapon and said, "Welcome to Canada."

Chapter 50

Clark and Martineau had been so deeply involved in a conversation about the assassination attempt on the president that they didn't even realize they were coming up on Detroit. The Secret Service agent had returned from the cockpit and said, "Have you ever seen anything like this?" Clark and Martineau quickly turned their attention to the port side window and gazed at Detroit below. "It's as if the Tigers, Lions, Pistons, and Red Wings won their respective championships on the same night."

The flashing lights of hundreds of police cars and emergency vehicles could be seen racing along the streets. Fires dotted the city landscape below, their flames illuminating the night sky. The agent leaned over Martineau, pointed toward Cobo Hall and said, "Look! It looks like half the cars in the rooftop parking lot at Cobo are on fire."

Clark again yelled to the cockpit, "Stryker, take us low over the riverfront."

Stryker swung the helicopter back around and dropped low over Milliken State Park, then flew southward on a course following the riverfront toward Cobo Hall. Clark and Martineau could see the Renaissance Center coming into view to the right, its buildings illuminating the downtown area. The beautiful, shining complex seemed out of place as fires lit up the sky in the surrounding area.

As they flew closely by the high-rise tower of the Detroit Marriott, bullets ripped through the side of the helicopter. The agent who was leaning over Martineau took a bullet to the throat that killed him instantly. His body snapped back against the other side of the helicopter and then slammed to the floor. As the helicopter spun around wildly, Stryker yelled out, "We're going down! Hang on!"

From their location on the roof of the Marriott, Jorge Delgado and his men laughed heartily as Delgado unloaded a clip of pot shots from his machine gun at the passing helicopter. They cheered in unison as heavy black smoke poured out of the engine and the helicopter spun out of control. Ironically, Delgado didn't even know whose helicopter he had just shot.

Delgado turned to his men and said, "Let's get going," then he and his men continued placing C-4 plastic explosives across the roof of the Marriott.

Clark, Martineau, and the other agent were knocked to the floor as the helicopter abruptly pitched to the right. The agent moved over and shielded Martineau's body with his own. "Stay down, ma'am!"

Clark slid over to check the pulse of the agent who had been shot. "He's dead!" Clark called out.

The helicopter started to drift away from the river and head toward the area surrounding the RenCen. Stryker was doing everything he could to regain control, but nothing was working. "We have lost all oil pressure! I'm going to try to put us down in the river!"

Clark and Martineau were now lying face to face. Clark took Martineau's hand and said, "Crashing into the river will be much better than crashing on land!"

"Well now that's very reassuring, Sam," said Martineau, as she buried her face under the agent's shoulder.

Stryker pulled hard on the cyclic stick and managed to turn the helicopter around, but he continued to lose altitude rapidly as he flew low and fast toward the Detroit River. "We're not going to make it!" he warned. A moment later the landing skids slammed into the pavement of Hart Plaza and the helicopter slid forward, bright white sparks spraying into the air. It slid over a hundred feet directly toward the river and then flipped over the embankment wall, sending the passengers and pilot down into the icy cold waters of the Detroit River.

Delgado and his men saw none of this as they were making their way out of the Marriott. They ran quickly to their truck and sped away from the towering hotel, heading down New Street. At the first intersection Delgado's driver pulled a quick U-turn and stopped the vehicle in the middle of the street.

Delgado opened the passenger side door and stepped out, looking down the center of the street from where they had come. He grabbed the sides of the opened door and placed his foot on the floorboard, then boosted himself up and onto the hood. From there he climbed on to the roof of the truck as he continued to gaze down the street. A block away stood the Marriott.

A rescue team that was in the RenCen area witnessed Clark's helicopter slide into the Detroit River, and they raced toward the riverbank. Within minutes the rescue team members were pulling the occupants of the helicopter crash to safety.

The surviving Secret Service agent onboard had received a strong blow to the head. The rescue squad wrapped him in blankets and stabilized him while they waited for an ambulance to arrive. Stryker was holding onto his forearm to elevate his right hand. "I think I broke my wrist," he said nonchalantly. Clark and Martineau were battered and bruised, but on the whole both were feeling quite blessed that that was the worst they had suffered.

Clark, Martineau, and Stryker stood shivering next to the rescue vehicle even though they were wrapped in blankets. "Man, that water sure was cold, wasn't it?" said Clark.

Martineau looked up at Clark. Her hair was matted down around her face, which was streaked with wet eyeliner. Her clothes had been torn in multiple places. She was shivering uncontrollably and her teeth were chattering. "We were just in a helicopter that was shot out of the sky and the most troubling part of that for you was the temperature of the water?" she asked.

"I'm sorry, Kenna," said Clark as he looked toward the Renaissance Center. "I think those shots came from the Marriott."

"You're probably right," replied Martineau as she too looked toward the RenCen.

Clark walked over to Stryker, placed his hand on the pilot's shoulder and said, "That was some amazing flying. You saved our lives."

"Whoever shot us was using some heavy firepower, sir, " said Stryker. "It takes a lot to bring down a helicopter of that size. It scares me to think that there are people out in the city with weapons that have that capability." He looked at the Marriott and said, "And you're right, sir, the shots had to have come from the Marriott."

Chapter 51

Thomas stepped back to the couch and said to Daniel, "A helicopter just crashed into the Detroit River. Witnesses are telling reporters that it looked like it had been shot down."

Daniel was busy tending to Ixchel and Thomas's words barely registered in his mind. "Here, let's sit her up," Daniel said. Together Daniel and Thomas gently lifted Ixchel so she was sitting upright on the couch. Daniel and Thomas had both taken a knee and were now facing Ixchel. Daniel kept brushing Ixchel's hair out of her eyes.

"Daniel, what happened?" cried Ixchel. "What happened?"

"Don't you remember? You saw President Bonsam and heard the shots, and you screamed. I think you fainted after that."

The sound of Daniel's voice started to fade as Ixchel once again felt her world slip into slow motion. Her vision focused like a laser on the television but everything else in the room was a blur. Her mind became flooded with the images of the symbols on the Maya tablet.

A CNN news reporter standing near the RenCen was describing what he had seen when the helicopter had crashed nearby. The camera shifted up to show a panoramic view of the RenCen buildings towering above. As the image of the Detroit Marriott tower came into view, Ixchel gasped. In her mind the image of the tower slowly morphed into the image of an ancient Maya temple.

Delgado stood on the roof of his truck staring at the tower before him. He was savoring the moment. He had blown up many things over the years, but tonight would be his crowning achievement.

He held his pistol in one hand and the detonator in the other. Slowly he raised his arms and opened them slightly. He flipped the cover off the detonator button with his thumb and took a deep breath. He smiled, and then firmly pushed the detonator button.

An enormous ball of flames erupted from the top of the Marriott. The explosion was so intense that the shock wave knocked Delgado back two steps. He could feel the blistering heat as the inferno climbed into the sky. Delgado's arms remained outstretched as he gazed in wonder at his masterpiece. *"Dios te salve María!"* he exclaimed.

Clark, Martineau, and Stryker were still looking up at the Marriott as the explosion blew the top two floors entirely off the tower. The force of the blast pushed them back against the rescue vehicle. Shattered glass and fiery debris from the torched tower rained down on the area surrounding the RenCen.

The rescue team leader had been loading the agent into the back of an ambulance when the blast occurred. He turned around quickly and said to Clark, "Got to go!" A moment later the rescue team and the ambulance took off toward the site of the disaster.

Clark was filled with fury as fire raged from the top of the tower. "That was not done by rioters!" he roared.

As Ixchel's eyes widened, Thomas looked at Daniel and said, "Uh oh." The image of the Maya temple glowed before Ixchel's eyes. The vision before her radiated evil and she sensed a tremendous atrocity was imminent. She again pulled her hands to her mouth and screamed. A violent blast of wind slammed into her body. She was shaking in apprehension. She stared at the temple as the glow became stronger and stronger.

Ixchel pointed to the television and screamed again. Daniel and Thomas turned to look at the TV. The CNN anchor announced, "We are receiving breaking new images of the rioting in downtown Detroit. This is coming to us live from a DMBC news helicopter that is hovering over the riverfront area near the RenCen." CNN went to a split screen, with the anchor on the left and the images coming from the helicopter on the right.

The helicopter swung around and aimed its camera directly at the Marriott tower. It hung there as the CNN anchor carried on excitedly about the assassination attempt on President Bonsam. A minute later a mighty explosion blasted from atop the Marriott, sending pillars of flames high into the sky.

Daniel and Thomas were both stunned by the sight of the explosion. The temple-fire symbol raged through Ixchel's mind. She let out another powerful scream and collapsed into Daniel's arms.

Chapter 52

Morning had come. As dawn broke, sunlight streamed through the smoke-filled air of Detroit. Delgado and his two agents were making their way back to their truck to pack up their gear and get out of Michigan for good. Their work was done here. They had incited so much violence that it would be weeks, maybe even months, before Detroit returned to normal. Delgado smiled. *Perhaps it will never return to normal.*

He was filled with adrenaline as he continued making his way through the back streets. He turned down an alley, still feeling extremely proud of himself for the operation he had organized and executed. It was flawless. The president was going to be so pleased.

As he approached the back of the truck, he heard strange thumping noises behind him. He snapped out of his daydream and turned to see where the noise came from. As he turned, he said, "Hurry up you g…" He stopped in his tracks, unable to complete his command. Less than ten yards behind him lay his two agents, blood pouring onto the asphalt from their freshly bashed in skulls. Over them stood two of the biggest black dudes Delgado had ever seen, each wielding an aluminum baseball bat.

Delgado knew right away that he was in deep shit. He had already broken down his assault rifle and he hadn't put a fresh clip in his pistol since he had fired victory shots into the air as the RenCen exploded. He turned to race to the truck, but didn't even get to take a single step.

"Mierda!" was all he got out of his mouth as the barrel of a .45 Glock was pressed against the center of his forehead. Delgado was overcome with shock. His shock was quickly replaced by fear.

The man holding the gun had seething hatred in his eyes. He pressed the gun harder against Delgado's forehead and said, *"Hola, amigo."*

Chapter 53

"*Que pasa*, George," said Clay, as he applied more pressure to Delgado's forehead with the barrel of his weapon.

"How in the hell...?" Delgado gasped as he slowly raised his hands.

Clay cut him off. "You should have counted the bullet-proof vests before you left, *muchacho*."

Since day one, Clay's instincts had told him that Delgado was not to be trusted. He had always sensed that Delgado was plotting something against him. Delgado's suave Hispanic charisma did not work on Clay and he had grown more suspicious of Delgado each and every time he was around him.

Clay's perception of Delgado had made him extra cautious. Clay had never turned his back to Delgado out of fear that the snake in the grass was patiently waiting for the right moment to strike. His distrust of Delgado prompted him to pick the lock of the SWAT truck a few days before the meeting with Lane. It wouldn't hurt to take a look inside, he had thought.

Upon entering the back of the truck, the first thing that had caught his eye was a large box of tranquilizer darts. He could not imagine why in the hell Delgado would need those. Whatever the reason, it had confirmed Clay's suspicion that Delgado had other plans for the Lane rendezvous that he had not shared with him.

As he continued to poke around the back of the tuck, he found a fireproof lockbox. He picked the lock in an instant, and discovered that it was full of fake driver's licenses, counterfeit passports, and real-world badges for several high-level government agencies. He helped himself to a few badges then returned the lockbox to where he had found it.

Next he popped the lock of an equipment chest, removed a bulletproof vest, and then relocked the chest. As he was exiting the truck with the vest and the badges, he grabbed a couple of boxes of .45 caliber rounds as extra insurance. He was going to be well prepared for the upcoming mission, much more prepared than Delgado realized.

Clay continued, "So, the president extends his thanks, huh?"

Delgado quickly regained his composure. His voice lowered, "You have no idea what you're getting yourself into, Clay."

With one quick nod from Clay, Isaac and Isaiah each grabbed one of Delgado's arms and twisted it up into Delgado's back, nearly dislocating both shoulders. Delgado let out an, "Ahhh," as the Grant brothers continued twisting his arms.

Clay narrowed his eyes and moved closer to Delgado. "No, it's Bonsam who doesn't know what he's gotten himself into, George."

Delgado let out a laugh. "What are you thinking? You think you're gonna kill the president? Bonsam will squash you like a *cucaracha*."

"Maybe you're right, George. Maybe I can't kill Bonsam." Clay moved directly in front of Delgado's face. "But I can kill you, *pendejo*."

Delgado's blood ran cold. His composure started to fade and his voice cracked with nervousness. "You don't have the *cojones* to shoot me, Clay."

Clay looked Delgado straight in the eye. "You're right, George," he replied, and with one swift move he pulled a ten-inch blade from his belt and plunged it to the hilt into Delgado's stomach. Delgado's eyes rolled back and a choking sound came from his throat as he took in his last breath. "*Adios*, George," said Clay, and he gave the knife a quick 180-degree twist.

Isaac and Isaiah let go of Delgado's lifeless body and let it drop to the pavement. "I told you we were gonna kill you, motherfucker," said Isaiah as he looked down at Delgado.

Clay bent down and wiped the blood from his blade on Delgado's sleeve. His hatred for the man he had just killed still remained. He stood back up and said to his brothers, "Come on, we've got some work to do."

Chapter 54

The command center that had been set up at City Hall was bustling with activity. Law enforcement personnel from a dozen different agencies were hastily coordinating their efforts to bring law and order back to Detroit. Messages cracked over police radios, phones were ringing off the hook, fax machines were churning out faxes nonstop, and so much documentation had been printed that it was necessary to send out for more print cartridges.

The main conference room was the command center's hub of activity. Within it many of the major players had gathered around the wall-sized projection of a map of Detroit. The Deputy Mayor, the Detroit Chief of Police, the Director of the Michigan State Police, and the Command Sergeant Major of the Michigan National Guard were among those listening intently to Lieutenant Governor Christopher Purnell.

Purnell had actually been in the Palace during the assassination attempt on the president. Luckily, he had managed to get out of the arena quickly. His instincts had told him that rioting was sure to begin. He quickly decided that the Secret Service and the FBI could deal with the assassination attempt. Detroit was his number one priority, so he had dashed straight down to City Hall.

Clark and Martineau had spent the early morning hours making their way to City Hall. They had to walk, understandably, since they weren't about to find a taxi downtown after the previous night's events. Along the way they had to stop a few times to give assistance to citizens who had been hurt by the explosion's falling debris. Finally they arrived at City Hall, haggard and tired. A police officer quickly escorted them to the main conference room.

Purnell stopped talking and raised his eyebrows as Clark and Martineau entered the room. Everyone at the map turned to see what Purnell was looking at and they too raised their eyebrows. "Uh, good morning, Governor," Purnell said.

"Christopher," Clark said with a nod to Purnell as he slowly limped toward a chair and took a seat.

Purnell looked at Clark's appearance and was baffled. "Well, how nice of you to join us," he said sarcastically yet politely. "So, how was Mackinac Island?"

"The flight back was a little bumpy," Clark replied. "But other than that…."

"Stop with the exchange of pleasantries already!" Martineau brashly said. "The president was almost killed, we were in a helicopter crash," she said as she pointed back and forth between herself and Clark, "and there was an explosion at the RenCen that you could feel in Toledo. What is wrong with you two?"

Purnell stared at Martineau for a moment then turned back to Clark. "Well your mother and I have been worried sick! You couldn't just pick up a phone and let us know that you were going to be…."

"Stop it!" yelled Martineau.

"Let's all try to remain professional, shall we?" the Deputy Mayor said diplomatically.

The Guard Command Sergeant Major stepped forward and said, "Governor, we have mobilized almost every Guard unit in the state. Many are already here, others are in transit, and others are standing by. The Governor of Ohio has offered us some troops as well. Lieutenant Governor Purnell's actions to integrate the Guard troops with the state and local police forces were extraordinarily successful. We now have hundreds of patrols systematically running throughout the city. Although the rioting had been heavy throughout the night, there have been few reports of any major violence this morning. We think the RenCen explosion had such a profound impact on the citizens of Detroit that even the worst offenders stopped what they were doing and simply went home to be with their loved ones."

Clark took a minute to let the information he had just received soak in. He then turned to Purnell and said, "Well done, Chris."

"I know," the lieutenant governor replied.

Calvin Hill, the Detroit Chief of Police walked over to Clark and shook his hand. "It's good to see you again, Governor."

"Good to see you, too, Calvin," replied Clark as he strained to get out of his chair.

"Don't get up, sir. But I think it is imperative that you get on television as soon as possible and speak to the citizens of Detroit. Make a call for calm. Let them know that we are doing everything within our power to bring civility back to the city."

"He's right, Sam. The people need to hear your reassurance that the situation is under control," said Martineau. "Thank you, Chief."

Thirty minutes later Clark was in front of the cameras, broadcasting a message stating he wanted to restore the people of Detroit's confidence in the state and city law enforcement personnel and other government agencies that were working diligently to reestablish peace within the city.

In the White House, President Bonsam watched Clark's appeal with disdain. He was certain that Clark's presidential campaign was now dead in its tracks. Delgado had exceeded his expectations, and he looked forward to thanking him in person. Bonsam was surprised though, that Delgado had not yet reported in.

Chapter 55

Later that afternoon Clark and Martineau returned to City Hall. They were both feeling much better now that they had had a chance to grab a shower, eat a hearty meal, and catch a couple of hours of sleep. Clark's key staff members from Lansing had arrived a few hours earlier and had just finished setting up a temporary Governor's office located down the hall from the command center.

Brett Mason and Emily Kates were all smiles as they greeted Clark upon his arrival to his new office. Emily rushed forward and gave Clark a big bear hug. "You're the first person I've met who has been in a helicopter crash," she said. "It's great to see you safe and sound!"

"It's great to see you, too, Emily," he replied. "Brett, nice to see you, too," he said as he reached out and shook Mason's hand.

"Welcome to your new digs," said Mason as he led Clark into his temporary office. "You've got a line of people waiting to see you, Gov. The FBI is here in full force. Before I go I need to pass on a message I just received that I think you'll find interesting. A superintendent from the Ontario Provincial Police wants you to call him. He says they nabbed the group of yahoos responsible for that horrific murder of the hardware store owner in Cass Corridor. He wants to turn them over to us, and these are his words, 'without all that mucking about with extradition.'"

Clark took the note and smiled. "Have Chief Hill give him a call. In the meantime go ahead and send in the FBI."

"They are in the command center, Gov. It would probably be easier if you just went to them."

Minutes later Clark entered the command center. He walked over to a bank of monitors where Martineau was standing. As he approached she said, "Governor Clark, this is Special Agent Kenneth Gibson. He is the lead investigator on the assassination attempt."

"Good to see you again, Sam," said Special Agent Gibson. "However, it would have been much nicer to see you under different circumstances."

"You two already know each other?" Martineau asked.

"We go way back," said Clark. He turned to Gibson and said, "What have you got so far, Ken?"

Gibson pulled out his notebook. "The three men killed by the Secret Service all belonged to a Michigan Militia organization."

"Funny how quickly the president's press secretary knew that," Martineau said.

"Their organization, however, operated independently of the true Militia. It had strong ties to the KKK. The leader was a man by the name of William Seward Lane. The other men have been identified as Bud Kenner and Spencer Boyd. All three are from Washtenaw County."

"An assassination attempt on the president seems like a pretty bold move for an organization such as this," Clark stated.

"That's where things fall apart. None of them ever even finished high school. Lane was the only one to get a GED. Boyd and Kenner couldn't even spell GED. They had no military experience or military training of any kind. They were just your everyday yokels," said Gibson.

"I think I see where you're going with this," said Clark. "Go on."

"To me it is obvious that there is absolutely no way these three hayseeds could ever get past the Secret Service operations, let alone the Palace's security force, heavily armed and loaded for bear. Not even with inside help."

Clark and Martineau exchanged glances. They were beginning to have the same suspicions.

Gibson continued, "And from what we can tell so far, the explosives used to knock out both the power and backup power to the Palace were uncommonly sophisticated and planted at the precise locations that would cause the most damage."

"I'll bet you'll find that the same types of explosives were used on the Marriott," said Martineau.

"We are already looking into that, ma'am," Gibson replied.

There was a long silence. Clark shook his head and said, "This doesn't add up."

Gibson paused. "I have something else you need to take a look at," he said as he moved toward a bank of monitors. "These monitors are synchronized to show the moments leading up to the assassination attempt from every possible camera angle. Watch this."

Gibson hit the play button and the footage of Bonsam's speech rolled across the monitors. Clark and Martineau stared at the screens. As the moment of the assassination attempt neared, they stepped closer to the monitors. Seeing the president come under fire was just as shocking now as it was the first time they had witnessed it.

"This time I am going to play it in slow motion. I'll also turn the sound up. Pay particular attention to Bonsam the moment before the bullets began to fly. Watch as he says the word 'election.'"

Clark and Martineau leaned even closer to the monitors. They watched intently as the slow motion voice of Bonsam spoke out, "...before... you... tonight... on... the... eve... of... history's... last... election..." A second later Gibson hit the pause button.

Gibson looked at Clark. "Did you see it?"

Martineau was puzzled and she looked back and forth between Gibson and Clark. "What?"

Clark slowly stood up straight and continued to look into the monitor. "He flinched," he whispered. He turned to Gibson and said, "He flinched before the shots were fired. He knew what was coming."

The three of them stood in silence for several minutes as they mulled over the significance of what they had just witnessed. Finally Gibson said, "Sam, the FBI is going to get to the bottom of this. My team will continue investigating this around the clock. But Sam, don't share this information with anyone. At this point, I don't trust anyone, especially the president."

Clark shook his head and said, "I understand."

Gibson started to turn to walk away, when Martineau piped up, "Wait, wait, wait! Play it again. Listen closely to what Bonsam says."

Gibson and Clark exchanged glances. Gibson hit the play button and the slow motion footage ran again. "...on... the... eve... of..."

"Listen, listen, listen!" whispered Martineau.

"...history's... last... election..."

Clark got it. "History's last election? What in the hell did he mean by *last* election?"

Chapter 56

Clark, Martineau, and Gibson left the command center and returned to Clark's office. Martineau could not get the phrase, "history's last election" out of her mind. "Sam, Ken, what do you make of Bonsam's use of the words 'last election?' He didn't say that by mistake, it had to mean something."

"I have to agree with you, ma'am," replied Gibson. "It seemed totally out of place."

Before Clark could reply, Emily entered the office. "Governor Clark, there is someone here to see you. He's sitting in the lobby."

Clark looked at Emily and waited. He waited some more. "Well, who is it?"

"He won't say, sir."

"What do you mean he won't say? I am way too busy to be meeting with strangers off the street, Emily. And how did he get past the Secret Service to reach your desk?"

"He has some sort of badge that made the Secret Service guys stand up straight and call him sir. They waved him right through."

Clark squeezed his eyes shut and pinched the bridge of his nose. He then looked up and said, "Okay Emily, bring him in."

As she left the office, Martineau looked at Clark. She shrugged her shoulders and stuck her hands out to her sides, palms up. Clark looked back, shaking his head in exasperation. Gibson took a seat on the couch so he could have a good view of the meeting.

Both Clark and Martineau were taken by surprise as the man entered the room. They were not expecting a young, handsome man who was dressed in jeans, a black t-shirt, and a black leather jacket. He was not someone you would expect to be carrying around a government badge of any kind, let alone one that would get you past the Secret Service.

He stopped in front of Clark's desk, but he didn't speak a word. Clark looked into his eyes, wondering what was going through the mind of this unexpected visitor.

Emily was standing next to the man, gazing at him adoringly. Clark broke eye contact with the man and looked over at Emily. "That will be all, Emily," he said as he returned to meet the man's stare. Emily gave the visitor a quick look up and down then turned and walked out of the office. At the sound of the door closing, the man spoke.

"Good morning, Governor Clark. My name is Clayton Jackson."

Clark was still perplexed. "What can I do for you, Mr. Jackson?"

"You can help me bring down Emmanuel Bonsam."

Chapter 57

Clark and Martineau looked at each other in disbelief. Gibson leaned forward.

"*Bring down* Bonsam? What is that supposed to mean?" Clark asked.

"Sir, President Bonsam orchestrated the assassination attempt. It was completely staged," Clay replied. "And his personal agents are responsible for running covert operations throughout Detroit during the night of the riots in order to escalate the violence. The explosion at the RenCen, that was all Bonsam's doing."

Clark leaned back in his chair. "That is quite a fascinating conspiracy theory, Mr. Jackson. Do you have any evidence to support this claim?"

Clay leaned forward as he reached into his jacket pocket. "I have a truckload of evidence," he replied, and he placed Delgado's truck keys on Clark's desk.

Special Agent Gibson took copious notes as Clay provided detailed directions to the location of the truck. "And this truck will contain evidence that will directly link President Bonsam to the assassination attempt, the riots, and the RenCen explosion," Gibson said skeptically. "Am I missing anything else?"

"No, I think that pretty well covers it."

Gibson pulled out his cell phone and placed a call to the lead FBI crime scene investigator in Detroit. "Get your best team together and have them meet me in the command center."

Gibson's skepticism remained. He looked at Clay and said, "So where are the agents who belong to this truck?"

"They are dead," Clay replied.

Gibson's eyebrows shot straight up. "And how do you know this?"

"I," said Clay as he dragged out the "I" sound, "saw them."

"You saw them? Where are the bodies?"

"Well, unless there was a trash pickup this morning, they are in a dumpster in an alley off Woodbridge Street."

Gibson stared at Clay. Without taking his eyes off him, he pulled out his cell phone and hit redial. "I'm going to need another CSI team."

Clay started looking around the room and whistled innocently.

"Come with me, Mr. Jackson. We're going to take a little ride on out to Woodbridge," Gibson said.

Martineau jumped up and said, "I'm coming with you."

"I'm sorry, ma'am, but you cannot come along. There have already been attempts made on your life," Gibson replied. "It's too dangerous, even with the Secret Service there. You should stay here."

Martineau took a step toward Gibson. She put her hands on her hips, cleared her throat, and said, "I'm coming with you."

Gibson looked at Martineau, and then over to Clark. Clark waved his hands in front of himself indicating that he was not getting involved in this discussion. Gibson looked back over at Martineau and said, "All right ma'am, you're welcome to come with us."

Clay looked over at Martineau and said, "Thank you, ma'am."

"Thank you, Mr. Jackson," she replied. "If what you say is true, I want to see it for myself," and together they walked out of the office with Special Agent Gibson.

As they exited the building, Martineau stopped, turned to Clay and said, "And one more thing, Mr. Jackson."

Martineau's expression was stone cold. Clay looked at her suspecting she was about to remind him that he could be facing serious jail time. "Yes, ma'am?" he replied nervously.

"I get shotgun," she said as she took Gibson by the arm and headed toward the investigator's car.

Gibson once again had his notebook out as he stood with Clay and Martineau behind the yellow crime scene tape. "Let me see if I got this straight. You were recruited by a secret agency, full of spies and assassins and whatnot. Am I right so far?"

"Yes," Clay replied.

"And you were on a covert mission to wipe out the Michigan Militia, but a secret agent named Jorge Delgado double-crossed you and tried to kill you."

Clay nodded his head once, "Correct."

"And so you went looking for Delgado, and you found him in this alley, lying there dead," he said as he pointed to the body bags lying in the alley, "along with two other secret agents who were also dead. That's your story?"

"That's the story I'm sticking to," replied Clay.

"Now wait a minute, Mr. Jackson," Gibson sternly said, but before he could continue his phone rang. He let out a sigh and answered it, "Special Agent Gibson."

Gibson's eyes remained on Clay as he listened to the CSI agent on the other end. The CSI team had located the truck that Clay had described. He continued to listen for several minutes as the CSI agent described the treasure trove of evidence within the truck. There were high-powered automatic rifles, handguns with laser sights, and military-grade explosives with electronic detonators. The agent also indicated that there were bloodstains on the floor, and they had already shipped samples to the CSI lab for DNA analysis. Gibson's expression never changed.

Finally he hung up his phone and looked at Martineau. "His story about the truck checks out. The CSI team leader can't believe what they've found inside."

He then turned his attention back to Clay. "Now, about these bodies...."

Before he could finish the sentence, Martineau cut him off. "Special Agent Gibson, I know how busy you and the entire Bureau have been since the president was nearly assassinated and riots broke out all over town. Mr. Jackson's story is convincing enough for me. It appears as though these three poor souls just happened to be in the wrong place at the wrong time. It would be impossible to find the culprits responsible for these deaths. I'd write this one off as a tragic act of random violence during the rioting. Let the Detroit police take it from here."

Gibson raised one eyebrow and stared at Martineau. "These three poor souls," he said as he again motioned to the body bags. "These three poor souls, who were found in a dumpster decked out in state of the art tactical uniforms, two with their skulls crushed and the third nearly disemboweled, were victims of random violence."

Martineau looked over at Clay, and together they nodded their heads in agreement with Gibson's assessment. Gibson's face remained emotionless as he clicked his pen and flipped his notebook shut. "Works for me," he said.

Chapter 58

The following afternoon Special Agent Gibson returned to City Hall. He entered the command center and was surprised to find Martineau inside. She was looking over the report that outlined the initial findings at the site of the Marriott explosion. "This is incredible," she said to herself.

"What's so incredible?" Gibson asked as he approached Martineau.

"People in Canada are finding pieces of the Marriott in their yards. It's a miracle that only six people were killed in an explosion like that. Lieutenant Governor Purnell's order to have the National Guard swiftly evacuate downtown saved a lot of lives."

"You're right," he replied as he thought about the magnitude of the explosion. He then asked, "Is Clark here?"

"He's in his office," Martineau replied.

"Come with me, I have more news about what has been discovered in Delgado's truck."

Clark and Clay were in a heated debate as to whether surviving gunshots to the chest at close range while wearing a bulletproof vest was more impressive than surviving a helicopter crash when Gibson and Martineau walked into Clark's office. "Don't get up," said Gibson.

"Hadn't planned on it," replied Clark.

Martineau and Gibson sat down in the chairs in front of Clark's desk. Gibson turned to Clay who was leaning against the windowsill and said, "Slide on over here, Mr. Jackson. You're going to want to hear this, too." Clay took a seat on the end of the couch closest to Clark's desk and sat up straight, still unsure of what Gibson had in store for him.

"The contents of Delgado's truck are truly unbelievable," Gibson began. "Delgado had enough military weapons and explosives to conquer a small country. Everything he had was state of the art."

"Not the kind of stuff you pick up from a local gun store, huh?" asked Clark.

"Not quite," replied Gibson, "but there is more. The phones that Delgado was using had an encryption system unlike anything the techies at Quantico have ever seen. They say it's highly unlikely that they will ever be able to determine who he was calling or who was calling him."

"Too bad," said Martineau. "That could have helped us root out even more of Bonsam's spies."

"On the bright side, we found Delgado's laptop computer," Gibson went on. "It also has a highly sophisticated encryption system, however, Quantico has already begun to decrypt some pieces of information."

"Anything useful?" asked Clark.

"Not yet, but Quantico believes that they will find more soon. The info uncovered so far appears as if it came from some kind of laundry list of Delgado's operations, operations that he had already carried out and operations that were yet to come. Much more time will be needed to piece it all together."

Gibson then looked toward Clay. "We did find a few nuggets of info regarding the Michigan Militia. It appears to corroborate what Mr. Jackson here has told us."

Gibson gave a nod of approval to Clay. Clay nodded back.

"There were other bits of information that completely puzzled the techies though. They found vague, cryptic entries about ancient Maya artifacts. Clay, does that mean anything to you?"

"Nope, it means nothing to me," replied Clay. "I never heard Delgado talk about Maya artifacts."

"What in the world does that have to do with anything?" Martineau thought aloud.

Gibson shrugged his shoulders and continued with his report. "Sam, here is the main purpose of this visit. We did discover information that is going to lead to some arrests. The warrants are being prepared as we speak."

"Arrests?" Clark was surprised to hear that. "Really? Who?"

"Well, the number one person we plan to visit first thing tomorrow is Mr. Darius Robinson. He is the newscast producer for DMBC."

Chapter 59

Special Agent Gibson fastened his seatbelt and made himself comfortable. "Thanks for the lift, Dave."

"Thanks for letting me come along for this arrest," said Detective David Delaney. Delaney was the head of the Detroit Police Department's Homicide Division. "For a *Federale*, you're all right."

Gibson laughed. "Well, I'm really going to need your help. This should be interesting. I can't wait to hear what Robinson has to say about Delgado."

"Me, too," replied Delaney.

"This Delgado character must have been pretty arrogant. He must have thought he'd never get caught."

"Ignorant is the word I'd use," replied Delaney. "He had the type of phones and a computer that you would only see in a James Bond movie, yet he left that information about Robinson and DMBC lying around his SWAT truck on a note pad, metaphorically speaking of course."

"Maybe it was false info planted to mislead an investigation if he ever got caught."

"Well, we're about to find out. We're here."

"Darius, your coverage of the rioting was phenomenal. People are already talking about a Peabody Award coming our way."

"Thank you, Marty," replied Robinson. Martin Schoenberg was the President of DMBC and Robinson's boss.

The two men were sitting in Schoenberg's office on the stately leather couches near the large picture window that overlooked the trees of Grand Circus Park. Schoenberg pointed toward the award display case that sat beneath an original Renoir that he had inherited from his grandfather. "I have a spot already selected for it," said Schoenberg eagerly.

Schoenberg looked up as he saw his secretary peering around the slightly opened door. "Come in," he said as he waved her forward.

She slid into his office, never fully opening the door, and then shut it quietly behind her. "Sir, the FBI is here to see you." Robinson's heart started to race, but on the outside he remained calm.

"Yes, yes. Send them in," he said. He then looked over at Robinson and said, "I'll bet that they request our assistance in their investigations of the riots."

The secretary opened the door and motioned to the visitors indicating they could now enter the office. Special Agent Gibson walked in first with Detective Delaney right behind. Schoenberg got up from the couch and approached Gibson with his hand extended. "Welcome gentlemen. I am Marty Schoenberg, President of DMBC. How may I assist you?"

Gibson took Schoenberg's hand and gave it a nice firm handshake. "Actually Mr. Schoenberg, we're here to see Mr. Robinson, or should I say, 'Lion One.'"

Delaney stepped toward Robinson and said, "Mr. Robinson I have a warrant for your arrest. You are being charged as an accessory to the murder of Joseph Franklin, Jr."

Delaney motioned for Robinson to stand up. When he did, Delaney stepped behind him and pulled his arms around his back. As he placed handcuffs on Robinson's wrists, he began to read him his rights. "You have the right to remain silent…"

Schoenberg looked on in disbelief. "What is the meaning of this?"

"Come on down to Police Headquarters with us Mr. Schoenberg, we'll tell you all about it," said Gibson.

Chapter 60

Clark and Martineau joined Chief Hill, who was standing at the window of the interrogation room where Darius Robinson sat alone. "He is one cool customer," said Hill as he looked in. "But we'll see just how cool he is after Delaney and Gibson are through with him."

"Thanks, Chief," Clark replied. He looked at Martineau and said, "I hope this interrogation will reveal who else was involved in this plot."

"I hope it verifies whether Clay's accusations that the president was somehow involved are true or not," replied Martineau.

"Excuse me, sorry to interrupt," said the chief. "They are about to begin."

Robinson remained calm as Delaney and Gibson entered the room. He sat at the table with his legs stretched out and his hands folded across his stomach.

As Delaney and Gibson pulled their chairs up to the table, Delaney said to Robinson, "Comfortable?"

"Very," replied Robinson.

"Okay, let's get right to business," said Gibson. "You ever heard of a man named Jorge Delgado?" He slid a picture of Delgado, one that had been taken by the CSI team when they first discovered his corpse, across the table to Robinson.

Robinson casually glanced at the picture, and then he looked up and shook his head no. Inside, his heart raced again. *They killed Delgado!*

"Recognize these guys?" asked Delaney as he slid four mug shots of the men accused of murdering Joe Franklin across the table. "Because this one here," he said as he tapped on the picture of Erik Torgersen, "sure seems to know a lot about DMBC. He hasn't stopped talking about it since he was arrested."

Gibson's turn. "And how was it that a mobile DMBC news team arrived so quickly at the scene of Joseph Franklin's murder?"

Over to Delaney. "DMBC was first on the scene at several murders that night."

"Right. Remember the Kaczmarek murders?"

"Yes, how horrific."

"Boy, whoever was involved in these murders will be going to jail for the rest of his life."

"You know, I hope they don't lock him up in one of those federal country clubs you call a prison," Delaney said as he looked over at Gibson. "I say put him in the Detroit Jail."

"I heard it was getting really crowded in there."

"Oh, the place is jam packed with the dregs of Detroit."

"And how's that been working out?"

"Well, the violence between inmates has been unbelievable. I'm not sure if they just didn't get enough of their frustrations out while they were tearing up Detroit or if they are dissatisfied with having eight men to a cell."

"You think any of those violent inmates might be from the Cass Corridor?"

"Oh, most definitely. We even locked up a number of gang members who were from Joe Franklin's neighborhood."

Gibson leaned forward. "You could be roommates with them, Lion One!"

"Oh, and by the way, the Detroit PD is currently out rounding up Lions Two through Six. Amazing just how many of them are reporters from DMBC. Can't wait to hear what they have to say."

There was a long pause as Gibson and Delaney stared at Robinson. Robinson lifted his hands from his stomach and clapped slowly. "Nice try guys, but you don't intimidate me. You got nothing and I have the best lawyer in town. By the time he is through with you, you'll be working parking lot security for the rest of your careers."

There was another long pause. Gibson then leaned back away from the table. He took out his notebook and opened it so that Delaney could see it. He used his pen to point to an item inside. "Hey, look at this, Detective. When we looked into Mr. Robinson's background, we discovered that he graduated from high school in the same class as President Bonsam."

"Now there's an interesting little coinkidink," Delaney replied.

Robinson's feet flew back and he sat up straight. He knew that if Bonsam found out that the FBI had linked them together, friends or not, it would mean certain death for him and his wife, his children, and probably his pets as well.

"What do you say we give the president a call, see what he thinks of all this."

"Yeah, he could be a character witness for you when you go to trial."

Gibson and Delaney pushed their chairs away from the table and stood up.

"Wait, wait, wait!" Robinson cried out. "I'll tell you what you want to know." He then looked at Special Agent Gibson and said, "But first, you need to tell me about the Witness Protection Program."

Gibson and Delaney exited the interrogation room and joined the group at the window. "Did you see his reaction when we mentioned Bonsam?" said Gibson. "He cracked like an egg."

"He sang like a canary," added Detective Delaney.

"He squealed like a pig," stated Chief Hill.

Clark wanted in on the fun. "He croaked like a frog," he said with a big grin on his face.

Gibson, Delaney and Hill looked at Clark, then at one another, without saying a word. Finally, Martineau said, "Sam, that makes absolutely no sense."

After an uncomfortable pause, Chief Hill turned to Detective Delaney and said, "Let's get him before the

Grand Jury. He's going to be indicted on a whole slew of counts, including accessory to murder." Then he turned to Clark and said, "We got it from here, Governor."

As Hill and Delaney walked off, Gibson said to Clark. "Oh, and in case you forgot, the presidential election is in four days. I think you might want to throw in a little campaigning between now and then. Chief Hill is right, we got it from here." Gibson's tone became serious. "Sam, you need to stay out of this. This is a criminal matter. If you focus on beating Bonsam in the election, we'll focus on bringing him to justice."

"Just be careful, Ken," replied Clark. "There is no way of knowing who else is working for Bonsam, and there is no way of knowing what else he has up his sleeve," said Clark.

"No worries, Sam," said Gibson. "Now you two run along. Back to Lansing, now," he said as he waved them away.

Clark gave him a handshake and then he and Martineau walked off toward the Secret Service agents who were waiting for them in the next room. "Croaked like a frog?" said Martineau as she slowly shook her head.

Once they were gone, Gibson walked down the hall and made his way to the office that the Mayor had allowed him to use. As he entered, Marty Schoenberg quickly got up from his seat. "Please, keep your seat, Mr. Schoenberg," said Gibson as he walked around his desk and took a seat.

Schoenberg was much too distraught to stay seated. "Where is Darius Robinson?"

Gibson paused for a second. "Right now I'd say he's either getting fingerprinted or having his mug shot taken, Mr. Schoenberg. He is under arrest for multiple charges, some of them very serious."

Schoenberg could not believe what he was hearing. "What has he been charged with?"

"As a newsman you must realize that I cannot discuss the matter with you at this time," said Gibson. "However, I can tell you that the investigation into his alleged crimes will begin at DMBC. He has DMBC so wrapped up in this mess that I'm afraid your network may never recover from the negative publicity. Even if he is proven innocent, which is extremely unlikely, the damage will be done. I'm sorry."

"No, this can't be happening!" Schoenberg began pacing back and forth. He kept running his hand from his forehead back through his hair. "DMBC has been my whole life. Has he incriminated DMCB?"

"As I said, Mr. Schoenberg, I can't go into details at this time," replied Gibson calmly. *Now for the big set up.* He leaned forward and said, "The only way DMBC will survive is if you come out with the whole story, Mr. Schoenberg. Robinson isn't the only one in your organization who's going down. It is up to you to make DMBC come clean and you need to do it fast, before the news of Robinson's arrest gets out."

"Come clean with what? I have no idea what's going on."

"Tell you what Mr. Schoenberg. I'll make you a deal. I'll give you the scoop of a lifetime and it will save DMBC," said Gibson. He paused for a second. "As long as I remain an unnamed source."

Schoenberg knew a good deal when he saw one. "Agreed."

Chapter 61

The next morning Clark and Martineau traveled back to Lansing. A little before noon, Martineau joined Clark in his office for a quick lunch. "You know what gets me the most about this whole assassination attempt fiasco," said Clark as he munched on a ham and cheese sandwich.

"No I don't, Sam," replied Martineau, "and stop talking with your mouth full. For heaven's sake you're about to become president. Please tell me you'll display a little more etiquette during state dinners." She then tossed a napkin across the desk to Clark.

"Sorry," he replied as he wiped his mouth with the napkin. He cleared his throat and continued. "What gets me is the brutality of Bonsam's henchmen. We lost four Secret Service agents that night, and one of them was from the QRF team. He was a young guy, newly married." Clark shook his head in disgust. "Security officers, state troopers, you name it. All had members killed or wounded. And it wasn't random gunfire that got 'em, they were specifically targeted."

"I know what you mean," she replied. "These shadow agents, whoever they may be, are modern day barbarians. To murder men that had sworn to protect the life of the U.S. President! It's incomprehensible."

"You're right," said Clark. "Even the reports on the deaths of the three militia members are horrendous. The two bubbas were shot over a dozen times each, and poor old Lane had nearly every bone in his body broken when he hit the floor. I mean the coroner said they had to scoop him up with a snow shovel. There was blood and brains and that cartilaginous goo covering a circle eight feet in diameter." Clark then slurped the remainder of his soft drink through a straw.

Martineau stopped what she was doing and looked down at the sandwich in her hands. She let it plop onto the wrapper in front of her and pushed it toward Clark. "Thanks, Sam," she said. "There goes my appetite."

Clark and Martineau looked up as they heard two quick knocks on the office door. Mason stuck his head in the room and asked, "May I come in?" and proceeded to enter the room before Clark had the opportunity to say no. "Good afternoon, ma'am, good afternoon, Gov. Glad to be back in Lansing?"

"Without a doubt," replied Martineau. "Detroit has definitely been removed from my list of vacation destinations for a while."

Clark laughed at Martineau's comment. He then turned to Mason and asked, "What do you have for me, Brett?"

Mason walked over to the television, picked up the remote, and hit the power button. "Sir, you need to start watching DMBC. They keep making special announcements saying that they have uncovered shocking new information about the Detroit riots. They are really hyping it up. They say they are going to go live with a special report at six o'clock."

Clark looked at Martineau for a moment, then back to Mason. "Thank you Brett, I look forward to watching it."

Chapter 62

Governor Clark was not the only one eager to watch the upcoming report. President Bonsam was caught completely off guard by DMBC's announcements and he too wanted to know what was in the report. He immediately contacted Agent Dolan in the Communications Office. "Have you heard from Delgado yet?" had asked with anger in his voice.

"No, sir," replied Dolan. "I have two teams of agents scouring Detroit, but so for they have been unable to locate him."

"Damn him!" shouted Bonsam. "Listen Dolan, get in touch with Darius Robinson and find out what the hell is going on!"

By 5:30 Dolan still had not reported back. "What is taking him so long?" Bonsam said to himself as he paced around the Oval Office. He could feel his temperature rising with every passing minute, and with it he felt the demons in the back of his mind waiting to attack. He lit a cigarette to calm his nerves. "I need to stay in control!" he said as he watched DMBC announce yet again that the special report was only minutes away.

By the time the phone rang at 5:55, Bonsam was furious. "What the hell took you so long, Dolan?" he screamed. "Where is Robinson?"

"Mr. President, I am afraid I have some bad news," Dolan replied nervously. "Robinson has been taken into custody by the FBI."

Suddenly, every nightmare Bonsam had ever dreamt struck his mind like bolts of lightning. He experienced his own private hell for less than a second, but his mind was clear now. He felt an incredible surge of power flowing through his veins. He glared at the television, knowing that whatever was reported would not affect him. *After all, I am Emmanuel Bonsam. No one can touch me.* "Stay on the line," he said to Agent Dolan as he placed the phone call on hold.

At the DMBC studio, Marty Schoenberg was going over his notes one last time. The speech he was about to give would either make him or break him, there was no in between. He looked over at Dean Reaves, who was getting one last blast of hair spray before they went live. Reaves had been fuming all afternoon, knowing that Darius Robinson had made a chump out of him. He was going to hit Robinson back and hit him hard. He brushed away the makeup artist and turned to Schoenberg. "We're live in 30 seconds, Marty," he said. "You're going to be fine."

"Thanks, Dean," he replied confidently, even though his stomach was in knots.

Schoenberg took in a deep breath and closed his eyes, going over his speech one last time in his mind. He heard the set director call out, "Cue the music," and ten seconds later they were live.

"Good evening, I'm Dean Reaves, and this is DMBC. Tonight, we have an exclusive report of unbelievable treachery that occurred during the Detroit riots. Shocking new evidence has come to light revealing a well-organized group of conspirators conducted covert operations to incite and exacerbate racial violence on the night of the riots. Here with me now is the Executive President of DMBC, Martin Schoenberg, with more on this chilling tale."

The camera panned back, showing Schoenberg seated at the news desk beside Reaves. Reaves turned to Schoenberg and said with pretended sincerity, "Mr. Schoenberg, welcome to tonight's program. I know that the information you are about to share with our loyal viewers must be extremely difficult for you to report." The camera then focused solely on Schoenberg, removing Reaves from view.

"Good evening ladies and gentlemen. As Dean just announced, a nefarious plot to stir racial violence throughout Detroit during the riots has been uncovered by

FBI investigators," said Schoenberg. He knew the eyes of the entire nation were upon him at this time, and he was determined to break the news of DMBC employees' involvement in the plot with conviction.

While Schoenberg paused to compose himself before continuing, Reaves was off camera pointing at the acting newscast producer with one hand while making the slit-your-throat signal with the other. The producer shook his head vigorously to show Reaves that he completely understood the signal.

"The FBI has even implicated employees of the Detroit Metro Broadcasting Channel in this plot," Schoenberg continued, knowing there was no turning back now. "Ladies and gentlemen, I assure you that those implicated by no means reflect the professionalism and dedication of the DMBC family. We are committed to assisting the FBI in bringing anyone involved in this plot to justice, especially anyone with ties to DMBC. I give you my solemn promise that DMBC will strive to continue bringing you the best news service possible. Thank you."

The camera pulled back to expose both Reaves and Schoenberg together. "Mr. Schoenberg, I must say that what you are doing is truly noble, and we here at DMBC offer you our full support."

Schoenberg smiled for the first time all day and replied, "Thank you, Dean."

As the camera switched to a close up of Reaves, Reaves gave one more glance to the acting producer. He then went off script, and started announcing the news that Schoenberg had forbade him to announce. "One of those implicated in these horrific crimes is Darius Robinson, newscast producer for DMBC," said Reaves in a deeply serious tone, his eyes glaring into the camera.

Schoenberg looked at the monitor in disbelief as a picture of Darius Robinson was splashed across the screen, with a DMBC logo prominently displayed in the lower right corner. He glared at the acting producer, who stood motionless behind the five-second delay button. *What is wrong with that schmuck?* Schoenberg motioned to him to hit it by pounding the desk three times with the palm of his hand, but the producer merely looked around like he was lost. Schoenberg could not understand why he was taking so long, but then again Schoenberg was unaware that Reaves had threatened the acting producer with castration should he even breathe on the button.

President Bonsam listened as Reaves gave a complete biographical rundown of Mr. Darius Robinson and his career with DMBC. With a picture of Robinson on the screen above his right shoulder, Reaves then went on to rehash the fact that Robinson had been taken into custody by the FBI and accused of participating in the riot plot.

Bonsam looked at the screen and said, "Humph. Robinson can kiss his family good bye." He then picked the phone back up, hit the hold button again, and said to Agent Dolan, "The Robinson family, take them out."

Chapter 63

The Bonsam political spin machine had kicked into overdrive following the DMBC announcement of the Robinson controversy. Every national news network picked up on the riot conspiracy and ran with it. The White House had been flooded by media requests throughout the night and into the next day, but Press Secretary Stratton turned them all away.

Bonsam had directed VP Holden to meet with him in the Oval Office first thing the next morning to discuss the DMBC announcement. "Mike, we need to come up with a plan to address this situation," said Bonsam calmly as he rocked slightly in his desk chair. "I need to make a strong, clear statement that the White House is doing everything it can to assist the FBI in its investigation into the riots."

Holden had to agree. He was pleasantly surprised that Bonsam was thinking about something other than himself. "You're right, Mr. President. With the election only three days away, it is now more important than ever that we show that this administration is committed to its promise to uphold the laws of this land and bring to justice anyone who threatens the safety of the American citizens."

Bonsam wasn't listening. "I mean it's not like the FBI can connect any of this to me," he said contemptuously. "I was nearly assassinated by the KKK! Why is the media giving so much attention to this petty violence when the horrendous crime was the attempt on my life? The deaths of pathetic rioters are inconsequential in comparison to the murder of the President of the United States!"

Holden thought he had heard it all, but Bonsam had an uncanny way of coming up with something more outlandish every time they met. "Mr. President, I don't mean to belittle the fact that you were almost assassinated," replied Holden, while having a hard time saying the word 'fact.' "But we must stand strong and show America that we will not back down in the face of adversity. That's what will get you reelected, Mr. President."

Bonsam still wasn't listening. "This was Clark's doing! It was in his state. He was conveniently on an island 300 hundred miles away from Detroit when I was nearly assassinated, wasn't he? Don't you see it, Mike? Michigan is crawling with KKK yet Clark turned a blind eye to the white supremacists when he became governor. And as soon as I mentioned that hate mongers were out to destroy us, they tried to kill me. Clark should be held responsible!"

Holden could take it no more. "Mr. President, you cannot go on like this! The election is almost here and you and I both know that Clark is ahead in the polls. To publicly attack Clark now would make you look desperate. Your appearance on *Meet the Press* tomorrow is your last major appearance before the election. You cannot go in there and start bashing Clark. You have to promote your accomplishments." Holden couldn't believe he had just said that, but he needed to get Bonsam's mind back on the political track. "You have to talk about your plans for your second term, in which you will continue to support legislation that is for the good of the people."

Bonsam could not be reasoned with. "He blew up the Marriott Hotel. I had just been there that morning. He wanted to kill me then!"

"Sir, you have got to pull yourself together!" Holden knew that the second those words had left his mouth he had crossed the line with Bonsam.

Bonsam's eyes narrowed. "That will be all, Mike."

Holden got up and marched directly to the door of the office. In his frustration he flung the door open and then slammed it shut hard behind him. The Secret Service agents at their post outside the office door were caught off guard as Holden stormed out of the office. They had never seen him angry before.

Inside the office, Bonsam let out a shout of anger and with one broad swipe knocked everything from the surface of his desk onto the floor. He would no longer hold back the maelstrom of hateful rage that swirled in the back of his mind. He now welcomed it.

He turned quickly and looked out the window behind him, clenching his fists and gritting his teeth as a powerful rush of heat flowed through the core of his body. The visions of flames slammed into his consciousness. Bonsam felt as though he were having an out-of-body experience as he floated away from the White House, slowly at first, then at a speed so fast that everything around him became a blur. In an instant he was standing between two towering mountain ranges that stretched out before him, the mountains themselves aflame. The heat scorched his skin and the wicked stench of burning sulfur permeated the air until his nostrils burned painfully. Within the inferno he heard the agonizing screams of millions as they cried out in horrific pain.

The two Secret Service agents who had witnessed Holden's abrupt exit stepped into the Oval Office, and found Bonsam standing in front of the window behind his desk. To the agents it appeared as if the president was staring into the Rose Garden, but in Bonsam's mind, he was staring into the gates of hell.

Chapter 64

President Bonsam's limo rushed through the streets of the capital as it headed toward NBC Studios. Bonsam sat alone watching Samuel Clark being interviewed on Fox News Sunday. His temperature rose as he listened to Clark express his views about the state of the nation's economy and his ideas for promoting economic growth. *What is wrong with my people? Can't they see that Clark is being deceptive? He will destroy America!*

Carl Worthington, host of Fox News Sunday, switched topics quickly and asked Clark questions about the Bonsam assassination attempt. Clark was not about to be led down that rabbit hole, and politely declined to comment on the grounds that the investigation into the incident was still in progress. Worthington then pressed Clark for his opinion regarding the controversy surrounding the Detroit riots. He went so far as to show a previously recorded interview from DMBC with Danté Franklin, the young son of Joseph Franklin, Jr., the man who had been burned alive in his hardware store during the riots. Clark would not reveal his personal opinions and steadfastly stuck to the facts about the tragedy, and then told the audience that he would personally see to it that Danté received a college education.

Bonsam became enraged when he heard Clark pander to the sympathies of the voters. *He is evil!* It felt as though the limo was on fire. Sweat poured from his forehead, and his hands shook nervously. Suddenly, horrific visions of cities on fire filled his mind. He heard the agonizing cries of pain coming from people trapped within the flames. He could not make the visions go away. As the torment gripped his mind, his limo pulled into the parking lot of NBC Studios.

In the *Meet the Press* studio, host Lawrence Sevnik prepared for his exclusive interview with President Bonsam in a coolheaded manner. Sevnik was one of the rare newsmen who never let his personal bias show in his reporting, which made him one of the most respected members of the political press community. He was thrilled that he had been chosen to conduct the last major interview with the president before Tuesday's election.

Bonsam had regained his composure by the time he took his seat across from Sevnik, yet Sevnik could sense that Bonsam was tense. "Welcome to the program, Mr. President," said Sevnik. He looked at the sling securing Bonsam's arm and said, "We appreciate you appearing on today's program so soon after the assassination attempt in Detroit."

"It's a pleasure to be here, Lawrence," replied Bonsam. To the television audience, Bonsam looked as distinguished as ever, however, his mind was still seething with anger from watching Clark's interview on Fox News Sunday. Sevnik wasted no time with small talk and got right down to business. "Mr. President, unnamed sources within the FBI are reporting accusations linking members of your administration to individuals who were arrested for their involvement in instigating racial violence during the Detroit riots. How do you respond?"

Bonsam remained calm and collected. "Lawrence, such accusations are preposterous. I won't dignify them with a response."

"But Mr. President," Sevnik continued, "Darius Robinson, a man you have known your entire life, was taken into custody by the FBI on suspicion of being an accomplice in the murder of Joseph Franklin, Jr. He and four other employees of the Detroit Metro Broadcasting Company have been arrested and charged with a multitude of crimes, including the murders of Stanley and Lidia Kaczmarek."

"What part of preposterous do you not understand, Lawrence!" yelled Bonsam. He was starting to feel hot again. Sevnik, however, remained in control.

"Robinson's wife and children were found murdered the day after the riots, and now Robinson has disappeared.

Are you saying your administration has no knowledge of either of these events?"

Bonsam's behavior became erratic, and his speech was bordering on gibberish. "Clark is responsible for the riots! They occurred in his state!" he roared. "He killed Senator Kirk and he tried to assassinate me! Clark is our enemy!" Bonsam's arm had come out of the sling and he was now out of his chair, pointing Sevnik in the face as he chastised Sevnik's insolence.

Sevnik remained emotionless as Bonsam continued to unravel in front of a nationwide audience. In his mind, Sevnik said a prayer of thanks. He then spoke to his sister in heaven and said, "This is for you, Lidia."

Chapter 65

The presidential election of 2012 was over. Governor Samuel Clark won decisively, capturing the delegates of 42 states. America showed that it had had enough of the Bonsam regime. The recent scandals, including Bonsam's belligerent outburst toward Lawrence Sevnik two days before the election, destroyed his credibility with the voters.

The media were euphoric in their coverage of President-elect Samuel Clark. Tonight their message was one of optimism, and they focused solely on the Clark victory and the impact that a new Republican administration would have on the government.

Spirits were high in the magnificent ballroom of the Lexington Lansing Hotel. Martineau had just finished giving Clark a big hug. She stepped back and looked at him with a big smile on her face, still holding onto his arms. She shook him back and forth, "You did it, Sam!"

"We did it!" Clark replied.

In the Oval Office, Vice President Holden was doing everything he could to calm down the president. Bonsam was pacing back and forth behind his desk as though he were a wild animal trapped in a cage. "I can't believe this. My people would never do this to me!" said Bonsam, as his walking pace increased. His voice was trembling.

"Sir, it's over," said Holden. "Now is the time to be dignified and make your concession phone call to Sam Clark."

"Clark!" Bonsam screamed. "This was all his doing! That racist had the help of the Klan. He manipulated the media and turned them against me. He stole the election from me! He wants to destroy my Providence!" Bonsam bolted through the office door and began running down the hallway.

Holden turned to the nearest Secret Service agent and commanded, "Get the entire West Wing Secret Service team down here, immediately!" and then dashed after President Bonsam.

Holden caught up to Bonsam just as he reached the Briefing Room door. "Mr. President, what are you doing?" he asked, but Bonsam ignored him and burst into the room.

The lead video technician was in the room winding up some cables when the president unexpectedly slammed through the doorway. He was so startled that he dropped the cables, then looked up and saw President Bonsam heading straight toward him. Bonsam grabbed the technician by the front of his shirt with both hands and lifted him up so his toes barely touched the ground. "Broadcast this immediately!" shrieked Bonsam. He dropped the technician and shoved him out of the way as he made is way to the podium.

By then Holden and a dozen Secret Service agents had arrived and they made their way into the Briefing Room. "Stand fast," Holden said to the agents quietly.

The technician was making his way back to the camera booth. As he passed Holden, Holden said discreetly, "Film this, but do *not* broadcast it."

"Don't worry, I won't. Not after that," replied the technician. He then took his place in the booth, put on his headphones, and motioned to the president that he was ready to go.

Bonsam nodded back to the technician. Bonsam's heart was racing and his body temperature was rising. He could feel the anger inside him intensifying.

Using his fingers, the technician counted down, "Three, two, one," and then pointed at the president.

"I do not accept the validity of this election!" Bonsam screamed into the microphone. "I am issuing an Executive Order, effective immediately, nullifying the results of this travesty!"

Bonsam grabbed the podium and with all his strength hurled it off the stage. He moved forward and jumped off the front of the stage to the floor. "Clark is our enemy! I am the one true leader!" he screamed.

Holden had seen enough. He patted the lead Secret Service agent on the back. The agent motioned to another agent and together they moved toward Bonsam.

Bonsam's movements had become spasmodic. His eyes rolled back into his head. He lunged forward toward the camera, but the two agents stepped in front of him and each placed a hand on his shoulder, stopping him in his tracks.

His eyes rolled back forward and they were filled with fire. Bonsam glared into the camera and screamed, "This is the last election! Repent! Repent!"

Bonsam pushed forward and yelled out, "Errrrrrraaaaaah!" as he thrust his arms into the air, sending both agents back a step. He reared his arm back then delivered a powerful blow to the lead agent's mouth with his fist. Blood gushed from the agent's lips and mouth. Bonsam spun around and jumped sideways at the other agent, kicking the heel of his shoe deep into the agent's stomach. More agents jumped into the fray as Bonsam continued to punch and kick anyone who came near him while furiously screaming, "Repent!"

In the end it took eight agents to subdue Bonsam. He was eventually worn down and reduced to sobbing. As Bonsam was wheeled out of the room with his arms and legs securely strapped to a gurney, his sobbing continued. In his head though, visions of ancient Maya symbols bombarded his mind. As always, the visions were accompanied by visions of flames.

Chapter 66

It was just past midnight and Team Clark was still partying the night away. Martineau was on her third glass of champagne and feeling quite festive. Emily was chatting up Clay, who she had dragged off to a secluded corner of the ballroom. Clark was standing in the center of the room with several of his old friends, yucking it up. "... and then I said, 'He croaked like a frog!'" and then he and his cronies burst into laughter.

Brett Mason was weaving his way through the crowd trying to locate Clark. "Excuse me, pardon me," he said as he tried to avoid spilling his drink on anyone. "Has anybody seen the president-elect?"

Clark looked up and said, "Mason, over here."

Mason made his way to Clark and said excitedly, "I have an important message for you, Mr. President-elect."

Clark looked at Mason, who was adorned in a Hawaiian shirt and two brightly colored leis, and said, "Nice shirt. What is it?"

Mason pulled a cell phone from behind his back and said loudly enough for everyone in the room to hear, "You have a call from the White House!" The crowd in the room cheered. "I think someone wants to make his concession phone call!"

Clark smiled and said, "I will take it in my office." He looked around the room for Vice President-elect Martineau and finally saw her standing at the drink table aimlessly trying to peel the label off a bottle of Dom Pérignon as she talked with Lieutenant Governor Purnell. "Kenna, come on."

Clark and Martineau made their way toward his office with Purnell and Mason close behind. Clark yelled, "Emily, come up for air and join us, I want you here for this!" Emily got up and took Clay's hand and dragged him along with her.

Once everyone was inside the office and the door was closed, Clark gave a big smile to those gathered and picked up the receiver from his desk phone. "Samuel Clark speaking."

"Sam, this is Mike Holden." The expression on Clark's face changed so drastically that everyone in the room froze.

"Yes, Mr. Vice President," he replied.

Everyone in the room mouthed "Vice President?" as they look around at one another.

Clark's eyes darted around as he listened intently to the words that the vice president was saying. After several minutes Clark said, "Okay Mike, we'll be on the first plane tomorrow morning." He slowly placed the receiver back onto the hook.

Martineau said, "Sam, what is it?"

"We've been summoned to the White House by Vice President Holden," Clark replied.

"Why? And why by VP Holden?" asked Martineau.

"I can't tell you right now." He turned to Lieutenant Governor Purnell and said, "Chris, you're in charge here again."

"Got it," replied Purnell, as he pulled out his cell phone and exited the office.

Clark then looked over at Clay and said, "Clay, you're coming, too." Then he quickly left his office to begin preparing for this unexpected trip.

Clay looked at Martineau and said, "Why me?"

"Obviously you're an important part of this team," she replied, realizing she was slightly tipsy.

His voice rose. "What part?"

Martineau walked to Clay, and put her arm around his shoulders, and turned him toward the door. As they walked out of the office, Martineau replied, "I am appointing you Deputy Vice President."

Mason and Emily stood at the door of the office as they watched Martineau and Clay walk toward the hotel lobby. The last thing they heard as Martineau and Clay rounded a corner was, "What the hell is a Deputy Vice President?"

"I have no idea, I just made it up."

Chapter 67

The limo carrying Clark, Martineau, and Clay stopped directly in front of the West Wing entrance of the White House. As soon as Clark and Martineau stepped out of the limo, Secret Service agents whisked them inside. By the time Clay got out, they were long gone. A Secret Service agent came up to him and said, "Who are you?"

"Clayton Jackson, Deputy Vice President," he replied.

"Yes and I'm Harald V, King of Norway. You wait here," he told Clay as he tapped the antenna of his radio against Clay's chest. The agent started to turn to walk away, but another agent came running up.

"President-elect Clark just ordered us to get this man a White House security badge, top level access," he said.

The first agent turned back to Clay showing no emotion whatsoever. Clay looked back and quickly smiled. "Come with me," said the agent, "I'll take you to get a badge."

"Thank you, Harald," Clay replied.

Clark and Martineau were led directly to the Oval Office. "Would you mind telling us what is going on here?" asked Clark. The agents remained silent.

The lead agent stepped into the Oval Office and closed the door behind him. Clark looked at Martineau as he shook his head in confusion. A minute later the agent opened the door and said to Clark, "You may come in now."

Clark looked toward Martineau and they moved toward the door. "Not you ma'am," said the agent. "Not yet anyway."

Clark was about to protest, but Martineau quickly said, "I understand," and motioned to Clark to keep going.

Clark entered the Oval Office and saw Vice President Michael Holden sitting behind the desk of the president. That made no sense at all.

Holden motioned Clark forward, so Clark proceeded ahead until he was standing directly in front of the desk. He noticed that Holden was intently viewing a document that lay on the desk before him. Holden looked up and greeted his visitor. "Clark," he said with a nod.

Clark returned the greeting, "Holden."

"That's Mr. President to you," Holden replied. He turned the document around and slid it across the desk to Clark.

Clark looked at Holden with bewilderment as he picked up the document and examined it. As he scanned the page, he started to realize what he was reading. "... and I am unable to discharge the powers and duties of the office of the President of the United States, and until I transmit a written declaration to the contrary, such powers and duties shall be discharged by Vice President Michael Prescott Holden as Acting President."

Clark's eyes darted to the bottom of the page, and much to his surprise he saw the freshly scrawled signature of President Emmanuel Bonsam. He looked up at Holden. "How in the world did you get Bonsam to sign this?" he asked.

"He didn't," replied Holden. "I did."

Clark stared at Holden with a blank look on his face. Finally he said, "Um, you can't do that." Holden folded his arms across his chest, tilted his head to the side, and glared at Clark. "Mr. President," Clark quickly added.

Holden stood up and looked Clark straight in the eye then said, "This stays between you and me, Sam." Holden then leaned over and pressed a button on his intercom. "Send her in."

Martineau entered the office and approached the desk, taking a position next to Clark. Holden's mood quickly turned jovial. "Ah, Madam Speaker, it is nice to see you again," he said as he reached out to shake her hand.

"It's nice to see you again, too, Mr. Vice President," she replied sincerely.

Clark leaned over toward Martineau and out of the corner of his mouth whispered, "That's Mr. President to you."

Martineau leaned back toward Clark and out of the corner of her mouth whispered, "What?"

"Enough with the formalities," said Holden. "Kenna, you and I have some important government business to take care of," he said as he held up the Acting President document, "but we will worry about that later. Let's make ourselves more comfortable." He set the document on the desk, then walked over to one of the couches and sat down, motioning for Clark and Martineau to take a seat on the couch across from him.

"Sam, Kenna, can I get you something to drink?" asked Holden. As Clark and Martineau sat down, Clark glanced at Martineau and then back to Holden and said, "No, we're good Mr. Pres—"

Holden cut him off. "Sam, you don't have to call me Mr. President," he said.

"Okay," replied Clark happily.

"You can call me sir."

Clark looked at Holden and blinked a few times.

"Just kidding," Holden said, and he moved forward to sit on the edge of his seat.

Holden reached out to a large screen laptop computer that was sitting on the coffee table between the couches. He tapped the mouse pad a few times until the screen came back up. "I have something you need to watch. You'll clearly see why I had to become the Acting President." He double clicked the play button icon on the screen and turned the screen so Clark and Martineau could see it as well. Clark watched Bonsam's meltdown with amazement. Martineau's mouth fell open.

At the point where the agents first began to do battle with Bonsam, Holden clicked the stop button. "That melee went on for another twenty minutes. Two of the Secret Service agents are still in the hospital. Another one was bitten on the hand and required stitches."

"Where is Bonsam now?" asked Martineau.

"He's resting comfortably," Holden said as he made quotation marks in the air with his fingers while he said resting comfortably, "and spending time with his family. The White House doctor said that the president is suffering from exhaustion and that he needs privacy."

"So you mean you've got him locked up somewhere," said Clark.

"Precisely," replied Holden. "But as far as the rest of the world knows, he's resting comfortably and spending time with his family."

Chapter 68

Holden went on. "By the time we got Bonsam to the hospital," he said, again making air quotation marks when he said hospital, "he looked like he had blown a major gasket. He was rolling his head from side to side and babbling incoherently. The first doctor to examine him lifted his eyelid and shined a light into his pupil, and the doctor nearly jumped out of his skin. His little flashlight went flying to the back of the room."

"What happened?" asked Martineau.

"I'm not sure, but whatever the doc saw really freaked him out."

"Could the doctors tell what was wrong with him?" asked Clark.

"No. Not initially. The doctor then hooked Bonsam up to an EEG to take a look at his brain activity," said Holden, "or lack thereof. You know you don't feel anything from an EEG right, but when the doctor flipped the switch Bonsam's body went rigid, which freaked out the doctor even more."

"What did the EEG tell them?" asked Clark.

"The doc looked at the results and said he was dumbfounded, said he had never seen anything like it before," replied Holden.

"What was so unusual about the results?" asked Martineau.

"He said the readings showed that Bonsam's brain activity was off the chart. Yet Bonsam was lying there like a total veg, drooling all over himself. The doctor was completely baffled."

All three sat in silence for a long time. Finally Holden said, "Anyway, President Bonsam will remain under observation and I will remain the Acting President. I will do everything within my power to ensure a smooth transition between administrations. I'll be working out of here, Sam, so you can use my office while you start getting things together. Meet me back here at 1:00 p.m. tomorrow and I'll introduce you to my transition team."

"Thank you, Mike," said Clark, "for everything. No VP has ever had to deal with a situation as bizarre as this. If there is anything I can do for you, don't hesitate to ask."

Holden thought about it a minute then said, "Sam, have you ever been to the Mediterranean?"

"Huh?"

"Oh, never mind."

Chapter 69

The next afternoon Clark and Martineau spent several hours interacting with Holden's transition team. There was much to do since Clark had been more than a little preoccupied with other matters in the days leading up to the election and hadn't had much of a chance to interact with his own transition team. It was late into the night when Martineau said, "We never had any dinner, Sam."

"I'm hungry, too," Clark replied. "Let's order a pizza."

"Does Pizza Hut deliver to the White House?"

"You know, I don't know. Add that to my list of questions to ask the transition team."

"You got it. I'll place it on the list between your questions regarding Homeland Security and the questions about the economic sanctions against Cuba."

"I'm pleased to see that we have our priorities straight!" Clark and Martineau sat back and laughed out loud. It had been a long day. A minute later Holden showed up.

"Hi, just wanted to stop by to see how things were coming along," said Holden. "Anything you need?"

"Yes," said Martineau, "can you tell us if Pizza Hut delivers to the White House?"

Clark burst out laughing. "Sorry, Mike, we're just kind of hungry."

"Come with me then," replied Holden. "I'll have the cooks whip something up. When you're done, let's take a ride out to check on Bonsam."

Clark and Martineau exchanged surprised glances. "Okay," Clark said hesitantly.

A light rain fell as the presidential limo pulled up to the front door of Bethesda National Naval Medical Center. Clark, Holden, and Martineau were ushered inside by Secret Service agents and led to the elevators. An agent pulled out his radio and contacted the agents upstairs to let them know that the visitors had arrived. When he was finished, he turned to the group and said, "Mr. Acting President, Mr. President-elect, Madam Vice President-elect, please follow me, I will take you to the president."

"That's a lot of presidents," Clark remarked as the elevator doors closed. Martineau rolled her eyes.

As the elevator doors opened at the eighth floor, another agent greeted them. He looked at Holden and said, "Right this way, sir." Holden and the agent walked down the main corridor with Clark and Martineau close behind.

Bonsam's doctor was waiting for them outside the door of Bonsam's room. "Any change?" asked Holden.

"No, sir," replied the doctor. "Please come in." Holden stepped into the room behind the doctor. Clark and Martineau cautiously followed, not at all knowing what to expect once they entered the room.

President Emmanuel Bonsam was sitting in a wheelchair and wearing a hospital gown. He was strapped across the chest to the wheelchair, but that was only to prevent him from falling out of the chair. His head was tilted back and off to the side and there was a vacant look in his eyes. He remained motionless as the party entered the room. It was an eerie sight to behold.

"Like I said before, I have never witnessed such a thing. His brain activity readings are unlike any I have ever seen," said the doctor, "but look at him."

The visitors turned their eyes to Bonsam. He looked like a hollow shell of a man. "Is he faking it?" asked Holden quietly.

"He couldn't be. Our top physicians have run a battery of tests that all indicate there is nothing physically wrong. But every test run to determine the cause of Bonsam's mental irregularities has been inconclusive. It is as though his body and mind are no longer connected. Watch this."

The doctor stepped over to the equipment tray, picked up a reflex hammer, and then walked over to Bonsam. He leaned over and tapped his knee twice, but nothing happened. "He's not even having monosynaptic reflex reactions."

Holden stepped forward and reached for the hammer. "Here, let me give it try."

The doctor quickly pulled the hammer up to his shoulder and turned halfway away from Holden. "No, no, no! I'm not about to let you to start banging on the president's knees with a hammer." Holden turned around and stepped back to Clark and Martineau, looking as innocent as an altar boy.

"There's something else," the doctor said. He paused as if he were searching for the right words to explain what he was about to say next. "The president continues to mumble now and then. Most of it is unintelligible gibberish, however he keeps coming back to the word..." he paused again.

"What?" Holden asked impatiently.

"Fire. At least that's what it sounds like."

"Fire?" whispered Martineau as she turned to Clark. "I wonder why fire?" Clark didn't know what to say, so he just shrugged his shoulders.

"Now here's the strangest part," the doctor continued. "One of the physicians who examined Bonsam this afternoon heard the mumblings. This physician had spent over a year in Honduras following the Hurricane Mitch disaster providing medical care to the Hondurans. He swears he recognizes some of the sounds coming out of Bonsam. He said that they sound exactly like some of the words he had heard spoken while he was treating sick and injured members of the indigenous population."

"What do you make of that?" asked Holden.

"I don't know. But we have contacted a linguist from the State Department who has conducted extensive studies on the languages used by the indigenous peoples of North and South America. He will be here tomorrow morning. I'm hoping he can shed some light on the subject."

Holden thought about what he had just heard. "Okay. Let us know what he finds."

They witnessed orderlies place Bonsam back on his bed. He remained motionless and silent, his eyes vacantly staring toward the ceiling as an orderly covered him with a blanket. Holden turned to Clark and Martineau and said, "Let's get out of here. This place is giving me the creeps."

The three made their way back to the elevator without speaking. As they began their descent, they had no way of knowing that at the same time a team of commandos had just parachuted onto the roof of the medical center.

Chapter 70

The rain started to come down much harder. It provided the perfect cover for the commandos as they went to work. A pair of the commandos dragged away the dead bodies of the two Secret Service agents who were guarding the roof, while others hooked up their rappelling gear to the ropes they had recently attached to the railing that circled the roof of the medical center.

The lead commando peered over the edge of the roof with his infrared binoculars and saw that the only commando on the ground at this time was in place by the hedges near the center's entrance. He then reached down and removed a rocket-propelled grenade launcher from the duffle bag beside him. It was a Russian made RPG-7, which was capable of firing shoulder-launched anti-armor warheads.

The presidential limo had been pulled to the entrance and Holden, Clark, and Martineau were escorted to the vehicle while Secret Service agents held umbrellas over their heads. They climbed into the limo and once seated the agents shut the door and notified the driver to take off. As they pulled away, Holden said, "Frankly, I'm not too surprised that Bonsam ended up this way."

The commander had loaded a warhead into the RPG launcher and was set to fire. As the motorcade pulled away from the hospital, he drew a bead on the Presidential limo, and a moment later he fired the missile. The missile streaked downward, but struck the ground about four feet behind the limo.

Inside the limo Clark was about to make a remark about Holden's last comment, when all of a sudden a large powerful blast exploded behind the vehicle. The force of the explosion lifted the rear of the limo into the air and propelled it forward. The momentum forced the limo to do an end-over-end roll. As it violently rolled onto its roof it continued its forward movement. The limo rocked upward so that its front end rose. It balanced on its rear bumper for a moment, its headlights shining straight into the sky. Then with a rush it tipped forward and slammed wheels down onto the road.

Inside Bonsam's room, the doctor had been leaning over his patient to examine him one last time before calling it a night. Bonsam's eyes were closed and his breathing had become deep and regular. The doctor looked down at Bonsam, still puzzled by his condition. Suddenly Bonsam's eyes flew open, his pupils raging with fire. Fear overwhelmed the doctor, but before he even had a chance to gasp, Bonsam's hand was clutched around his throat, cutting off his airway. Bonsam slowly pulled himself out of the bed and stood up, his grip on the doctor's throat becoming stronger. The doctor was horrified as Bonsam's fiery eyes stared into him and his grip intensified. Bonsam let out a deep strong yell as he crushed the doctor's windpipe, and then threw him to the floor where he slowly suffocated. Bonsam quickly spun around to face the window, and a moment later he heard the sound of the missile exploding on the ground below.

Holden, Clark, and Martineau lay in a twisted heap on the floor in the back of the limo. Clark was the first to come around and he clambered up onto a seat. The limo was surrounded by smoke and in the heavy rain it was impossible to see anything on the outside. His ears were ringing but as he looked down at Holden and Martineau he was still able to hear them groaning. *They are alive!*

Moments after the missile exploded, the team of commandos rappelled their way down toward the eighth floor. Inside the medical center, panic had broken out. The explosion shocked everyone. Even the Secret Service agents on the eighth floor were moving about haphazardly as they tried to get a grip on the situation. Just as the lead agent was about to order his team to move to protect the president, commandos burst through the windows. The commandos fired their machine guns on full automatic, spraying bullets down the corridors. The Secret Service agents drew their weapons, but they were no match for the heavy firepower of the commandos. The agents went down like flies. One tried to make a call for help, but was shot before he could speak.

The lead commando burst into Bonsam's room. "Time to go, Mr. President," he said as he tossed Bonsam an assault rifle.

Bonsam caught the rifle with one hand. He looked at the commando and said, *"Kamoasumnida."*

"Aneiyo," responded Commander Gu Limja. Commander Gu then raced back into the hall and shouted out orders in Korean to the rest of the commandos.

Most everyone in the medical center was reacting to the disaster happening out front and was completely unaware of the events taking place on the eighth floor, however, two Marine MPs who had been on the ninth floor had heard the gunfire directly below them. Knowing that the president was on the eighth floor, they reacted quickly and raced down the stairs to the floor below.

As they approached the eighth floor door, one of the MPs whispered, "There should be Secret Service here."

His partner was thinking the same thing. He then said, "Look!" as he pointed to smoke coming under the door into the stairwell. He slowly opened the stairwell door and peered cautiously around the corner.

There in the smoke-filled air stood President Bonsam. He remained standing there motionless with his hands behind his back. The MPs looked at one another, then moved into the hallway and slowly approached Bonsam. The MP who had opened the door spoke first. "Mr. President, are you all right? What has happened…"

Before he could say another word, Bonsam pulled the rifle from behind his back and fired at the MPs. He slowly walked toward them, unloading his entire clip. The anger was back, and so were the visions of flames. He kept firing into the bodies of the MPs long after it was obvious that they were already dead.

Commander Gu was revolted by the sight of the bloodbath that Bonsam was unleashing. When Bonsam ran out of bullets he let out a yell through his clenched teeth, and reached for another magazine. Commander Gu stepped up and grabbed Bonsam's arm before he could get another magazine, "Sir, we need to get out of here."

Bonsam spun around and faced Commander Gu, still burning with anger. Gu Limja was momentarily speechless. He had experienced the horrors of war many times over the years during his covert operations south of the demilitarized zone, but nothing that compared to the horror he felt when he looked into Bonsam's eyes.

Clark had leaned over to check on the condition of Martineau. "Kenna! Kenna! Can you hear me?"

Martineau's eyes fluttered open and she rubbed them with her fingers. She looked around the haze of the limo trying to get her vision to return to normal. When she was finally able to focus, she looked at Clark and said, "Holden?"

"He's right here, Kenna." Clark slid over in his seat so he could check on Holden. He cautiously turned Holden over so they could see his face. Martineau gently stroked his cheeks and said, "Mike, are you all right?" Martineau started to smile as she saw Holden open his eyes and look up at her, but at that instant they were struck by a blinding flash of light as a stun grenade exploded next to the limo.

The commando who had been hiding in the bushes was now at work. The noise that came from the flashbang he had tossed next to the limo was even louder than the missile explosion. He followed the flashbang with several smoke grenades. Everyone in and around the limo was now totally disoriented. The commando sprang from his hiding place and raced toward the limo. His protective mask and earplugs allowed him to move freely about the smoke-filled area while those around him rolled on the ground gasping for air.

The commando was searching for one person in particular and he located him in less than a minute. He walked over to the president's military aide who was sprawled out face down on the ground and coughing heavily. The commando then pulled out a two-foot long machete from the sheath attached to his belt and swung it down with tremendous force, striking the aide where he lay.

Commander Gu and his team led Bonsam out a side door of the medical center and onward to the rendezvous point. Bonsam caught a glimpse of the crumpled presidential limo through the rain and the smoke as he raced on. He shouted to Commander Gu, "They're dead! They're dead!" Gu wasn't so sure, but there was no way to find out at this time.

A moment later the ground commando came sprinting to join them. Commander Gu took the satchel that the ground commando was carrying and handed it to Bonsam. Bonsam let out a wicked laugh as he took the case and then he and the commando team boarded the stealth helicopter that had just moments before landed at the rendezvous point. The helicopter took off, and along with President Bonsam, vanished into the night.

As the smoke cleared, medical personnel stormed out of the hospital to treat the victims of the attack. The seriously injured were rushed inside while others received treatment at the scene of the incident. The rain continued to beat down making everything more difficult. QRF agents had swarmed the facility in search of President Bonsam but came up empty-handed.

In the midst of the chaos, QRF agents and medical personnel who were working together to treat the wounded pulled Holden, Clark, and Martineau from the limo. They were placed on blankets beneath a makeshift shelter just as two doctors arrived to conduct triage. All three had been pretty banged up when the limo flipped end-over-end, and the effects of the flashbang still lingered. Holden and Clark awkwardly stood up, much to the dismay of the medical personnel who were treating their injuries. Both men were still feeling woozy and they steadied each other as they stood. The doctor treating Martineau looked up and said, "She was knocked unconscious, but it appears that she has suffered no serious injuries."

Clark was relieved as he knelt down beside Martineau. Suddenly, the yells of a Secret Service agent pierced the air. As Clark and Holden looked toward the source of the disturbance, they saw an agent frantically waving for assistance and other agents racing toward him. "This looks serious," said Holden. "Let's go."

Clark and Holden pushed their way through the crowd that had gathered. They looked down and saw the presidential military aide lying face down in the wet grass. His hand had been cut off at the wrist. The agent who had discovered him looked up and yelled, "We've lost the football! We've lost the football!"

The paranoia that had always been a part of Bonsam's character had led him to develop a variety of plans for an escape should he ever be taken captive, and tonight those plans paid off. The stealth helicopter landed at a deserted airfield, and Bonsam quickly hopped out of it and boarded his getaway plane. This was no ordinary plane. Bonsam had had the plane secretly built for his personal use, and it was capable of reaching speeds over Mach 2. The plane took off the second Bonsam sat down, and headed due east.

Bonsam had also developed a myriad of contingency plans should his power as president be threatened. One such plan called for the sabotage of all the government computer network systems. Should the government leaders ever turn against him, he would retaliate with a nationwide cyber attack. Bonsam's hackers had been persistently placing both software and hardware bugs throughout the government networks for years, patiently waiting for the day that they would be discharged. Now it was time to turn them loose.

As Bonsam's getaway plane streaked across the Atlantic, he placed a call to the mastermind of his cyber attack. "It is time," he said. "Execute the attack." As he hung up the phone he looked at the nuclear football and smiled. Minutes later, computer network systems across the United States started crashing.

Chapter 71

That same night, Ixchel tossed and turned as images of the third and fourth symbols flashed over and over in her mind. It was the image of the fourth symbol that she found so disturbing. She had seen it before, she was certain. *But where?*

The fourth symbol flashed in her mind again and it made her tremble. *Why do I feel so frightened every time I see it?* Frightened was an understatement. What she was feeling was closer to sheer terror. She lay there trembling, but eventually drifted off to sleep.

Hours later, Ixchel awoke with a start. The room was freezing cold and a light breeze blew through the air. She looked around quickly, and then she heard someone call out her name. The voice was soft and distant, but it still felt like it came from within her room.

She nervously stepped out of her bed. Suddenly a ghostly figure passed before her dresser mirror then disappeared into the darkness. She gasped as her eyes widened. *I must be dreaming.*

"It is not a dream Ixchel, I am here." This time the voice sounded as though it was very near. *This can't be happening, I must be dreaming.*

She remained motionless, gazing into the shadows. She felt a spiritual presence there in her room. Goosebumps covered her skin and a chill ran down her spine. Her heartbeat raced as she waited, wondering if she would hear the voice again.

"Come, Ixchel. I am here," the voice gently called out. Ixchel remained paralyzed with fright. "Come, take my hand."

Slowly a colorless hand emerged from the shadows. Moments later, the rest of the specter slowly materialized before her eyes. Ixchel stood frozen in fear. She was unable to move and unable to take her eyes off the figure looming before her. She was now looking into the eyes of her great-grandmother, Ixazaluoh.

Ixazaluoh appeared as though she were floating across the floor as she approached Ixchel. She wore a long white gown that flowed in the breeze. Her hand was still extended toward Ixchel.

Ixchel took her great-grandmother's hand and stepped toward her. *How can this be? I must be dreaming. I want to wake up.*

Together they stepped into the shadows, and Ixchel was instantly hit by another blast of wind that shook her to her soul. The blast took her breath away.

Ixchel's head spun and she felt as though she were being transported to somewhere far away. *I am still in my room. I can still see the bed. Please let me wake up.*

Still, she could not escape the feeling that she was somewhere else. It was somewhere distant, yet somewhere familiar. Unearthly surroundings appeared before her eyes and enveloped her. She felt as though she were entering another world.

This world was warm and filled with sunlight. Bright green parrots could be seen in the branches of the nearby trees as they squawked at one another. The screeches of howler monkeys could be heard coming from the faraway forests. Ixchel could smell the delicious scent of *hilachas* simmering in a cooking pot. She soon recognized everything around her. Her heart raced as she realized where she was. She was in Sacatepéquez, the Guatemalan village in which she had lived as a child. In her mind she heard Ixazaluoh's voice again, "Look, Ixchel."

Ixchel stepped further into her village and saw a little girl. The girl was sitting on the ground, drawing pictures in the sand with a small stick. "That's me!" she gasped.

She was transfixed on the vision before her. Next she saw an old woman approaching the little girl. It was Ixazaluoh. She was dressed in a traditional Maya *huipil,* a boldly colored blouse designed with intricate embroidery along the edges. Maya women had been wearing these ancient garments for centuries.

Ixazaluoh joined the little girl by sitting on the ground facing her. Ixazaluoh then took the stick from the little girl's hand and wiped the sand between them smooth. Now it was Ixazaluoh who drew in the sand.

Ixchel moved further into the scene as an unseen force continued pulling her forward. It was as if she were an invisible observer who had traveled back in time. She kept hearing Ixazaluoh's voice echo through her mind. This time the voice called out, "It is one."

She was deep within the apparition now, standing directly behind the little girl. Ixchel had to see what her great-grandmother had drawn. Ixchel could no longer see the spirit of Ixazaluoh but she could still feel her presence. Again she heard Ixazaluoh calling from far away, "It is one."

She leaned over the back of the little girl's head and gazed down at the ground. What she saw made her blood run cold. It was the third and fourth symbols, just as they appeared on the tablet.

The force pulled on her again. She moved slowly in a wide circular path from behind the little girl toward the back of her great-grandmother. As she reached the midway point between the two, the force seemed to stop. Ixchel had a much better look at the symbols as she stood halfway between the little girl and Ixazaluoh.

She could now see the third symbol in much greater detail. It was no longer just a plain circle. Within the ring outline she could see several other small markings. As she stared at the symbol, images of celestial objects started flashing through her mind. The images slowly faded away, except for one. The image that remained was Earth. "That is it!" she said. "The third symbol represents Earth!"

Deciphering the third symbol sent a rush of happiness through Ixchel. Then she slowly felt the force pull her onward. Moments later she was standing directly behind Ixazaluoh. For the first time she could see the symbols drawn on the ground from her great-grandmother's perspective.

From this angle the fourth symbol was now above the third symbol, the Earth. As Ixchel stared at the fourth symbol, she felt the sensation that images were again going to flash through her mind. She closed her eyes and waited. It seemed like an eternity passed before an image finally developed in her mind. It faded in slowly. When it fully appeared, Ixchel was aghast by what she saw. It was a nuclear mushroom cloud.

Ixchel opened her eyes and saw that the little girl was looking up at her. "It is one," the girl said. Ixchel looked back down at the symbols and finally realized that the two symbols were actually one. It was shaped exactly like an enormous nuclear mushroom cloud over the Earth.

Earth-fire! She looked back at the little girl, who was now standing up. Ixazaluoh was no longer there. The girl's arms were outstretched, as if she wanted a hug from Ixchel. Ixchel hesitated, not knowing what to do.

Ixchel's vision became very blurry. For a few seconds the image of the little girl was fading away. In an instant, Ixchel's vision cleared. Where the little girl had stood now stood a spectral image of Ixchel herself. The image stretched out her arms toward Ixchel. Then, Ixchel screamed in horror as her mirror image suddenly burst into flames.

Ixchel shielded her eyes with her arm as a blinding flash of light ripped through the air. She could still hear the sounds of the roaring fire before her, and caustic smoke burned her lungs as she tried to breathe. Slowly she lowered her arm and in terror peered back into the fire. Within the flames stood a laughing Emmanuel Bonsam.

Chapter 72

Daniel awoke to the sound of his cell phone ringing. As he lay there on his stomach, he opened one eye and looked at the clock on the nightstand next to his bed. *5:30, what the hell?*

He threw his hand onto the nightstand and fumbled around for his cell. He finally found it, picked it up, and rolled over onto his back. His eyes were barely open and he didn't even see the caller's name as he pressed the answer button. He put the phone to his ear and paused for a minute as he cleared his throat. He was barely awake as he said hello.

"Earth-fire!" screamed Ixchel. "The symbol stands for Earth-fire!"

Daniel bolted upright. "Ixchel, what's wrong?"

"We were looking at the symbols upside down. It is one. It's Earth-fire, Daniel, Earth-fire!"

"Ixchel, please calm down. You're not making any sense."

"It's Bonsam! The sky-fire was Kirk's plane crash. The temple-fire was the Marriott explosion. Bonsam is connected to both. The last symbol is Earth-fire! He's going to set the world on fire!"

"Ixchel, listen. Stay where you are. I'm coming right over." Daniel tossed the phone back onto the nightstand. He jumped out of bed and threw on a pair of sweats. Then he grabbed his phone and his car keys and shot out of his apartment. Fifteen minutes later he was banging on Ixchel's door.

"Oh my God, Daniel," said Ixchel as she threw herself into his arms. "Oh, my God! Bonsam is going to destroy the world."

"Ixchel, explain to me what you are talking about."

"Come to my computer, I'll show you."

Together they quickly went to Ixchel's computer desk. Her hands were trembling as she shook the mouse to wake up her computer. On the screen was an image of the tablet. She moved the cursor over the rotate button and clicked twice, and the image rotated 180 degrees.

"See this Daniel," Ixchel said as she pointed a pen at the last symbol, "the third and fourth symbols are actually one symbol. The bottom part is the Earth, and the top part…"

"Is a mushroom cloud," said Daniel. He stared at the screen. "I see it."

"Daniel, every time I looked at the symbols on the tablet I had nightmares. Horrible nightmares! And Bonsam was always there. I even had nightmares when I was awake. Remember when I saw the assassination! Remember when I saw the Marriott explosion?"

"Yes, I remember."

"And I never told you this, but I had a nightmare when I was studying the sky-fire symbol. And Bonsam was in it. I passed out in the UVA lab and didn't wake up until hours later."

"What? Why didn't you tell me?"

"The nightmares were terrifying. I began seeing visions and hearing voices in my head. I kept seeing bright flashes of light and feeling strong blasts of wind. I thought I was losing my mind, Daniel."

"Ixchel, do you really believe that the final symbol represents some kind of all out nuclear war?"

She paused for a moment. "Yes, I can feel it, Daniel. I'm certain it will take place and it's going to happen soon, unless we can find a way to stop it. To stop Bonsam."

Daniel thought for a moment. "We need to tell somebody about this."

"But who? Who is going to believe us?"

"President Clark," said Daniel. "If Bonsam needs to be stopped, he's our only hope.

Chapter 73

"Sir, I can't explain it," said General Miguel Arroyo, Chairman of the Joint Chiefs of Staff. "The system has locked us out. We can't shut it down and we can't override it. The football is still active!"

"How can that be?" shouted Holden. He could not comprehend that the president's Emergency Satchel was not only missing but also still capable of authorizing a nuclear attack.

Everyone who had gathered around the conference table in the Situation Room was anxiously awaiting the chairman's reply. "Last night, shortly after President Bonsam broke out of Bethesda, STRATCOM was hit by an enormous cyber attack. A tidal wave of powerful viruses has managed to infiltrate our most secure military systems."

Clark looked at Martineau. "My God!" she whispered.

"Even if we are locked out, how is it possible for Bonsam to start shooting off nukes? Even if he has the codes that could authorize an attack, the attack order would still need to be confirmed by the Secretary of Defense," said Holden.

"Sir, we must assume that if President Bonsam has the ability to lock us out of the emergency launch system, he has the ability to override the SECDEF's confirmation," General Arroyo replied.

Holden paused for a moment. "Just how extensive is this cyber attack?"

"The viruses are spreading throughout the Combatant Commands at lightning speed. CENTCOM reported that communication systems throughout Afghanistan are beginning to crash, putting the troops there in mortal danger. PACOM reported that they have lost contact with over half of the *Ohio* class subs in the Pacific, meaning that there are about a hundred Trident nuclear missiles out there that we can't find. This is just the tip of the iceberg, sir."

Before Holden could respond, the Deputy Administrator of NASA leaned over the table and announced, "General, Mission Control Houston is reporting that our space communication systems are failing. We have lost all contact with the International Space Station."

Even before the murmuring following NASA's announcement had died down, the Deputy of Homeland Security yelled to the chairman, "General Arroyo, the viruses have spread to networks beyond the military networks. The Treasury Department is reporting breaches of security in the Federal Reserve. We could be looking at an economic meltdown if this gets out and there is a run on the banks."

The Under Secretary of the Commerce Department elbowed her way to the table and announced, "General, sir, NOAA is reporting disastrous malfunctions within its science satellite services. We can no longer monitor any oceanic or atmospheric weather conditions. Commercial shipping vessels worldwide are in grave danger."

The noise level throughout the Situation Room climbed as the country's top leaders redoubled their efforts to keep up with the disastrous intelligence information that kept pouring in. Holden pulled the chairman away from the conference table to speak in private. Martineau motioned to Clark to come close, "It is a miracle that Holden has been able to keep a lid on the news of Bonsam's escape and the events happening here. If the public were to find out, there would be a worldwide panic."

"He won't be able to contain it much longer," Clark replied. "Too many things are going wrong, and most of the people in this situation room are part of the problem. Holden needs their help, but they're only making things worse."

"I'm afraid you're right, Sam."

Clark paused for a minute and said, "Let's get out of this goat rope for a few minutes so we can hear ourselves think."

Clay looked out the window as his driver headed toward the White House. He was still astounded by Clark's news that Bonsam had shot his way out of Bethesda and disappeared without a trace. "And to think that I once admired the man," he said aloud.

"You say something to me, sir?" asked the driver.

"Uh, sorry. No. I was just talking to myself."

"Well, as long as you don't start answering yourself, you'll be fine," said the driver. "We'll be there in a few minutes."

Clay smiled. "Thanks." He turned back to the window, and then something strange caught his eye. As they passed the White House visitors' entrance he saw a group of National Park Service rangers standing around a young couple. The woman was obviously upset about something and she waved her hands around forcefully as she spoke to the rangers who had encircled her.

Clay tapped on the back of the driver's seat and said, "Pull over, let me out here."

"Here?" replied the driver.

"Yes, hurry." Once the vehicle stopped Clay jumped out and crossed the street, and then made his way to the visitors' entrance.

"He must have started answering himself," the driver said aloud. "Oh God, now I'm doing it," he said as he drove away.

As Clay reached the crowd he heard the woman exclaim, "You don't understand. I have got to see the president!"

A ranger replied, "President Bonsam is resting comfortably and spending time with his family."

"Not President Bonsam," yelled Daniel, "President Clark!"

"Actually, he's not the president yet," the ranger explained. "You see, after an election the winner becomes…"

"I know! Whatever! I have to see President Clark, now!" shouted Ixchel.

Clay stepped forward and said, "What seems to be the problem here?"

Both Ixchel and the ranger turned to Clay and at the exact same time said, "Who are you?"

"I am a member of Clark's staff. Maybe I can help."

Ixchel said, "Give me a break" at the same time that the ranger said, "Sure you are."

Clay took out his White House badge and held it in front of the ranger's face, and the ranger and his cohorts snapped to attention. The ranger said, "By all means, sir. Please feel free to assist this young lady."

The rangers quickly moved back to their positions. Clay looked at Ixchel and Daniel and said, "So tell me, why is it so important for you to see President-elect Clark?"

Clark stared at Ixchel. He was flabbergasted by what he had just heard. "The symbols on an ancient Maya tablet predict that doomsday will come at the hands of Emmanuel Bonsam, in the form of a nuclear holocaust?"

"I know it sounds crazy, but the sky-fire and temple-fire prophecies have come true. It was Bonsam who had both Kirk's plane and the Marriott tower blown up," Ixchel said, "and I have seen visions of Bonsam in the flames of these acts of destruction."

"Visions?" said Clark. "I'm supposed to believe this because you are having visions?"

"Wait a minute, Sam," said Martineau. "Now, I'm not a big believer in this kind of stuff either, but look at what is happening." She got up and paced around the room. "Bonsam has stolen the nuclear football and it can't be shut off. We are under a cyber attack of epic proportions and we don't know who is responsible."

She started speaking excitedly, "Remember when Special Agent Gibson said that the FBI had discovered bits of information on Delgado's computer about Maya artifacts? And remember the last time we saw Bonsam. Remember what his doctor said? The only word that he had said was fire."

She turned to Ixchel. "The Maya people, they are found throughout Central America, yes?"

"Yes," replied Ixchel.

"Including Honduras?"

"Yes, there is a very large Maya population in Honduras."

"Sam, do you remember what else the doctor said?"

Clark stood up. "Yes, his mumblings. Are you saying that Bonsam was mumbling in the language of the ancient Maya?"

"What are you talking about?" asked Ixchel.

"Sam, think about it," Martineau pleaded.

Clark turned to Clay. "Clay, I need you to get with the tech shop and get them to set up a computer station in this office for Ixchel and Daniel. Top level security."

"You got it, Sam," Clay replied. "Daniel, come with me. I need you to make sure that the tech nerds get you everything you need." Clark watched the two men as they left the room, not quite knowing how to react to being called by his first name by Clay. He just shook his head and smiled.

Martineau looked at Clark, "We need to share this with Holden."

"He's kind of busy right now, Kenna," he replied.

"Sam, he has to know."

As Clark and Martineau approached the Situation Room guard station, they saw Holden heading their way. "Hello," he said as walked between them and continued down the hall. Clark and Martineau spun around and followed after him.

"Mike, I know you're swamped, but I need thirty seconds of your time, no more," said Clark.

"Then come in here," replied Holden as he pushed open a men's room door. "I've got to pee so bad my eyes are tuning yellow."

Martineau looked at Clark, motioned toward the door and said, "Be my guest."

Holden went straight to the nearest urinal. "Ahhh. I needed to get out of there for a minute," he said as he stared at the wall in front of him.

"How are things going?" asked Clark.

"Terrible. You now have 25 seconds."

"Mike, now hear me out," Clark said hesitantly, "and keep an opened mind."

"Twenty seconds."

"Okay, okay," said Clark. "Mike, archaeologists have discovered an ancient Maya artifact with carvings on it that predict the world's devastation, and the archeologists believe that the prophecy is linked to Bonsam. They think that he will somehow cause a cataclysmic event that will annihilate the entire planet." Clark replayed what he had just said in his mind and realized just how ridiculous it sounded when spoken aloud.

Holden zipped his pants and turned around to face Clark. "I believe you, Sam."

"What?" said Clark.

"I believe you," Holden repeated. He walked to the sink and turned on the faucet. "This cyber attack is a runaway train. All of our systems are failing. Bonsam is responsible for all of this." Holden looked up at the mirror as he washed his hands, making eye contact with Clark who was standing behind him. "And Bonsam has disappeared with the nuclear football. So, yeah, I think Bonsam is capable of anything."

Holden pulled a paper towel from the dispenser and began drying his hands. "I need to get back to the Situation Room," he said, then tossed the paper towel into the trash bin. He walked past Clark and pulled open the door, and as he entered the hallway said, "27... 28... 29... 30."

Clark followed Holden out of the restroom and saw Martineau watching Holden walk back toward the Situation Room. "Well, what did he say?" she asked.

"He believes us!"

Chapter 74

Two men stood in the blazing heat, waiting for a visitor who they had never imagined they would meet. They watched as a sleek plane landed on the nearby runway. It turned around at the end of the runway and taxied toward their location. Once the plane stopped, they looked at one another and then proceeded toward the hatch. As they approached they saw the hatch open and the airstairs lowered. They halted and looked on, waiting for their visitor to deboard.

Moments later, Emmanuel Bonsam, former president of the United States, appeared at the top of the airstairs. To the two men waiting, he no longer looked like the leader of a great nation. A day-old beard covered his face and his eyes were hidden behind mirrored sunglasses. He sported an old, faded army jacket, black denim jeans, and worn hiking boots.

Bonsam walked toward the men who were waiting. Once he reached them, he stopped and looked at one man, then the other. He slowly removed his sunglasses and said, *"As-salaam alaikum."*

Bonsam climbed into the back of their SUV, and in less than a minute was on his way to meet an old friend. He was still pissed off from the news that Holden, Clark, and Martineau had survived the RPG blast. Gu would pay dearly for that mistake.

An hour later Bonsam was ushered into the grand hall of a magnificent palace. As he looked at the ornate surroundings, he tried in vain to comprehend why anyone in their right mind would choose to build such a majestic home in the middle of a miserable, desert wasteland.

The escort said, "The Sheikh will see you now."

"Thank you, Hajji," Bonsam replied respectfully. His escort then pulled open the ten-foot-tall doors leading into his master's office.

Sheikh Abdul-Qadir Aziz had a wide smile on his face as he walked swiftly toward Bonsam, his *keffiyeh* flowing behind him. *"As-salaam alaikum,* Emmanuel. It is good to see you again."

"Wa alaikum as-salaam. It is good to see you, too, my brother."

"I am thrilled you have made it here safely. Our friends from the Korean People's Army are to be commended for their daring rescue. You have been in the air now, for what, 12 hours?"

"Seven, actually," Bonsam replied.

"Oh my brother, you must promise me that someday you will take me for a ride in your jet plane," Aziz said with excitement in his voice. "To travel over 6,300 miles in seven hours is truly amazing."

"Of course, my brother," replied Bonsam. "I would be honored to have you as my guest on a flight. Anyone within *Enkhtuyaa* is welcome on my plane."

"Shokran jazeelan, Emmanuel!"

"I apologize, my brother," replied Bonsam, "but I have forgotten how to say 'you're welcome' in Arabic."

"Do not worry about that, Emmanuel," Aziz replied. "Ah, you must be hungry. We shall have a feast in your honor."

"You are most gracious, my brother. However, it is urgent that I begin my work. May I see the computer that you so generously offered for my use?"

"Of course, Emmanuel, I understand. We shall go now."

Sheikh Aziz led Bonsam to the rear of the office where an open elevator awaited. They stepped inside and Aziz closed the door and pressed the down button. "I am certain that my computer will be to your satisfaction."

The elevator descended slowly. After three minutes, Bonsam said, "Just how deep is this bunker?"

The Sheikh smiled and said, "We are almost there."

Once the elevator stopped, Aziz opened the door and led Bonsam down a short, dark hallway. When they reached the end, Aziz flipped a huge power switch that illuminated the bunker before them.

There in the bunker stood the largest computer Bonsam had ever seen. It was mammoth, nearly 20 feet tall and covering an area larger than two tennis courts. Bonsam was astounded. He stepped forward and put his hand against the side, then turned to look at Aziz.

The Sheikh could tell Bonsam was very impressed. "This is China's Tianhe LS-3000 Supercomputer. Very few people know that it exists. It is so powerful that it can carry out over eight trillion calculations per second. I also have 150 North Korean technicians at your disposal. With the information that you possess, we will be able to break into any network in the world. Once inside, there is nothing we cannot do."

Over the next six hours Bonsam directed the upload of over 11 terabytes of the most sensitive digital information that the United States government possessed. As the data uploads were taking place, Bonsam asked Aziz to meet with him out of earshot of the technicians. "My plan is to use the LS-3000 to break into the cyber networks of every industrialized nation in the world," said Bonsam in a menacing tone, "and seize control of their weapons systems. Someday we may need to use their own weapons against them." Aziz was elated as he heard Bonsam's words, though strangely, as he imagined death raining down on the infidels, Bonsam was imagining wiping out Aziz and the rest of the camel-jackers from this shit-hole corner of the world.

In the late hours of the evening, Aziz accompanied Bonsam on the trip back to the airfield. Before Bonsam boarded his plane, he expressed his gratitude to Aziz. "And remember, my brother, I owe you a ride on this jet," Bonsam said with a forced smile. When Bonsam reached the top of the airstairs, he stopped and gave one last wave to Aziz, then turned around, rolled his eyes, and entered the cabin of his jet.

The pilot, who was waiting at the cockpit door, knew how much Bonsam despised Aziz. "How was your visit with the Sheikh?" he inquired.

"Fantastic," Bonsam replied sardonically. "Aziz gave me total access to his supercomputer, but the dumb-ass has no idea that I have locked him out of it for good." He sat down in his recliner and said, "Please, just get me the hell out of here."

The pilot laughed. "Where to, sir?"

Bonsam looked out the window and said, "Mexico."

Chapter 75

In the early hours of the morning, Professor Jameson was jolted awake as he felt his bed begin to shake. Before he even had the chance to say, "Oh, no," he heard a low rumble and his bed shook even more.

"Earthquake! Everybody out!" he yelled. Jameson clambered to his feet and made his way out of his tent.

"Is everyone out, is everyone out?" He called as he frantically looked around the encampment.

"It's all right Professor, everyone is here," said Jesse as he walked toward the professor. "Are you ok?" he asked.

Professor Jameson was still a little shaken, but he bobbed his head affirmatively.

Everyone stood still and silent, waiting for the next tremor. Jameson was actually holding his breath. After several minutes, the students relaxed and began moving around and speaking to each other but still in hushed tones, as if speaking loudly would somehow trigger another tremor.

Jameson and the students made their way over to the main cabin. As they filtered inside and looked around, they found that there was almost no damage to the cabin. Jesse turned on the radio that was sitting on the bookshelf. "Shhh! Listen to this," he said. The message was in Spanish, but everyone on the team knew enough to understand. The report said that a 2.9 magnitude earthquake had hit the area.

"A 2.9, that's nothing," said Jesse with a smile.

"It felt like something to me!" exclaimed Jameson. He tried to laugh it off, but still he was very uneasy.

Next the team went to the excavation site to see what damage had been done by the earthquake. As they looked around, they found that several pieces of equipment had been knocked from their stands, but other than that there was little disturbance to the site.

Jameson was still shaken from the earthquake. He was breathing hard and sweating much more than normal. He kept nervously wiping his brow with his handkerchief. Something else was bothering him, something other than the earthquake. He mind was elsewhere, and he couldn't control it.

Jameson finally snapped out of it and saw the team members looking at him with concern on their faces. He coughed a little and said, "We need to clean this place up." As the students began picking up the equipment, he walked toward the one section of the site that they had yet to excavate. It was as if he was being drawn there.

One of the students called out, "Be careful, Professor." Jameson turned and looked back. His eyes met the gaze of the students. They still had that look of concern on their faces. Jameson turned back around and took one more step, and as he did the ground beneath his feet crumbled away, plunging him into a chamber beneath the surface.

Chapter 76

The students gasped as they saw Professor Jameson tumble into the hole in the ground. "Oh shit!" yelled Jesse, and he and the rest of the students scrambled over to the hole.

Fortunately, the hole was less than five feet deep. Jameson had landed flat on his ass. He sat there with his arms on his knees, shaking the cobwebs out of his head. He heard Jesse call out his name, and looked up to see him with his arm outstretched. "You okay, Professor?" Jesse asked.

"I'll be all right," he said as he took Jesse's hand and pulled himself up.

"Go get the ladder," Jesse yelled to his friend nearest the equipment racks.

Jameson stood now, shoulder deep in the ground, looking around at the students. Jesse lowered the ladder into the chamber. "Watch your step, Professor," he said. He could see that Jameson had not fully recovered from the shock of the fall.

Jameson was indeed still shaken, both from the fall and the strange feelings he was having. His stomach churned and his mind was still spinning. He placed his hands on the sides of the ladder, and then let out a large breath of air as he prepared himself for the climb. He looked up and took a step backward, and as he did he felt something hard move beneath his feet. He looked down, but it was too dark to see what it was.

"Ready, Professor?" asked Jesse.

"Hold on, there is something down here." He reached down to his feet and felt around. His hand soon hit something hard. He felt around it. It was not very big, and obviously made out of stone. He stood upright and lifted it into the light.

"Wow!" said Jesse, as he saw the relic the professor was holding.

The professor smiled. It was the missing piece of the tablet.

Chapter 77

Early that afternoon, Jesse stopped by the cabin in search of Professor Jameson. He knocked lightly and he slowly pushed open the door. "Professor Jameson, you in there?"

"Yes, Jesse. Come in and join me," Jameson called out.

Jesse looked around as he joined Jameson at the main table. "What an amazing find today," he said. "Can I take a look at the artifact?"

"I have already locked it in the safe, Jesse," Jameson replied. "Tomorrow, after I contact Ixchel Cobán, I will put it on display for the entire team to view."

"Okay, Professor. I'll talk to you later," said Jesse as he reached out his hand toward Jameson.

Jameson reached out and gave Jesse a firm handshake and replied, "Talk to you later, Jesse. Thank you for all your hard work."

Jesse exited the cabin and made his way back to his tent. When he reached the encampment he continued walking past, following the path deep into the wilderness. After walking nearly twenty minutes, he came to a large, steep hill. He stopped and looked toward the top, took in and let out a large breath of air, and began his climb

By the time he reached the top he was nearly out of breath and he felt his legs cramping up. "If I can't get reception up here, I give up," he said as he pulled out a satellite phone and placed a call.

Jesse was shocked when the person on the other end answered. Whoever it was had no Spanish accent, and he obviously was not the same person who had paid him to call and report on any unique discoveries at the dig. Jesse paused then asked, "Who is this?"

"Never mind who this is," Agent Dolan said in a low voice. "Have there been any developments at your location?"

"Yes, sir," Jesse proudly replied. "We have discovered another artifact. It's the missing piece of the tablet."

Jesse listened intently for several minutes as he received further instructions from the unknown man. He smiled as he received praise for reporting the information. His smile went away quickly, however, when the stranger shared a surprising piece of news. He was stunned. "President Bonsam is here in Mexico and heading this way? You've got to be kidding!"

Chapter 78

Ixchel had arrived at the White House even before Clark or Martineau had arrived. She was eager to get back to her research on the Maya prophecies. She was searching for some verifiable proof linking Bonsam to the symbols on the tablet. She sensed that Clark still had some doubts about her visions.

Clay and Daniel arrived a short time later. "Good morning, Ixchel," said Daniel. He walked up behind her chair and put his hands on her shoulders and slowly massaged the base of her neck.

She reached up and put her hand on Daniel's hand and softly caressed it. "Good morning, Daniel. Good morning, Clay."

"Good morning, Ixchel," said Clay.

Daniel looked over her shoulders at the screen. "Have you been able to reach Professor Jameson?"

"No. Not yet."

"The cyber attack has screwed up communication systems everywhere," said Clay.

"I know. I just want to tell him what I have seen in my visions. Remember when we were at Chacchoben, Daniel? He said that the symbols were a warning. He knows more about the Maya prophecies than anyone alive. If only I could tell him about my visions."

Clark entered the office and went straight to his desk. Martineau followed closely behind and approached Ixchel. "Any luck?"

"No. Nothing." Ixchel replied as she glanced over at Clark. Clark looked like his mind was elsewhere.

"Mr. Jackson," Clark said, causing Clay to straightened up in his chair. "I know that you provided everything you know about Delgado and his connection to Bonsam to the FBI. The information you provided was invaluable, but what you gave them were facts. I want to hear your feelings. You're the only person we know that isn't sitting in jail right now who worked for Bonsam's minions. What is your gut feeling about Bonsam and this doomsday prophecy?" Clark glanced at Ixchel.

Clay glanced at her as well. "Sir, my gut feeling is that if there is anyone in this world who is capable of bringing it to an end, it would definitely be Bonsam."

Ixchel gave him a smile and mouthed, "Thank you."

"Delgado worshiped Bonsam. And he was more than just a sick, twisted murderer. He was a diabolical psychopath. He was like some sort of demonic offspring of Bonsam's. I wouldn't be surprised if the medical examiner that performed his autopsy discovered he was cloven-hoofed." He paused then said, "I'd be inclined to think that Bonsam is much, much worse."

"I'd have to agree with that," Martineau added.

"Thanks for your input Clay," said Clark. "You paint a very vivid picture."

Unexpectedly, the office door opened and everyone looked up in surprise as Holden walked into the office. A few steps in he stopped and looked around, noticing that everyone was staring at him. "As you were," he said sarcastically then continued on toward the desk.

Holden looked exhausted. "Have you gotten any sleep in the last three days, Mike?" Martineau asked.

"No. Not really," he replied as he walked behind the desk. "Excuse me, Sam," he said as he leaned in front of Clark and pulled open the top center drawer of the desk. "I think I left some Pepto-Bismol in here."

"Have you had anything to eat?" asked Martineau with marked concern.

"On Saturday I had a cookie."

"Mike, come on, you're going to kill yourself."

"Oh I'm just kidding," he replied as he took a big swig of Pepto-Bismol right out of the bottle. "Seriously, we have regained significant control over the systems that were attacked," Holden said, "and thank God we reestablished contact with our missing submarines. But every time we solve one problem five more pop up. We are still extremely vulnerable right now. Another cyber attack of that magnitude would shut us down completely."

"How is the rest of the world responding to this?" asked Clark.

"Remarkably, our allies have offered unlimited support. The UN is doing everything it can as well. Even Russia and China are sympathetic to our plight and have promised not to cause any trouble while we try to get back on our feet."

Clark was surprised. "Do you believe them?"

"Yes I do. If the cyber attack had come from either of them we would have known. But no one has been able to figure out where this attack came from. They are spooked and worried that the same thing could happen to them."

"What is the latest from the Joint Chiefs?" asked Martineau.

"They are taking us to DEFCON 3, and preparing to drop to DEFCON 2 as we speak. As long as we cannot disarm the football…" Holden didn't finish his sentence. He didn't need to. There was silence in the room for several seconds as everyone considered the seriousness of what Holden had just said.

Finally Ixchel blurted out, "What about Bonsam? Will you be able to find Bonsam?"

Holden paused. "I don't know. The deeper we dig into his shadow network, the more intricate we realize it is. There are layers upon layers of complexity to the protection of this network."

Daniel stood up quickly. "Sir, please forgive me for interrupting. Ixchel, look!" He pointed to her computer screen. "Professor Jameson has gotten through. He's inviting you to webcam."

Ixchel spun around and gasped. She grabbed the mouse and quickly clicked accept. Daniel slid his chair beside Ixchel's. Clay and Martineau got out of their seats and moved to stand behind them. Holden looked over at Clark. He gestured toward the computer and moved next to

Clay. Clark quickly joined him by standing next to Martineau.

"This thing is so slow," said Ixchel in frustration.

"Just be glad we're able to connect. With all the network problems out there it's a miracle that he got through. Just pray that the connection doesn't drop," said Daniel.

Everyone stared at the screen in anticipation. Finally, Jameson's image appeared. It faded in and out a few times, but finally the picture remained clear.

"Professor Jameson. We have been trying to reach you for days. I have something I need to tell…"

Jameson cut her off. "Miss Cobán, please listen. I have important news that I must give you and I am afraid we may lose this signal at any moment." As if on cue Jameson's image faded in and out again.

"There was a small earthquake here yesterday morning. It opened up a hidden chamber at the excavation site. In it we found the missing piece of the tablet!"

Daniel and Ixchel looked at one another with astonishment. "What does it look like? Can you tell what it says?"

"It doesn't say anything. It's a map," replied Jameson.

Ixchel and Daniel were taken by surprise once more. Jameson's image flickered again. "A map of what?" asked Ixchel.

"It appears to be a map of Tikal, in Guatemala," he replied. "It shows the causeways, the Central Acropolis, and the Plaza of the Seven Temples."

Ixchel felt a shiver run down her spine. She was getting an eerie feeling again. "Professor, please wait just one second." She minimized the webcam window and quickly popped open her database of Maya images. She typed Tikal into the search field and hit enter.

"What are you doing?" asked Daniel.

A thumbnail entitled "Tikal" came up. Ixchel double clicked the thumbnail and an image of Tikal's Temple I appeared. Ixchel's mouth fell open and her body trembled.

The temple she saw on her screen was the same temple she had seen the night of the Marriott explosion.

Daniel had come to know the warning signs that preceded Ixchel's episodes of delirium. He placed his hand on the small of her back and rubbed gently. "You're going to be okay," he said softly.

She quickly maximized the webcam window. "Professor Jameson, what do you think it means?"

"What do *you* think it means?" he replied. "I'm emailing you a digital picture of it now. Tell me what you think."

"Okay, thank you," she replied. Martineau and Clay exchanged glances, and Holden stepped closer to the desk.

"But Ixchel, I must warn you. I was drawn to the map by forces I could not control. Every time I look at it I am struck by feelings of terror. Please be cautious. I remember what happened to you when you first viewed the tablet."

Ixchel lowered her eyes. She hadn't known that Professor Jameson realized that she was struck with terror as well the first time she saw the tablet. "I'm okay Professor, please send it."

A moment later the message popped up. She quickly opened the message and downloaded the photo. Her heart raced as she pulled it up. It looked exactly as the professor had described. Everyone standing behind Ixchel and Daniel leaned forward for a closer look.

"Professor, please hold on for another second." She minimized the webcam window again. She took a digital photo of the original tablet and placed it next to the photo of the map on her screen. Then with a few quick mouse clicks, she fused the images together.

Ixchel was instantly struck by a blinding light and blast of wind. She felt herself being transported back to the village of her youth. Suddenly she was standing face to face with her great-grandmother. Her great-grandmother called out, "Come, Ixchel."

Another flash of light and blast of wind struck her. She was no longer in Sacatepéquez. She slowly spun around and looked at the strange environment surrounding her. She was now standing in the ancient city of Tikal. She stood at the base of the great temple, looking up at a dark figure standing high atop the stairs. She watched in horror as the figure burst into a pillar of flames.

The flames spread outward rapidly. As the flames approached her, she saw the shadowy figure standing directly in front of her. It was Bonsam! His eyes were filled with fire. Soon they were both engulfed in the blazing inferno. She screamed in agony, "Bonsam! Bonsam!"

The others in the room watched helplessly as Ixchel's entire body began to thrash about. She whipped her head back and forth uncontrollably, her long black hair twisting from side to side. "Bonsam! Bonsam!" she screamed again.

Clark and Holden looked at each other with blank expressions. They did not know what to make of Ixchel's sudden breakdown. Martineau moved forward to help Daniel restrain Ixchel. She was still shaking incredibly. "Ixchel are you all right?" called out Daniel.

Ixchel continued to scream in horror as the fire spread rapidly through the ancient city of Tikal. The temples, the trees, and the land were all on fire. She saw Bonsam throw his head back as he let out a bloodcurdling scream. An instant later, Ixchel heard the sound of thunderous explosions echoing through the air. The flames that engulfed her turned white and the heat became so intense that she felt her entire being ignite.

Suddenly she awoke from the nightmare. Sweat was pouring down her cheeks and her mouth was frozen open. She turned to the computer screen. "Oh God, I saw it!" she screamed as she pointed to the map. "That is where it will end. That is where the world will end."

Clark leaned forward. "Ixchel, what do mean? What do you mean when you say, 'That is where the world will end?'"

"I don't know, but that is where it will end. I am certain," said Ixchel excitedly. "I was just there, in Tikal. I heard loud explosions like bombs going off. I saw the world on fire. And Bonsam was there! He was there! It was him!"

Holden spoke softly, trying to get Ixchel to calm down. "Ixchel, if what you are saying is true; that the symbols on the tablet represent the end of the world via nuclear bombs and the symbols on the map point to ancient Maya ruins, then there would be some kind of connection. But it doesn't make any sense. I assure you there are no nukes in Guatemala."

"I know, it makes no sense," Ixchel said.

"Now wait a minute, Mike," said Clark. "Bonsam still has the football. He could order a nuclear attack on any place in the world, including Guatemala."

"I don't see the rationale behind that," replied Holden.

"We're talking about Bonsam here, he is not a rational person."

"You've got a point there."

"Wait!" Martineau cried out. "Listen. It's not that Bonsam can order an attack *on* any place in the world, it's that Bonsam can order an attack *from* any place in the world."

Clark finished her thought, "Including Guatemala!"

The room fell silent. Holden's mind raced as he considered the idea of Bonsam being in Guatemala. There was a worldwide manhunt for Bonsam taking place, but he was positive that no one was looking in Guatemala. His mind reeled with possible courses of action to search out Bonsam in this unexpected location, but with all the disastrous events occurring in the world and the extreme strains already being placed on the military, he could not come up with a decisive plan at the moment.

Daniel minimized the pictures and maximized the webcam image of Professor Jameson. "Are you still there, Professor?"

"Yes Daniel, right here."

"Professor, Ixchel thinks…"

The professor cut him off. "I heard it all. She may be right. I don't fully understand what is happening with

President Bonsam, but I can tell you that I was drawn to the map by unseen forces. Both the tablet and the map are menacing. There is evil in the air, I can feel it."

Suddenly the sound of a door slamming could be heard in Jameson's cabin. Then two gunshots fired in rapid succession cracked from the computer, and Jameson slammed face first onto the table in front of him.

Everyone jumped at the sound of the shots. "Oh my God!" Ixchel screamed. There was mass commotion in the room as the others reacted to the sight of Jameson being shot.

Daniel yelled into the microphone, "Professor Jameson! Professor Jameson!

Everyone held their breath as they stared at the screen. Daniel watched and waited, but Jameson did not move. "Professor Jameson!" he yelled again.

Everyone was fixated on the image of Jameson lying across the table. Clay leaned in closer and shouted, "Look!" A shadow had fallen across the professor. Slowly a hand came into view from the right side of the screen. It reached forward until it was resting on Jameson's shoulder, then it gave him a shove. Jameson slid to the left and his arms dragged papers off the table as he collapsed to the floor. The hand then reached over and picked up the stone map, and a deep voice was heard saying, "I'll take that."

Seconds later the face of Emmanuel Bonsam leaned in from the right and stared into the webcam. He glared frighteningly as his hand moved slowly toward the camera lens, and before anyone watching had a chance to say something, the screen went blank.

Chapter 79

Everyone was still in shock when suddenly the office door opened and the Air Force Chief of Staff quickly entered the room. He didn't know what to make of the clamor in the room. Holden looked up and said, "What's wrong, General?"

"Space Command has just reported that TacSat-3 is falling out of orbit and will hit the atmosphere at any moment!"

"What will that do to our military intelligence gathering?" asked Holden.

"That satellite provides the bulk of our tactical imagery," said the general as he walked toward Holden. "Its destruction will have ripple effects that will leave us virtually blind."

"We have lost our ability to see what our enemies are doing? They could be moving against us and we'd have no way of knowing."

"It gets worse. We're also losing control of the satellites that make up our Strategic Missile Defense system."

Holden knew that if the military lost control of the space-based weapons systems that protect the country from nuclear attack, then there would be nothing to stop Bonsam from dropping a nuke anywhere within the United States. "Tell the chairman I am on my way. Make sure the Joint Chiefs are there."

"Yes, sir," said the general as he quickly left the office.

Holden turned to Clark. "Sam, I have to get back to the situation room."

"I'm coming with you," replied Clark.

"No, you're not. You need to go find Bonsam and stop him. We don't have the time to get a team briefed and up to speed to go searching for Bonsam across Central America." Holden stopped and looked around the room at the others present. "If we're lucky, Bonsam didn't hear what Jameson was saying before he killed him, and then he won't know where the map leads. But he *will* figure it out sooner or later. You may be able to get to Guatemala before Bonsam does and stop him."

"Us, really?" said Martineau. "Don't you think this is a job for the military?"

"The military is in disarray and we're going to drop to DEFCON 2. There is too much confusion right now," replied Holden. "You're the only ones who know about this Maya prophecy. Take Marine One over to Andrews. While you're in transit I'll find you a flight to Guatemala. Clay, grab the Secret Service agent outside the door and have him load you up with weapons."

Clay rushed out the door, with Martineau right behind. Daniel held his arm around Ixchel as he led her out. She was still in shock from seeing Professor Jameson killed. Holden then turned to Clark and gave him a firm handshake. He grabbed Clark's forearm with his left hand and said, "Sam, I'm counting on you."

Chapter 80

Lieutenant Colonel Dembe Kybiroa shielded his eyes as Marine One touched down. As he ran toward the helicopter he saw the door begin to open. By the time he arrived, the airstairs had been lowered and the passengers had begun to file out with Clark in the lead.

"Welcome to Andrews Air Force Base, Mr. President," said Kybiroa as he gave Clark a salute.

"I'm not president yet," Clark replied, as he looked up at the 6 foot 2 airman.

Kybiroa ignored the comment and called out to the others, "Welcome to Andrews Air Force Base. I know you are in a hurry and so am I. Please follow me." He turned toward the nearby runway and began taking long, quick strides across the airfield. Clark almost had to run to keep up with him.

"I'm Lieutenant Colonel Dembe Kybiroa, sir. Just call me Kabaka, that's my call sign."

"Kabaka?"

"My parents were from Uganda," explained Kybiroa. "Kabaka is the Bantu word for 'king.'"

"I like it," replied Clark as they swiftly made their way to the flight line.

"Thanks. I'm piloting a flight heading to Guatemala. Well, not Guatemala actually, but close enough. We'll be glad to swing on over and drop you off. You were lucky that you caught us. We were already taxiing to the runway when we got the call saying you needed a lift."

They rounded the corner of a hangar and stepped onto the flight line. "There's our ride," said Kabaka as he headed toward the plane. It was a C-17 cargo jet.

Martineau raced to catch up to Clark and Kabaka. "We're going to fly there in that?"

"Do you want to get there fast or do you want to get there in comfort, ma'am?" replied Kabaka. "Who knows when there will be another flight going anywhere near

Guatemala." Martineau knew he was right, so she stopped and waited for the others to catch up.

"Kabaka, do you have any idea what is going on up there?" Clark said as he pointed toward the sky.

"Pardon my French, sir, but air traffic control is becoming one big clusterfuck," Kabaka replied. "There are communication problems across the country. Planes trying to take off or land are periodically losing communications with the towers. Same thing is happening to planes in the air. It's only a matter of time before we start having accidents."

"Are we gonna be safe?" Clark asked. "You really think we should do this?"

"Sir, we have dropped to DEFCON 2. Commercial flights are being stopped so it will only be the military that's in the air. We'll be all right."

Within five minutes everyone had gathered at the base of the rear cargo door, which had been lowered to the tarmac. Clark could see that Martineau still had a look of uncertainty about the aircraft. "Kenna, trust me. I've flown on these babies dozens of times. We'll be fine." Martineau shook her head in despair knowing that Clark had certainly jinxed them.

Clay and Daniel wheeled their weapons lockers to the base of the door and stood by for further instructions. Clark put his hands on the backs of Martineau and Ixchel and said, "You go first." As the women climbed the ramp, Clay and Daniel lifted one locker while Clark and Kabaka lifted the other.

Kabaka was surprised by the weight of the locker. "What do you have in here?" he asked Clark.

"Weapons," Clark replied.

"You planning on invading Guatemala, Mr. President?"

Clark laughed. "No, we just have some important business to take care of."

"Yes, sir. You're the president," said Kabaka as he smiled at Clark, and together they carried the weapons onboard the plane.

Clark and Kabaka made their way to the front of the cargo area where everyone else was already waiting. "Make yourselves comfortable, we've got a long flight," said Kabaka as he reached the stairs to the cockpit and climbed upward.

Once Kabaka reached the top of the stairs, he heard his copilot call out, "Welcome back your highness. 'Bout time."

"Talk to me, Costner," replied Kabaka as he slapped the back of the seat in which his copilot, Captain Kevin "Costner" Carson, was sitting while watching the news on his iPad. Carson had been Kabaka's copilot and friend for the last two years. Carson received the call sign "Costner" from his buddies during his first assignment. He was stationed in Germany at Ramstein Air Base, and every time he introduced himself to cute young *fräuleins* and said his name was Kevin Carson, they would always reply, "Oh, Kevin Costner."

Costner plopped his iPad down onto of his flight bag and proceeded to prepare the plane for takeoff. "Sir, the chatter coming from the tower is kinda alarming. They keep losing comms. And by the way, who was so damned important that we had to stop a takeoff so they could hitch a ride?" asked Costner.

"You wouldn't believe me if I told you, Costner" replied Kakaba as he taxied the plane to the end of the airstrip.

"Fine, then don't tell me," Costner replied. "Oh, and while you were gone, I was watching the news. There is some freaky shit going down out there. Reports are coming in from all over the country saying that the crashing computer systems are causing widespread panic."

Kabaka gunned the throttle and the C-17 hurtled down the airstrip. "I hope we can make it to Guatemala!" Kabaka yelled as the plane lifted off and banked to the right. As they climbed higher, the minds of both men envisaged the problems occurring below. They flew in silence for several minutes. Once they reached cruising altitude, Kabaka reached over and slapped Costner on the shoulder. "So what kinda freaky shit did you see on the news?" he asked.

"Oh man, people are acting like a Category 5 hurricane is coming," Costner replied. "They're mobbing the stores for bottled water, canned goods, generators, you name it. People are filling up their gas tanks and then bolting out of the service stations without paying. There have been break-ins at several national banks because their ATMs had shut down."

"This is going to get worse before it gets better," Kabaka said as he shook his head despairingly.

"No doubt," Costner replied. "And that's just the minor stuff. Computer malfunctions opened about twenty dams in Central Texas and now Austin is underwater. Power grids throughout Southern California are dying and there was a report out of LA that said that a computer glitch at Cedars-Sinai killed 17 people who were hooked up to life support." Costner reached over and slapped Kabaka back. "And get this, out in New Mexico someone hijacked a Virgin Galactic space-plane."

"Get the fuck outta here!" Kabaka said in disbelief.

"I shit you not," Costner replied.

Kabaka couldn't believe it. "Damn, I want to party with that dude."

Costner continued. "A drawbridge in Connecticut opened on its own with no warning. Four cars and some poor dude on a motorcycle plunged into the river. And sir, brace yourself. There was a horrible story out of St. Louis. Anheuser-Busch is reporting that computer viruses have shut down their breweries in Missouri and Virginia."

"Noooooooo!" screamed Kabaka as he shook his head back and forth.

Costner laughed at Kabaka's pain, but he knew it was time to be serious. "Sir, no more jokes. There has also been major rioting across the country, and widespread looting in many major cities." Costner hesitated before he went on. He had hoped to avoid this conversation, but now he felt it was necessary. "Sir, I hate to tell you this, but Atlanta has been hit the hardest. Gangs have taken over the streets and half of downtown is on fire. Hundreds of people are trapped in the underground rail system. And if that wasn't enough, computer malfunctions at the Atlanta Federal Pen opened the cell doors and prison gates and over 2,200 prisoners stormed out."

Kabaka stared straight ahead without saying a word, and there were several seconds of uncomfortable silence. "Kabaka, I'm sure your wife and daughter are okay," Costner said reassuringly. "They are all the way out in East Point. I'm sure they're safe."

"Thanks, Costner," Kabaka finally replied. "Okay, we are the Air Force's finest and we are on a mission, let's focus on that. By the way, the passenger we picked up was President-elect Clark."

"Oh, bullshit," Costner laughed.

Chapter 81

Kabaka stuck his head out of the cockpit. "Sir, we are beginning our descent. We should be on the ground in ten minutes. We'll be landing at the airport in Belmopan, the capital of Belize. Actually, airport is kind of a strong word. Airstrip is more like it. But it is the closest landing site to your destination."

"Okay," Clark said to the others. "That should put us less than 70 miles from Tikal. We'll need to find some transportation once we land. It may not be easy, seeing that the entire trip will be along dirt roads through mountain passes."

"I can help us," said Ixchel. "I have been to Belize many times. The people are friendly and helpful. We should be able to find someone to transport us to Tikal without any problem. It is becoming a popular tourist destination. It will not cost very much, the dollar goes a long way in this part of the world."

Clark removed his wallet and looked inside. "That's good," he said, "because I only have 22 bucks on me."

Suddenly the engines whined and the plane picked up speed. They could feel the plane begin to climb. Martineau looked at Clark and said, "What's happening?"

"I wish I knew," he replied.

A few minutes later the plane leveled out. "I wonder what is going on," said Clay. "They obviously had to abort the landing. Oh, look." Clay pointed to the cockpit stairs. Kabaka climbed down and joined his passengers in the cargo hold.

"What's wrong, Kabaka?" asked Clark.

"Sir, I got some good news and I got some bad news."

"What is it?"

"Central America just got hit by an 8.2 earthquake. It hit Belize, Guatemala, and Honduras with tremendous force. The airfield that we were heading to has been destroyed and there is no way we can land there. We are running out of fuel and there aren't any airfields within range that aren't damaged and have a runway long enough to accommodate an aircraft of this size. The last radio transmission we received before our radio died said that several air traffic control satellites had started to malfunction, which means there is no way an aerial refueling plane can find us. It looks like we'll have to ditch the plane in the Caribbean Sea."

Clark stared at Kabaka. "So what's the good news?"

"That was the good news, sir. The bad news is, there are only two parachutes on board and me and my copilot claim those. The only way you're going to get out of here is in one of these," Kabaka said as he slapped his hand against a giant wooden cargo crate.

Oh shit! Clark very slowly turned his head toward Martineau. She folded her arms across her chest and said, "Trust me. I've flown on these babies dozens of times. We'll be fine."

Kabaka led them to the crate furthest back in the cargo hold. It was nearly eight feet high, ten feet wide, and six feet long. "These crates can hold several tons of cargo. Fortunately, this one is empty. You five together weigh less than a thousand pounds. With this huge chute you'll float down like a feather and land as softly as can be," he said. "But we gotta hurry. We got enough fuel to get you to your temple but we won't have enough to circle. We get one shot at this."

"If we bail out in this box, do you think you can get us to land close to the temple?" asked Clark.

"Well, normally for this type of drop we have a loadmaster in charge, but we weren't expecting to make any drops on this flight. But don't worry, I'll have my copilot drop us down to 1,500 feet and I'll release the crate right over the temple. I can drop these bad boys directly on target every time," Kabaka said as he smacked the side of the crate. "Well, most of the time. Actually, I'm batting about .500 these days."

Clay dropped his head and looked down at the floor, and Daniel rubbed his eyes with his thumb and forefinger. Ixchel observed their reactions and asked, "What does 'batting about .500' mean?"

Daniel moved his hand away from his face and replied, "You don't want to know."

Kabaka handed a crowbar to Clark and another to Clay. "Pry it open from this side." He then turned to Daniel and said, "I'll help you bring back your weapons," and together the two of them worked their way toward the front of the cargo bay.

Ixchel said, "I need to sit back down." She was still bereaved by the death of Professor Jameson. She closed her eyes and tried to relax, but it was proving to be difficult. *Patrick was murdered, Professor Jameson was murdered. What next?* As worry set in, she unexpectedly heard her great-grandmother's voice call out, "I am here."

As Clark and Clay finished prying off the side of the crate, Clark turned to Martineau and said, "We're lucky this one was empty."

Martineau put her hands on her hips. "Lucky? This is your idea of lucky?"

Clark spun around quickly and examined the inside of the crate. Clay looked over at Martineau, who shot him a wink.

"Okay, everybody in," said Kabaka. Once everyone was inside he said, "Stand back, I'm going to nail the crate shut now." He began lifting the heavy wooden side of the crate up into place. The passengers watched intently as the side opening was about to close off. At the last second Kabaka dropped the side back to the floor, startling everyone in the crate and causing them to gulp in a breath of air.

"Oops, almost forgot. You'll need these," he said, as he handed in hammers and crowbars. "You won't be able to bang your way out without them."

Clark and the others let out a gigantic sigh of relief, imagining what it would have been like to be locked in the crate with no way of escape.

As soon as Kabaka finished nailing the crate shut he pounded the side and said, "If I were you I'd lay down on my stomach."

"Get down," Clark said to the others as he dropped to the floor of the crate. Everyone followed suit.

Moments later they heard a strong rush of wind as the aft cargo bay door opened. "Bon voyage!" yelled Kabaka.

As the crate began sliding backward, Clark yelled, "Hold on!"

The entire group buried their faces into their arms and called out, "Ohhhhhhhhhh!" as the crate moved down the rollers and shot out the back of the C-17. Martineau, Ixchel, and Daniel each held their breath as they anticipated plunging rapidly to the ground below, however the crate drifted downward slowly just as Kabaka had promised. One by one they lifted their heads and looked around at one another, relieved that they were not plunging rapidly toward the ground below.

"We'll be hitting the ground in just a few minutes," said Clark. "Everyone stay down. Even though this is a light load, there might be a slight bump when we land." No sooner were those words out of Clark's mouth than the crate slammed into the top of a tree in the center of a large forest.

The crate rocked hard to the left, sending each passenger into a log roll against the weapons lockers that had been placed against the left wall. Ixchel held tightly onto Daniel and prayed that the crate would not roll to the right, because the lockers would surely crush them. Branches could be heard snapping as the crate continued its downward path. It crashed into one last big branch, which righted the crate just before it pounded into the ground with a loud whump. As the passengers in the crate untangled themselves, Martineau could be heard saying, "You call that a slight bump?"

Chapter 82

Clark and Clay quickly went to work banging the side off the crate. Once the nails became loose, Clark looked at Clay and said, "On three we kick." They took a step back and on three they each slammed a karate kick against the wood. The side fell outward and crashed to the ground, revealing their location inside a shadowy forest.

Martineau exited the crate first, while Clark and Clay moved to the rear of the crate to retrieve the weapons lockers. Ixchel had smacked her right thigh on the corner of a locker when the crate came crashing down and had suffered a serious bruise, so Daniel helped her up and assisted her as she limped her way out over the side of the crate.

Martineau turned around and saw Ixchel limping her way. "Are you okay, Ixchel?"

"I think it's just a bruise. I'll be okay," she replied, noticing that Daniel was looking all around. "Daniel, what is it?" she asked.

"Look," he replied.

The three stood in awe as they gazed at the forest before them. It was filled with tall, straight trees with smooth, gray bark. Their long, leafy branches spread open near the top of the trunk, creating a spectacular canopy high above them. "These are Ceiba trees," said Ixchel. "Ancient Maya cultivated them in the plazas of their cities for shade. You'll find these near many of the ancient ruins in Guatemala."

"This means we could be close to Tikal," said Daniel.

Ixchel slowly scanned the forest. She began experiencing a strange feeling that she had been here before. Moments later she heard the voice of her great-grandmother in her mind, "I am here."

She turned excitedly to Daniel and said, "We *are* in Tikal! I can feel it."

Clark and Clay pulled the weapons lockers over to where Martineau, Daniel, and Ixchel had gathered and plopped them to the ground, causing small colorful lizards to scurry away.

Daniel looked at Clark and said, "Ixchel is certain that we are already within Tikal."

"Well, chalk one up for Kabaka. This should improve his batting average," said Clark. He paused, and then said in almost a whisper, "Man, I hope those guys made it out okay."

There was another long pause as everyone thought about Kabaka and his copilot bailing out over the sea. "There are enough backpacks in here for each of us," Clark said as he reached toward a locker, breaking the silence. "Let's load up. Men, grab a weapon and as much ammo as you can carry. There are rifles and pistols with holsters, feel free to grab one of each."

Martineau looked at Clark and loudly cleared her throat. "But be sure to give Kenna first dibs on the weapons," Clark quickly added.

Once everyone had their backpacks situated and weapons loaded, Clark looked at Ixchel and said, "Which way?"

She closed her eyes for only a moment, and then motioned with her head toward the east. "This way," she replied softly.

As they started to move, Clark turned to Daniel and quietly asked, "How does she know this?"

"I don't know," he replied, "but I trust her instincts. He looked over at Ixchel and then turned back to Clark. "I'm going to stay in the rear with Ixchel, if that's okay with you."

Clark could sense Daniel's affection for Ixchel and his concern for her safety. "Okay. Be safe."

Clay called out, "I got point," and began leading the group single file through the dense forest. The group marched slowly and silently. Spider monkeys could be seen swinging through the trees above them. Somewhere in the distance a jaguar roared, causing everyone's eyes to momentarily widen. Large beetles constantly flittered about as the expedition moved on.

Clay had led the column over a hundred yards when suddenly he froze, putting his hand up in a fist, signaling to everyone to stay still. Nobody moved. He pointed toward the ground to signal that everyone needed to get down. As everyone crouched low, Clark made his way to Clay's position and whispered, "What do you see?"

"I don't see anything," Clay replied, "but listen."

The underbrush had become very thick and they could only see a few yards ahead, but they could hear that something or someone was up there. Clark and Clay strained to hear the strange, faint sounds that were definitely not the natural noises of the forest.

Both men nearly jumped out of their skin when, from out of nowhere, Martineau appeared between them and placed her hands on their shoulders and quietly asked, "What's going on?"

Once Clark's heart resumed beating, he turned to Martineau. "We think there is someone up there," he said, pointing his rifle toward the brush in front of them. Martineau squinted her eyes and peered into the brush, and a moment later Daniel and Ixchel joined her.

"So much for stealth, guys," Clay whispered to the group.

As Clay and Clark discussed the concept of covertness with Martineau and Daniel, no one noticed that Ixchel had moved five yards ahead. She stood motionless and closed her eyes, listening to the sounds that were coming from the other side of the brush. The sounds became clearer, and she soon realized that they were voices, voices speaking the language of the ancient Maya.

As the others came to an agreement on the benefits of furtiveness in their near-term travels, Daniel looked up just in time to see Ixchel disappear into the wall of brush ahead. "Wait!" he cried out as he ran after her.

"Ixchel!" cried Clay as he dashed after Daniel, with Clark and Martineau hot on his heels. The thick brush made their progress difficult, but a few minutes later the three plowed through the brush and, much to their surprise, found themselves standing in a vast, sunlit clearing. They could once again see the sky, which was crystal blue and spotted with large, white cumulus clouds. Lush green grass covered the rolling hills that stretched out before them, and white and purple orchids were scattered throughout the clearing. They were speechless as they beheld the breathtaking panorama in wonder.

"Unbelievable!" whispered Martineau. "It's like the garden of Eden."

Daniel and Ixchel were standing at the crest of a small hill midway into the clearing when they saw Clark, Clay, and Martineau come crashing out of the forest. "This way!" yelled Daniel as he waved them over. Clay sprinted ahead and joined them, while Clark and Martineau climbed the hill at a much less strenuous pace.

As Clark and Martineau continued to approach the trio, Clark noticed that all three had bright smiles on their faces, and Daniel and Ixchel were holding hands. "Sam, Kenna, hurry," shouted Clay. "Check this out!"

"I'm running out of breath here," Martineau shot back as she latched onto Clark's shoulder for the last few yards of the trek to the top of the hill.

"That's okay," Clay replied, "because what you are about to see will take your breath away!"

Clark stepped up next to Daniel and Ixchel and said, "So, what have you…" but he was too surprised to finish his sentence.

Martineau joined Clark and had a similar reaction. "My God, where did *they* come from?" she gasped.

Just beyond the base of the hill, a caravan made up of dozens upon dozens of Maya slowly passed by. The sight captivated Clark and the others. Men, women and children dressed in traditional Maya outfits made of bright, beautiful cloth sang and danced as they marched onward. Lovely melodies could be heard coming from the children as they played their *Ocarina* flutes. The sweet smell of delicious *Brazo de Reina* filled the air. Martineau pointed to a group of plump, buxom women wearing round, colorful *toyocal* hats that were common in Maya cultures throughout Central America. Clark, Clay and Daniel laughed as the women clapped their hands and blew kisses their way.

Ixchel squeezed Daniel's hand and placed her head on his shoulder as she watched the Maya parade pass by. "Oh Daniel, this is beautiful."

Daniel turned to face Ixchel, and he put his arms around her waist. He pulled her close and rested his forehead against hers. "You are beautiful, Ixchel," he replied. Ixchel wrapped her arms around Daniel's neck and smiled. Daniel smiled back, and then gently kissed Ixchel's soft lips.

Martineau elbowed Clark in the ribs and whispered, "Look," as she pointed her head toward Daniel and Ixchel, who remained engaged in a long, passionate kiss. "Let's give them some privacy." Clark looked over at Clay, who wolf-whistled approvingly at Daniel and Ixchel's warm embrace.

Clark, Clay and Martineau walked to the base of the hill and continued to observe the procession as it passed by. "I wonder what's going on," said Clark. "Is it a holiday or something?"

"Perhaps it is a Guatemalan Carnival celebration," replied Martineau. "Every Latin American country celebrates Carnival in its own way. But Carnival is in the spring, not November."

Clark looked on. "I wonder where they are going?"

"My guess," said Clay as he pointed far off into the sky, "would be there." In the distance an ancient Maya temple peaked above the tall trees of the surrounding forest. Bright sunlight reflected off the giant gray edifice.

Daniel and Ixchel walked toward the base of the hill to join the others. It was slow going since Ixchel was still limping, but Daniel supported her as they moved on. When they reached the base they saw Clark, Martineau and Clay admiring the spectacular view of the temple.

"That is Temple IV," said Ixchel. "It is the tallest pyramid in Tikal."

"You mean there are more than one?" asked Clark.

"Yes, there are several," she replied. "But Temple IV is the largest. It marks the western boundary of Tikal. From there it is a short journey to the Great Plaza, the center point of Tikal.

"Do you think that is where the Maya pilgrims are headed?" asked Martineau.

"Yes," replied Ixchel, as she gazed at the ancient marvel. She felt herself being drawn toward the plaza.

"Why?" asked Clark.

"I can't explain it," she said, as tears welled up in her eyes. "But Tikal beckons us. I can feel the spirits of our ancient ancestors all around us. It is as if they are calling out for us, calling for us to return."

"Return where?" asked Daniel softly.

Ixchel paused as a single tear ran down her cheek. "Home," she replied.

The group stood silently as they watched Daniel pull Ixchel into his arms. "Everything is going to be all right," he said as he rocked her from side to side.

She looked up into his eyes and replied, "I know, I can feel it."

"Um, I hate to break this up, really," said Clay, "but have you all forgotten that we are here to find Bonsam? The Maya are heading to Tikal, we are headed to Tikal, so it's pretty likely that if Bonsam is around, he'll be heading to Tikal, too."

"He's right," said Clark. "Let's go."

Chapter 83

Clay was out in front again as the group hiked toward the temple with the Maya. Strangely, the Maya seemed to take no notice of the weapons that Clark, Clay and Martineau were carrying. Ixchel suddenly realized that the pain in her leg had gone away, and she walked briskly as the group closed in on the center of Tikal.

"Ixchel, does it appear to you that the Maya are behaving differently than when we first saw them?" asked Daniel. "Their mood has changed." Ixchel lightly shook her head yes.

"I feel it, too," Clark said to Daniel. Clark was slipping back into sniper mode. His senses were heightened and he started moving as though he were stalking prey. The natural sounds of the wilderness had disappeared and there was no sign of wildlife moving about. He could sense a presence in the thick forest, something that did not belong there.

The Maya were now speaking very little, and when they did it was in hushed tones. As they passed beneath Temple IV, their pace slowed dramatically. They continued moving forward in a zombielike trance. For Clark, the presence he had been feeling was growing stronger with every step.

Clay turned around and waved the others forward. When they reached him, they saw that they had reached an open area. "This is the Tozzer Causeway!" said Ixchel. It will lead us directly to the Great Plaza."

Clark gazed ahead and said, "We need to keep our guard up. Keep your eyes and ears open and move forward cautiously." Clay could tell that Clark sensed danger, so he trotted several yards down the causeway to scout the route ahead. Anyone or anything that tried to get to his friends would have to get past him and his rifle first.

"Sam, what is the matter?" asked Martineau.

"There is something out there," he replied and he scanned the area.

"Bonsam?" she asked.

"I don't know. Maybe," Clark said. "But I feel a presence out there, unlike anything I have ever felt before."

Martineau turned to Ixchel, but she didn't even have to ask the question. "I feel it, too," said Ixchel. "We are almost there. Soon we will see Temple II. That will take us into the Great Plaza. On the opposite side of the plaza is Temple I." She paused and looked over to Clark. "That is where the Maya are heading, I can feel it."

"So is Bonsam," Clark thought.

Ten minutes later they were standing to the rear of Temple II. "This is known as Temple of the Masks," said Ixchel. "On the other side is the Great Plaza." She watched as the Maya trod onward around the north side of the temple. She looked at Clark and said, "They are heading to Temple I. It is the foremost temple in Tikal."

"No they're not," said Clay as he walked toward Ixchel. "Come with me," he said to the group. "I have something to show you. Hurry."

As they rounded the northwest corner of Temple II, Temple I came into view. "Temple I is called the Temple of the Jaguar," said Ixchel. "It was built as a tomb for an ancient Maya king."

"Yes, but still the Maya are not heading there," said Clay. "Trust me." As they rounded the northeast corner of the temple and entered the Great Plaza, Clay pointed ahead and said, "Look."

An ancient acropolis lined the entire north side of the plaza. Layers of interconnected stone fortifications covered the hillside, many with huge stone staircases running up through their center. Clay pointed toward a large jagged gap that had opened in the face of the enormous citadel next to Temple I, revealing a cave that had been hidden for thousands of years. "That's where the Maya are heading."

Chapter 84

The five of them stood there in the shadow of the Temple of the Jaguar, staring at the opening to the cave. "What is this place?" Daniel asked, as he looked around in astonishment.

"The earthquake must have opened this," said Martineau.

The cave was eerie, yet something about it was spiritual. Maya descendants young, old, and infirm continued to march toward the darkness of the cave. As they got closer, they started shuffling forward slowly and speaking in a language that had not been used in a hundred generations. Ixchel listened to the whispers of the Maya as they passed by, and she kept hearing a phrase being repeated over and over. It was nothing she understood, but she could tell that it must have something to do with the cave.

"Daniel, listen. The Maya keep repeating a phrase over and over," said Ixchel.

"I noticed. Do you know what it means?" he replied.

"No, but something tells me it's important. It must relate to the cave."

"Maybe one of the Maya can translate it for you."

Ixchel walked over to several Maya women who were standing nearby. She tried to inquire as to the meaning of the phrase, but none of the Maya seemed to speak English or Spanish. When Ixchel returned to the group she said, "This is odd, but it seems as if everyone is speaking in the ancient Mayan language."

"We don't have the time to worry about that now," said Clark. "We have to find Bonsam."

"If Bonsam is in there, we may never find him," said Martineau.

"Come on," said Clark. "We have to try."

Each grabbed their gear and headed toward the cave. They paused once they were about fifty feet into the cave because it became extremely dark. Martineau was the only one with a flashlight, so she set her backpack down to dig for it. Clark and Clay went several steps farther and peered into the pitch-black darkness.

The cave gave Ixchel a strange feeling. She was feeling drawn forward by a force, just as she had been in her dream. Inside, she was trembling with fear; fear of the unknown. Daniel was watching Ixchel's changing expressions as he dug through his backpack. She looked so beautiful, but she looked frightened as well. "I'll get you through this, Ixchel," said Daniel as he looked up from his backpack. "You'll be safe as long as I'm with you, I promise."

Suddenly, there was a commotion in the crowd. People at the entrance of the cave could be heard screaming and many started to run forward into the cave. Everyone looked up, but it was Daniel who first saw the source of the disturbance. It was Bonsam, and he was heading into the cave, stone map in one hand and machine gun in the other. He was pushing people out of his way as he moved forward.

"There he is!" yelled Daniel. Clark and Clay spun around and drew their weapons. When Bonsam heard Daniel's yell, he dropped the map and leveled the machine gun, all in one motion. His weapon was aimed directly at Ixchel. Daniel saw what was about to happen, so he quickly leaped in front of Ixchel just as Bonsam fired.

Daniel took a bullet in his lower right leg and another in his right side as he fell to the ground. Ixchel screamed in horror, "No!" She dropped to her knees and pulled Daniel's head to her lap. "Daniel! Daniel!"

Martineau quickly grabbed her rifle and popped off a few shots in Bonsam's direction, but she saw the bullets bounce off the cave wall behind him. The crowd scattered in every direction and several of the Maya crashed into Bonsam.

Clark and Clay raced toward Bonsam, but there were too many people in the way to get a clear shot. Bonsam was filled with fury as the Maya kept jostling into him. In frustration, he screamed and fired his weapon into the air, scattering the people even more. He fired until he had emptied his magazine. When he saw that Clark and Clay were heading his way, he let out another scream and then fled from the cave, pulling out another magazine and popping it into his weapon as he ran. As he raced across the Great Plaza toward the Temple of Masks, visions of fires flooded his mind, and he felt his body temperature rise.

Clark and Clay weaved their way through the panicking crowd in the cave, which severely hindered their progress. As they raced past Martineau, Clark yelled, "Kenna, help Daniel!" They finally freed themselves from the crowd and exited the cave, then saw that Bonsam already had a good lead on them as he sprinted past the southeast corner of the temple toward the forest.

Clay dropped to one knee and pulled his rifle to his shoulder and yelled, "I got him!"

Clark ran up and pushed the barrel of the rifle downward just as Clay was taking aim. "No, that's the football," Clark said, motioning to his own backpack. "We can't take a chance on shooting it." Clay stood up and indeed saw the top of a black satchel sticking out of Bonsam's backpack, just as Bonsam disappeared into a grove of trees near the rear of the temple. Clark slapped Clay on the back and said, "Come on!

Martineau desperately wanted to join in the hunt for Bonsam, but she knew that Daniel was seriously wounded. She grabbed her backpack and ran to where Daniel lay. Ixchel was there, still holding Daniel's head in her lap and crying out his name.

Martineau dug through her backpack but found nothing that could be used as bandages. "Ixchel, do you have anything in your backpack for first aid?" she called out quickly.

"No. Nothing!" Ixchel called back. The women looked at each other as fear started to set in. Ixchel was losing all color in her face. "Daniel! Daniel!"

As Martineau desperately tried to stop the bleeding with her bare hands, she was startled as she heard a man's deep voice call out. She stood and quickly turned around, and saw two Maya men approaching. One of the men kept repeating a word over and over. Martineau looked at Ixchel and asked, "What is he saying?"

Ixchel cried out happily, "It's the ancient Maya word for medicine man. He's a doctor!

Clay had dashed ahead of Clark and was first to reach the grove of trees that Bonsam had entered minutes ago. "Sam, come on!" he yelled to Clark, but he saw Clark quickly put his finger to his lips to signal for him to be quiet. Clay moved to a tree on the edge of the grove and crouched down.

Clark reached Clay seconds later and crouched down beside him. He looked into the shady darkness of the woods, his eyes slowly scanning back and forth. "He's in there waiting for us," Clark whispered to Clay. "Let's spread out, but stay within visual distance. Stay behind cover as much as you can, and move forward stealthily."

Clay moved down 20 feet to Clark's left, and waited for Clark's lead to enter the forest. Clark moved forward slowly with his rifle to his shoulder, moving the barrel's aim back and forth as he looked to his left then his right. Clay stepped gingerly as he proceeded forward, his eyes darting about in search of Bonsam. He had only progressed a few yards into the forest when he saw Clark freeze, then crouch down. He followed his lead immediately.

Clark was in the zone. He heard none of the sounds of the forest and his eyes focused on a large Ceiba tree 75 yards ahead of him. As he pulled the stock of his rifle tightly against his shoulder and aimed at the tree, time seemed to stand still. The next few seconds seemed like an eternity. A sliver of Bonsam's head came into his view as

Bonsam slowly peeked around the side of the tree. Clark fired three shots in a quick sequence, but all three bullets struck the tree. Bonsam threw himself to the ground and did a barrel roll to his right, then jumped to his knees and fired wildly. Bullets tore into the branches above Clay's head, causing him to dive to the ground and put his arms around his head. Clark lowered his rifle and scrambled over to see if Clay had been hit, and out of the corner of his eye he saw Bonsam tramp through the brush taking him deeper into the forest.

Kenna and Ixchel stood up to watch the men who had come to their assistance. The medicine man laid down his pouch and began pulling out cloth to dress Daniel's wounds. His partner pulled out a small drinking flask and poured water over the wounds and wiped them clear with his handkerchief. As they watched the medicine man sprinkle ground herbs over the wounds, Martineau and Ixchel unexpectedly heard a voice behind them say, "Hello."

They spun around quickly. There stood a young man who was pointing a handgun directly at Ixchel. "Set your rifle down on the ground, lady," said Jesse as he looked at Martineau. He moved the gun closer toward Ixchel. Ixchel gasped as she looked into the barrel of the gun. Martineau slowly squatted down and set her rifle at the man's feet, then slowly stood back up again, raising her hands toward her shoulders and taking a step back.

Jesse's eyes narrowed as he glared at Ixchel. "President Bonsam wants to meet you, Moon Goddess. You're coming with me." He continued to point his gun at Ixchel as he slowly reached out with his left hand toward Ixchel's arm. Just as he was about to grab her, a surge of Maya travelers barged through, pushing Jesse aside and taking his aim off of Ixchel.

Martineau delivered a quick uppercut slap to the bottom of Jesse's pistol, knocking his hand upward. As a shot went off hitting the ceiling of the cave, Martineau drove a knee kick deep into Jesse's groin, causing him to double over in extreme agony and drop his gun. Martineau bent down to reach for her rifle, but Jesse kicked her hard in the shoulder, knocking her face first to the ground.

Jesse let out a shout of anger as he pounced down on Martineau's back. He wrapped his hands around her throat and squeezed tightly as he pounded her face into the dirt. Martineau reached down deep and with all her strength did a quick rollover move that made Jesse fall to the ground by her side. She crawled away and grabbed her rifle, then she and Jesse stood up at the same time, their faces a mere three feet apart. Martineau yelled through clenched teeth as she flung the stock of her rifle around and butt-stroked Jesse's left temple with all her might. Jesse slumped forward, and was dead before he hit the ground. Martineau looked down at the man who had just attacked her, then turned her head to the side and spit the dirt out of her mouth.

Martineau wiped her lips as she walked back over to Daniel. The two men who were treating Daniel looked at her with respectful admiration. "How's he doing?" she asked Ixchel.

"Kenna, you just killed a man!" Ixchel replied.

"That's not important right now," she replied coolly. "We need to take care of Daniel."

Chapter 85

As Bonsam led Clark and Clay deeper into the forest, visions of a black jaguar flickered through his mind. He was confused by the visions. *A jaguar? Why?* He continued lumbering onward, clumsily tromping through the brush. He was well aware of Clark's past service as a sniper in Vietnam, and he knew it was only a matter of time before Clark would catch up to him. "Clark is the enemy!" he yelled.

Clark heard Bonsam's yell and stopped in his tracks. "Clay, did you hear that?"

"Yes, it sounded like Bonsam," he replied.

Clark could not imagine what Bonsam was doing by giving his position away. "He's pretty far ahead of us, we need to pick up the pace."

Bonsam looked around for a possible hiding place, but saw nothing that could conceal him from Clark. He was about to run deeper into the forest, but another vision of a black jaguar appeared in his mind. He froze as he stared at the vision. *Temple of the Jaguar! That's it!*

He felt a powerful force enter his body from the vision of the jaguar, and soon he was moving though the forest with the cunning of a cat. *Clark will not find me now!*

He doubled back and headed toward the Great Plaza, totally undetected by Clark and Clay. He cleared the trees and looked ahead to the ancient Temple of the Jaguar rising above the Great Plaza. As he ran toward it, visions of fire grew stronger in his mind. A whirlpool of flames surrounded the temple, drawing him into the spiraling vortex.

In his mind he saw his mother, her skin melting away. All that remained were sinewy strands of bones and cartilage. Her eyes were dark and sunken deep into the hollow sockets, and her teeth were protruding from her bleeding gums. Her ribs became skeletal as the skin on her torso constricted inward. Her hair was straggling behind her, ratty and gnarled. He watched her scream out as flames slowly consumed her hollow body.

Bonsam breathed heavily as he raced on, almost to the point of hyperventilating. Spittle flew from his mouth and his eyes began to water. His mind screamed in horror as he watched his mother flail about in abject misery as the flames continued to scorch what remained of her body and soul.

Bonsam ran to the front of the temple and stopped to catch his breath. As he stood there panting, visions of the ancient Maya carvings flooded his consciousness. There was a symbol flashing painfully over and over in his mind. It was the symbol of the Earth-fire. He looked at the temple steps leading upward, and was again racked by torturous visions of fires. His body trembled fiercely as he witnessed a vision of his own body immolating in the flames of hell. He screamed in panic, his eyes widening in terror.

He was struck by a blast of blinding light and a powerful gust of wind roared past him, and the visions disappeared. He stared at the top of the temple high above him, still breathing heavily. He smiled, then recklessly climbed the gigantic stone steps of the ancient Temple of the Jaguar. Once he reached the top step, he quickly moved forward and started to scale the rock wall of the funerary shrine that formed the pinnacle of the colossal temple.

At the midway point, one of the stone bricks he pulled on to raise himself gave way and crumbled down the side of the temple. Inside the space where the brick had been was a solid gold panel containing a carving of the Earth-fire symbol. As Bonsam stared at the symbol, his mind was deluged by visions of fire. He was enraptured, for he finally realized the meaning of the message hidden within the symbols of the ancient Maya calendar.

By the time Clark and Clay realized that Bonsam had doubled back and they had returned to the Great Plaza, they saw that Bonsam had already climbed the temple steps and was standing at the apex of the towering temple looking down at them with contempt. Bonsam paused for a moment as he stared at Clark with hatred in his eyes. He then ripped off his backpack and threw it to the surface of the shrine, never taking his eyes off of Clark.

Clark and Clay watched helplessly as Bonsam withdrew the satchel from his backpack. He flung it open, exposing the interactive console that controlled the entire nuclear arsenal of the United States.

"Come on!" yelled Clay, as he moved toward the temple.

Clark reached out and grabbed him by the shoulders. "We'll never make it in time!"

They saw Bonsam pull cards from the satchel and begin to punch numbers into the console. "Shit!" yelled Clay.

Clark grabbed Clay and pulled him in front of him. "Clay, I need you to stand perfectly still," whispered Clark from behind. He then placed the barrel of his rifle on top of Clay's left shoulder. Clay knew what was coming, so he took a deep breath and held it.

Bonsam punched in the final codes, activating the launch system. He only needed to push the blinking button on the console that displayed 'Launch' in large red letters to initiate a nuclear attack.

Clark placed his fingertip on the trigger and softly leaned his face against the stock of the rifle.

Bonsam stood up and looked around. Everything in his field of vision was on fire. The land, the trees, the temple, they were all on fire. It was magnificent!

Clark zeroed in. His breathing slowed down as his body relaxed. His mind flashed back to the jungles of Vietnam, then to the woods of Michigan.

Bonsam raised his hands toward the heavens, as he looked skyward. Even the sky was on fire. The revelation was clear. The dawn of his Divine Providence was now at hand, at this time and in this place.

Bonsam threw his head back and let out a powerful, primal scream, then quickly dropped to one knee in front of the console. Clark slowly followed his movement and placed his aim on Bonsam's midsection. As Bonsam moved his hand to push the activation button, Clark gently squeezed the trigger.

The recoil from the shot caused the rifle barrel to rise. Clay twisted hard to his right, clenching his teeth as he covered his left ear. The bullet ripped through Bonsam's chest, blowing him backward and knocking him over the backside of the temple along with the satchel. He bounded end-over-end down the sloped stone wall and landed in a heap on the ground below, the satchel landing nearly twenty feet away.

Clark let go of the rifle with his left hand and lowered it to his right side. He turned to Clay. "Let's roll," he said as he took off toward the rear of the temple. Clay was right behind him. As they rounded the corner of the temple, they saw Bonsam lying there with the satchel nearby. Bonsam's body was violently contorted and covered in blood.

They slowed to a walk. As they got closer, Clark put his hand on Clay's shoulder and said, "Go make sure Bonsam is dead."

"Okay," said Clay, continuing to look at Clark as they walked.

Clark said, "I need to get the football to…" Then without warning, Bonsam jumped up and pointed a pistol directly toward them. Clark forcefully pushed Clay to the ground and yelled, "Look out!" Clark turned back toward Bonsam, but he knew he would have no chance to fire his weapon. He stood up straight, pulled back his shoulders and threw out his chest, and dropped his hands to his sides. Bonsam smiled as he pulled the trigger, sending a bullet directly into Clark's stomach.

Clark doubled over and fell to the ground. Bonsam staggered around and laughed hysterically. As Clay attempted to get to his feet, Bonsam yelled, "Hold it!" and pointed his gun at Clay. He let out another hysterical laugh and then pulled the trigger, but all that was heard was a click. Bonsam laughed again and then staggered backward a few steps and fell flat on his back.

Clay got to his feet and ran to where Bonsam lay. Bonsam's mouth was filled with blood and he was having trouble breathing. His face was streaked with dirt and blood, and his eyes were rolling back into his head. Clay was filled with disgust as he looked at Bonsam's grotesque, hideous face. He put the barrel of his pistol to Bonsam's forehead and screamed, "You're going to hell!"

Bonsam laughed again, choking and coughing from the blood seeping into his lungs. This laugh was not hysterical like the others. It was monstrously low and macabre. Bonsam's eyes rolled forward, and they were filled with fire. He looked like Satan himself.

Bonsam looked up at Clay and laughed. "It's too late," he said, "we're all going to hell," and he spit a mouthful of blood into Clay's face. Clay was consumed with rage and before Bonsam had the chance to laugh again, he pulled the trigger, and the fire in President Emmanuel Bonsam's eyes was no more.

Chapter 86

Clay spit back onto the face of Bonsam's corpse and then kicked it in the ribs for good measure. He then ran over to Clark and dropped to his knees beside him. Clark was lying on his back with his blood-soaked hands covering his stomach. His skin was pale and he was having difficulty breathing. "Sam, how you doing, buddy?" asked Clay. He lifted Clark's hands away from his stomach and saw that the bullet had torn him wide open.

"Belly wounds, they're the worst," replied Clark. He was gasping for breath.

"Don't be such a wuss, you're gonna be fine," said Clay. He was nervously trying to decide what to do to help Clark.

"No, I'm not," he said as he started coughing. "Did we stop Bonsam?"

Bonsam's chilling last words ran through Clay's mind. "Yeah, you did it, man. Nice shot. You hit him smack in the breadbasket. He never stood chance," he said enthusiastically, but deep down he was filled with uncertainty.

Clark closed his eyes and smiled, "Ah, that's great." His coughing became worse.

Clay started to tear up. He could see Clark beginning to fade. "Sam, stay with me, man."

"Make sure you call Kenna 'Madam President' the next time you see her," Clark said as his voice became faint. He then took in a large breath of air and held it, his body becoming rigid. The air then slowly escaped from his lungs as his head fell to the side. He had stopped breathing, but with a peaceful smile on his face.

Clay hung his head in sorrow. He tried to hold in the tears but it was no use, and he began to cry. As he wiped the tears from his eyes, Clark's phone started ringing. Clay was startled, but he quickly pulled the phone from Clark's pocket and looked at the screen…VP Holden.

"Oh God, please God, let this be good news," he whispered to himself. He took in a deep breath and let it out slowly, clicked the answer button, then put the phone to his ear.

Holden was frantic. "Sam, have you found Bonsam? We have lost all control of our weapons systems. Our nukes are arming and can't be stopped!"

Clay began walking back toward the cave. "China and Russia are claiming the same thing is happening to them. And there are reports coming in that say two nuclear explosions were just detected in Pakistan. Sam! Have you found Bonsam?"

Clay dropped the phone and kept walking.

Chapter 87

Ixchel was holding Daniel's head in her lap as the Maya medicine man put a pressure bandage over Daniel's side wound. Ixchel had tears running down her cheeks as she stroked Daniel's hair. "Do not be afraid," said the medicine man to Ixchel, "he will live."

"Thank you," said Ixchel through her tears as she looked down at Daniel's face. She quickly looked back at the medicine man and cried out, "You speak English?"

The man shook his head yes as he continued to treat Daniel's wounds.

"Please, tell me. The phrase that the people here keep saying, what does it mean?"

He stood up and wiped the sweat from the back of his neck with a handkerchief. He looked at Ixchel for a moment, then pointed into the darkness of the cave and replied, "Shield Place."

Martineau had moved to the cave entrance to look for signs of Clark and Clay. Minutes later she saw Clay weaving his way through the crowd of Maya. She ran to Clay and asked, "Where's Sam?" Clay didn't need to answer, the look in his eyes said it all. Martineau buried her head into Clay's shoulder and started crying.

She looked up with tears in her eyes. "Did you stop Bonsam?" Again, his eyes said it all.

"We can't stay here," he said as he brushed past her on his way to check on Daniel. The medicine man and his companion had already lifted Daniel and placed themselves on either side to hold him up. The medicine man was on the left and he motioned to Clay that they would help Daniel move on, and then they slowly turned around and made their way further into the cave.

As Daniel and the Maya men faded into the cloudy darkness, Clay turned to Martineau and gently took her hand. "Come on Kenna, we need to go."

Martineau wiped the tears from her eyes as she walked with Clay toward Ixchel. She noticed that Ixchel had a confused look on her face. "Are you okay, Ixchel?" she asked.

Ixchel peered into the darkness of the cave. As she took a few steps forward, she heard her great-grandmother's voice call out, "I am here."

Ixchel smiled, for she finally understood why her great-grandmother had been calling for her all this time. Somehow she knew she would be safe within the darkness of the cave. She looked over her shoulder at Clay and Kenna. She smiled again and said, "I know the way."

With Ixchel in the lead the three walked deeper inside the mysterious cavern, knowing they had to go, but unknowing of what they would find inside. Clay, Kenna and Ixchel slowly disappeared into the shadowy abyss, and in the skyline beyond the ancient temples of Tikal, the sun set for the final time.

Epilogue

Nothing survived the nuclear holocaust that was unleashed on that fateful day. The entire planet was dead. As the end came sweeping across the Earth, humanity cried out for its final time, begging for a second chance. But all life was gone, everywhere.

Just like every other place in the world, the sky over Tikal was dark and cold and filled with acrid smoke. This is where it had ended. Yet deep beneath the surface a secret lay. Perhaps this was the second chance.

Acknowledgements

I want to express my appreciation and thanks to the family members, friends, and comrades who supported me during the creation of *The Last Election*. A very special thanks goes to Tamara Hoffer, for her unbelievable patience while editing my story. Thank you Dave Macintosh, wherever you may be, for telling me years ago that I should write a book. Six-two, thanks for the awesome cover.

About the Author

Kevin Carrigan is a former elementary school teacher and a proud member of the U.S. Army Reserve. He lives in Portsmouth, Virginia. This is his first novel.

the.last.election@hotmail.com